THE VIRTUAL TRAIL

J.C. FIELDS

Sharon Kizziah-Holmes, Publishing Coordinator
Jaycee DeLorenzo, Cover Design

Paperback-Press
an imprint of A & S Publishing
A & S Holmes, Inc.

ISBN -13: 978-1-951772-84-0

OTHER PUBLICATIONS
By J.C. Fields

The Sean Kruger Series:
The Fugitive's Trail
The Assassin's Trail
The Imposter's Trail
The Cold Trail
The Money Trail.
The Dark Trail

The Michael Wolfe Saga:
A Lone Wolf
The Last Insurgent

ACKNOWLEDGMENTS

Once again, as with my other books, I am indebted to a group of talented individuals who lend their assistance in my pursuit to produce as good a novel as possible. Over the course of my nine books, the contents are on me, but how the story is presented to you, the reader, is aided by the following:

To the members of my critique group, I cannot thank you enough for the brutal honesty you share with me every Friday. I have learned so much from each of you that I must tip my hat and express my gratitude to Shirley, Sharon, Lori, Heather and Conetta.

Sharon Kizziah-Holmes, owner of Paperback Press, continues to be a steadfast partner as my publishing coordinator. She has been by my side since the first novel and I cannot thank her enough. She is the one who deals with all the final formatting for both my eBooks and paperbacks. Her wise counsel has helped me achieve success as an Independent Author.

To my developmental editor, Kate Richards, thank you for taking me on as a client. Your edits and suggestions were spot-on. I appreciate your efforts on my behalf and look forward to working with you on future projects.

Shirley McCann and Tina Vyborny, thank you for fine tuning the final draft. It never hurts to have several final read-throughs before sending the manuscript off to the publisher.

Jaycee DeLorenzo, I am indebted to you for your continuity in producing covers which convey the theme of both The Sean Kruger Series and The Michael Wolfe Saga. Everyone who previewed your effort enthusiastically approved. Plus, your process for producing the images is both seamless and uncomplicated.

Nikki McSorley, the theme music you composed for

both The Sean Kruger Series and The Michael Wolfe Saga were both outstanding. Your talent as a composer and musician help make my Audiobooks a more enjoyable experience. Thank you.

Paul J. McSorley, continues as the voice of Sean Kruger. Over the past four years, he has become both a friend and a fantastic business partner. Due to the huge success of our audiobook version of *A Lone Wolf*, we are both able to pursue our passions full-time. He as an audiobook narrator and I as an author. While there is always a bit of sadness when I complete a new book, the excitement returns when Paul produces the audiobook.

And again, I have to thank my wife and best friend, Connie. Her encouragement to pursue my goal of becoming a full-time author has been unwavering since the beginning of this journey. We finally did it. I am blessed to have both her love and support. Not sure where I would be without her.

CHAPTER 1

Cambridge, MA

Due to the migratory nature of the neighborhood's residents, the presence of large moving vans or trucks seldom drew special attention. Less than a quarter of a mile from the main campus of the Massachusetts Institute of Technology, students were constantly moving in and out, particularly this time of year as the spring semester came to a close.

The man sitting behind the steering wheel of the truck kept his eyes on one particular door, one hundred feet from where he waited in the idling vehicle. His broad shoulders tapered to a narrow waist giving him the appearance of a Y.

Dusk settled over the street, but the man kept the lights off. As his target exited the office door, he slipped the truck into gear in preparation for the task ahead.

***

Danny Barton removed his wire-rim glasses and rubbed

his weary eyes with the palms of his hands. After twelve hours of crunching voter registration data from various southern states, it was time to call it a day and head home to his small apartment not far away.

As the Director of Voter Insights for President Roy Griffin's re-election committee, Barton's paycheck over the next six months would fund his doctorate post-graduate work through the following year.

He checked his cell phone for the time and realized he would be late for his eight o'clock dinner date with his fiancée. As he slung his backpack over his shoulder, he pressed the send icon on his phone.

Natalie Hart answered the call and said, "Let me guess, you're going to be late."

"You got it."

She chuckled. "That's okay, I'm running a few minutes behind myself. When can you be there?"

"Ten after."

"You'll probably beat me. See you then."

After the call ended, Barton set the alarm and locked the door to the campaign office. The small workplace was in a street-front building on Main, seven blocks from the apartment he shared with Natalie. Both were post-graduate students at MIT. She in biotech, and he in Predictive Analytics.

Streetlamps now offered additional illumination to the fading day as he approached the curb to cross the street. Traffic was light as he looked both left and right to check for oncoming vehicles. Not seeing any, he prepared to cross the avenue to the side where their apartment was located. He planned to drop off his laptop, feed the cat and then rush to meet Natalie.

After stepping onto the street, he froze. Bright lights and a deep rumbling sound hurtled toward him. Unable to move, his feet felt encased in concrete. Danny stared at the oncoming lights realizing he had made a fatal error. The last thought of his life, which occurred as the delivery truck bore down on him was, *Natalie is going to be so pissed at me.*

***

EMTs worked feverishly to resuscitate Danny Barton as Cambridge police detective Ginger Bell listened to the young male standing in front of her. "The guy works a few doors down at the president's campaign office. I see him leaving every night, sometimes at six and sometimes later. Tonight, it was just before eight when I saw him."

"Do you know his name?"

The man shook his head.

"The office is down the street?"

"Yeah." He pointed to his left, "Fourth door that way. It's President Griffin's campaign headquarters for Boston and Cambridge."

Ginger stopped writing. "Really?"

"Yeah, really."

"What kind of vehicle hit him?"

"One of those big rental trucks, the kind you move with."

"Did you by chance get the license?"

He shook his head again. "Sorry, but the front passenger quarter panel had a huge dent in it."

"That helps. Thank you, uh…?"

"Newcome, N-E-W-C-O-M-E, Barry Newcome."

"Thank you, Mr. Newcome."

Bell walked toward the indicated office door and stopped in front to see if there was a contact phone number painted on the window or door. There were two, she made note of each. Turning back toward the accident scene, a uniformed officer hurried toward her.

"Detective?"

She glanced at his name badge. "Yes, Officer Garcia."

His words were garbled as the ambulance spooled up its siren and drove away. "I'm sorry, what did you say?"

"One of the EMTs said they had a faint heartbeat, but his breathing was shallow and erratic. They don't expect him to make it to the hospital."

"Which one?"

"CHA Cambridge."

"Thank you, Officer Garcia."

As he hurried off, she referred to the phone number on her notepad and dialed it. After six rings, it went to voice mail, and a female voice told her the office was currently closed. She then called the other number listed on the door.

This time the call was answered on the fourth ring by a female voice who sounded on the verge of tears. "Griffin campaign, Chloe speaking."

"This is Cambridge Police Detective Ginger Bell. May I speak to the manager of the Cambridge campaign office for President Griffin?"

With total silence as her response, Ginger took the phone away from her ear to make sure the call had not dropped. It was still active. "Hello?"

"I'm sorry, who—who is this again?"

Bell picked up on the stress in the woman's voice and repeated her request. Immediately she heard a mournful sob.

"Uh—Chloe, are you okay?" Silence returned to the call. Bell heard another sniff, so she repeated her question. "Chloe, are you okay?"

"No, I'm not. What's this about?"

"One of your campaign workers had an accident outside your office, and I'm trying to identify who it might be."

"Oh dear. When did this happen?"

"About fifteen minutes ago. Who would have been working this late?"

Another cry of pain. "Oh, no, not Danny, too."

"Danny? What do you mean not Danny, too?

"Danny Barton…" Her crying intensified.

"Chloe, try to calm yourself. I really need to speak to the manager of the office."

The young woman took a deep breath. "You can't." Chloe wailed even harder. "She was killed in a drive-by shooting at her house earlier this evening."

CHAPTER 2

Springfield, MO

Sean Kruger, retired FBI profiler and current bored homeowner, sat behind his home office desk staring at his laptop computer screen. For the fourth time in an hour, he clicked the refresh key on his email service. This action brought a new message from Pete's Premium Performance Auto Shop. Since the Krugers were loyal and valued customers, Pete's was offering a limited-time discount on tires. As he read the new email, another appeared. This one came from a local handyman service telling him he and Stephanie needed to remodel their outdated kitchen.

His wife breezed by his open office door, stopped and smiled. "What's ya doing?"

"Amazed at how the Internet thinks we need new tires and our kitchen remodeled."

She chuckled. "I hope you're resisting temptation."

He looked up and smiled. "Don't worry, I've already resisted the urge to join a brand-new health spa, get six months of HBO free, and trade in our perfectly good cell phones for the latest and greatest ones."

"Why don't you find something to do around here?"

"What? I've tightened every screw, oiled every hinge, and painted every wall I can find."

"Then go read or watch TV. Sitting around waiting for emails does not become you, Mr. Kruger."

He let out a sigh. "Okay, turn on the TV. I'll be there after I shut the computer down."

Just as he shut the lid on the computer, he heard Stephanie yell out, "Sean, you need to get in here and see this."

"What?"

"Something just happened to the Griffin re-election campaign."

He rose and walked toward the living area where Stephanie stood, her focus glued to the television. "What's going on?"

She pointed at the screen. "Just watch."

He saw an ambulance's flashing lights disappear off camera. The talking head said, "Police have not commented on any connection between the hit-and-run accident of a Griffin campaign worker and the death, earlier today, of the national director of the campaign. The hit-and-run victim has not been identified at this time, but we can tell you that Loretta Floyd was shot and killed around five-thirty this evening as she exited her car at her home in Newton, Massachusetts."

Kruger took off his glasses. "Have they said anything besides this?"

Stephanie shook her head. "Not that I've heard. I just turned it on."

"Two accidents several hours apart, there's a connection."

Stephanie Kruger looked at her husband. "As you have always said, *coincidence does not exist, there are only connections.*"

He nodded as he continued to stare at the television screen.

***

President Roy Griffin paced in front of the Resolute Desk. National Security Advisor Joseph Kincaid sat on one of the sofas in the Oval Office watching him.

Griffin said, "This is not a coincidence. Someone targeted them." He stopped pacing and stared at Joseph. "Why?"

"Don't know, Mr. President."

"Is the FBI getting involved?"

"I doubt it. At this time, it would be a local law enforcement issue. Why?"

"Because, I don't trust the acting director of the FBI."

"I don't either. Paul's cancer treatments are going well. He's supposed to be back at his desk in a couple of weeks."

"That day cannot come fast enough." Griffin took a deep breath and leaned against the desk facing Joseph. "Remind me to discuss with Paul why Todd Perkins was made deputy director."

"I can explain. When Deputy Director Alan Seltzer was murdered, Associate Director Perkins was named acting deputy director. Paul didn't realize how controversial the man would be as deputy director."

"Do I have the power to fire him?"

Joseph nodded once. "You do, but Congress would call for hearings. Which would, in today's hyper-partisan atmosphere, jeopardize the goodwill you have established within the halls of the Capitol."

"Shit." The president started pacing again. "Then what do I have the power to do?"

The national security adviser smiled slightly. "Appoint an independent investigator."

Griffin stopped pacing, stared at his advisor, and tilted

his head. "Excuse me? An independent investigation?"

Joseph nodded. "Yes, into the deaths of the campaign workers. Article II of the Constitution states in Section 3, and I quote, *he shall take care that the laws be faithfully executed.* He being you, Mr. President."

"How does that give me the power?"

"From an interpretation of the document by prominent constitutional scholars, two Republicans and two Democrats. I believe that makes it a bipartisan agreement."

"Huh." Griffin folded his arms. "I take it you have something in mind. You're always two steps ahead of everybody else."

With a shrug, Joseph said, "Let's put it this way. When I first took this job, it was my responsibility to be prepared to advise you about all threats to the nation. You need to appoint an adviser to investigate and determine if this is a threat to the country or just a coincidence. That someone would then report back to you. Then you could ask the DOJ to get involved, which would cause the FBI to get involved."

"I take it you have someone in mind for this investigation."

A nod was his answer.

"Who?"

"The same someone who saved you and your wife's lives seven years ago."

A smile came to the president's lips. "Call him."

***

The digital alarm clock showed 11:22 when Kruger's cell phone vibrated. Not quite asleep, he grabbed it and stared at the caller ID. An all-too-familiar number appeared. He pressed the accept icon and said, "Kind of late for you, isn't it, Joseph?"

"Sorry about the time, Sean. Have you been watching

the news tonight concerning the president's campaign office in Cambridge?"

"Yes."

"What do you think?"

"With no more than I saw on the news, I would bet the two deaths are related."

"The president and I agree with you."

Taking a deep breath, Kruger let it out slowly. "You're not calling just to get my opinion, are you?"

"No, we need you in Washington DC tomorrow."

"Joseph, I'm retired, remember?"

Ignoring the comment, Joseph continued. "There will be a first-class ticket waiting for you at the airport for a noon flight to DC. Can you make it?"

"For what?"

"A meeting with the president."

"About?"

"He would like for you to look into the two deaths. He's convinced they aren't a coincidence either."

"Joseph, under whose authority would I be conducting this inquiry?"

"The president's."

Kruger thought for a moment before commenting. "Yeah, I'll be there. Give me the details." He ended the call several minutes later and lay back down, realizing it would be difficult to get to sleep.

Stephanie rose to one elbow next to him in bed. "That was Joseph, wasn't it?"

"Yeah."

"He has a distinct voice. I heard every word."

"Are you good with me going?"

"Very. You need something to do besides refreshing your email every two minutes."

"What if the two deaths are a coincidence and unconnected?"

"What're the odds, Sean?"

"In my experience, zero."

"Then, you need to pack for an extended stay. I'm sure you can figure it out. If you determine they are connected, you'll be properly prepared to stay for a while and advise the president. He can then make an informed decision. The kids and I will still be here when you get back."

He chuckled. "That's good to know."

She smiled and leaned over to kiss him.

***

The American Airline flight landed at Reagan National Airport a little after five p.m. the next day. Since this was not his first time in Washington DC, and there would be a need to get around town, he made the executive decision to rent a car. To his surprise, when he checked his cell phone, there was a text message from Joseph instructing him to go to the Budget counter where a car had been reserved for him. Once there he discovered, with a sense of familiarity, his rental car would be a Ford Mustang.

With a smile, he took the keys and headed toward the car's locale.

DC traffic delayed his arrival at Joseph's condo until a little after seven. The invitation to join Joseph for dinner had arrived just before his plane took off from the Springfield-Branson National Airport.

Joseph met him at the door. "Sean, good to see you. Come in, please."

Kruger took in the front room of the condo and recognized some of the furnishings from Joseph's place in Christian County, Missouri. "I thought this was a temporary gig. You've moved some of your furniture."

"Well, it was supposed to be. But Roy can be very persuasive."

"You're enjoying it, aren't you?"

The older man nodded. "Yes, I must confess I am. Mary

has fallen back into her old social circle, so she's happy as well."

During the short walk toward the kitchen, Kruger realized his friend, Joseph, had not changed in the past decade. He still wore a white Oxford shirt, navy blazer, pressed khaki pants, boldly colored socks, and scuffed brown loafers. Plus, his resemblance to the actor, Morgan Freeman, grew more pronounced with each passing year.

"I'm sorry Mary won't be joining us tonight. She and the First Lady are at one of their charity functions."

"I was looking forward to seeing her."

"She sends her regrets."

Joseph went to a stand-alone pantry and extracted two crystal tumblers. "Can I fix you a scotch?"

Kruger nodded. "Make it light, I have to drive later."

"Got it." He poured two fingers from a bottle of Glenfiddich into the glasses. Once completed, he stepped over to the refrigerator and withdrew a Ziploc bag of ice from the freezer. After placing a few cubes into each glass, he replaced the bag. Turning to Kruger, he handed him one of the glasses. "There's been a development."

CHAPTER 3

Georgetown

After taking a sip of scotch, Kruger raised an eyebrow. "A development?"

Joseph nodded. "It appears one of the secure email servers at the White House has been hacked."

"How bad?"

"We don't know yet. With the permission of the president, I'm bringing in an expert to examine it and determine how bad the breach is."

"Someone from the NSA?"

Joseph shook his head. "No, I needed someone with a top-secret security clearance and independent of the government."

"I know someone like that?"

Glancing at his wristwatch, Joseph said. "His plane landed an hour ago. I sent a car to pick him up. He'll be joining us shortly."

"Why didn't you tell me? I could have waited and let him ride with me."

"Because I need to talk to you before he gets here."

Kruger furrowed his brow. "That doesn't sound good. What's going on?"

"There's another reason Mary isn't here tonight."

"Now you have me concerned, Joseph."

Taking a deep breath, Joseph took his first sip of his drink. "I haven't even discussed this with the president."

Kruger remained quiet.

"I still have a few contacts at the CIA."

"Gee, I would never have guessed."

Joseph gave Kruger a guilty grin. "Sarcasm does not become you, my friend."

"Go on."

"I have an assistant, Jerry Griggs."

"I've met him."

"Jerry and I had a brief meeting with someone this afternoon at a Starbucks in Arlington. What this individual told me made the hairs on the back of my neck stand up."

Once again, Kruger did not respond.

"Did you know President Griffin has a primary challenger?"

"No."

"He does. However, his name did not appear on any of the state primary ballots until Super Tuesday back in March. Of the fourteen states with primaries that day, his name was only on seven. The news media is ignoring him, as are the voters. He only garnered less than one percent of the votes."

"Sounds like a long shot."

"As a rule, I would agree. However, there's more to the story."

Kruger studied his old friend and took another sip of his drink.

"We're three months from the convention, and there will be a challenge to the legitimacy of the Griffin administration."

"How's that possible?"

"In reality, it isn't. But the CIA operative told us the challenger will be presenting proof the death of Vice President Donald Pittman was not a suicide and that Bryant didn't die from an aortic aneurysm."

Kruger sipped his drink again.

"The challenger will be accusing Griffin of having Pittman murdered and Bryant poisoned."

Kruger shut his eyes and shook his head. "That's an old conspiracy theory. One that's been debunked hundreds of times."

"I'm aware of that, Sean. The CIA operative told us the challenger is planning to bring these charges up at the convention. Since we now know the server has been hacked, what's to stop someone from planting bogus emails proving the theory?"

Returning his focus to Joseph, Kruger said, "I'm stating the obvious here, but if somebody has tried to plant fake ones, you need to find them."

"That's the reason we need JR. To make sure any emails they release can be shown to be fake."

"Why wait till the convention? Tell the news media now."

"According to the CIA source, the challenger will start releasing electronic mail three weeks prior to the convention."

"Joseph, you and I both know the best defense is a strong offense. Tell the media about the hack now."

"Yes, but if the challenger tries to prove his theory with the counterfeit messages, the public might believe it. People tend to believe lies once they've been repeated enough times."

"So, that's why you've asked me to look into this. You want someone outside of government to stop the challenger. What's his name?"

"Derick Thorton."

"Never heard of him. Where's he from?"

"He's the current attorney general of Illinois."

"Not a real high-profile position, Joseph. Why are you and the president so worried about him?"

"You and JR were responsible for uncovering Pittman's complicity with the Russians. We believe you can do it again."

"So, you think Thorton's been compromised by the Russians?"

"That's our working theory at the moment. I can't emphasize enough it is only a theory. We can't prove it."

"Are you sure this isn't a case of sour grapes because someone is mounting a challenge to a sitting president? Something that rarely happens."

Shaking his head, Joseph said, "No, we expected one. After all, like Gerald Ford, Roy was appointed vice president and then vaulted to the presidency when Bryant died. What we didn't expect was for Roy's campaign workers to be targeted or the White House email server to be hacked. Someone is orchestrating this behind the scenes. Like I said before, we think it's the Russians."

"Then that means Thorton's in on it."

"That's what caused the chill to travel down my spine. The Russians aren't content with using social media to assist a candidate they think is more favorable to them. They're now directly trying to get their own guy elected."

***

JR Diminski stared at the condominium in Georgetown and then turned back to his driver. "Where'd you put my bag?"

"Trunk. Joseph asked me to drop it off at your hotel and check you in. Kruger has a car. He'll take you there later."

"Sounds like I'm going to be here for a while."

The driver grinned. "You know Joseph. He likes to

talk."

"Yeah. I know." He opened the door and offered his hand. "Thanks, Jerry. It was nice meeting you."

"Nice to meet you, too, JR. Joseph speaks of you often."

JR frowned.

"Don't worry. He's always discreet when he's praising your abilities."

JR turned and walked toward the condo's front entrance. After pressing the ringer, it only took a few moments for a smiling Joseph Kincaid to open the door and usher him in.

Getting right to the point, JR asked, "What's the big emergency?"

"In a minute. Let's go to the back of the house."

As they entered the kitchen, JR stopped and grinned. "You didn't tell me Sean was involved." He shook Kruger's hand and turned to Joseph. "Whatever it is, it must be serious."

"It is. The president requested a meeting with both of you."

Looking at Kruger and then back at Joseph, JR folded his arms. "How bad is the computer breach?"

"Good question, JR. We don't know at this point how bad or who is responsible. That's why you two are here."

Kruger handed JR a beer and said, "Joseph, you've got a whole group of talented computer geeks at the NSA and the FBI. Surely they could tell you."

"That's the problem, Sean, we don't know who we can trust. The president trusts you and JR. We also need to keep this quiet as long as possible."

With a frown, JR asked, "What do you mean, you don't know who to trust? As far as I've seen, Griffin is one of the most popular presidents we've seen in my lifetime."

"I know. But there's more to the story."

After taking the first sip of his beer, JR looked over his wire rim glasses. "Before I commit to helping, you might want to fill me in."

Taking a sip of his scotch, Joseph started. "The general public and most government workers don't know how sophisticated the cyber-attacks on this country have become. There may actually be some we've not detected at this point. Plus, the frequency of these attacks has shot up recently."

"Since when?"

"Since the first of the year."

"Are we counter-attacking?"

"Yes."

"But it's not affecting them, is it?"

"No, it's like playing whack-a-mole. You take one site down and another one pops up in a different country."

"That confirms something my company has been seeing recently. An increase in the number of attacks from all over the globe."

Having stayed quiet during this exchange, Kruger said, "For instance?"

"With the proliferation of social-media platforms, some of my larger clients are experiencing phishing attacks after an employee checks their Facebook, Twitter, or Pinterest account. For example, one company received emails from a thought-to-be trusted source addressed to a number of upper management associates. Every single one of them had recently checked social media on their company cell phones. Since those cell phones have access to company emails, the phishing attack grabbed their work email addresses. Then the unsuspecting employees received an email, clicked on the links, and all of a sudden, the network had keylogging software downloaded. Keystrokes started being recorded, which included company passwords and additional email addresses."

He paused to take another sip of beer. "It was a mess to clean up, but we did. That particular client now has a strict rule about social media use on their company cell phones and computers. Plus, they now ban company emails from being accessed by anyone's personal cell phone. Alexia Gibbs traced the source to a group of hackers in Vietnam." He smiled as he took a long pull from his beer. "She reverse-engineered the malware and sent it back to them. We knew every company or government agency they'd hacked." With a chuckle, he paused. "When she found they had infiltrated a large Chinese conglomerate, she quietly let the company know. The Vietnamese site disappeared a week later."

Joseph said, "That's what President Griffin wants. To find the hackers responsible for the White House breach and shut them down. Do we need Alexia?"

JR pursed his lips. "Maybe. Let's see what I can determine before we get too far ahead of ourselves."

Joseph glanced at his watch. "I have a catering company scheduled to serve us dinner at nine." He looked at his two friends. "Jerry Griggs will pick you two up at 9:30 in the morning at your hotel and drive you to the meeting. But now, it's time to put business aside and catch up with each other. I'll open some wine."

CHAPTER 4

Illinois Attorney General's Office, Chicago, IL

"Where's the money coming from, Mike?"

"Relax, Derick. Our fund-raising efforts are uncovering a surprising number of disenchanted former Griffin supporters."

Derick Thorton, the current attorney general for the state of Illinois stood from behind his desk and started to pace in front of the large window overlooking the city hall of Chicago. "Then why am I getting only 1 percent of the primary votes?"

"Because we are only just now getting your name out. Remember, we started late."

Thorton stopped pacing and stared at his campaign manager. "I don't see how we overcome the popularity of Griffin. He has a 62 percent approval rating."

"When we start releasing the emails, that will change."

"Why aren't we releasing them now? I don't want to look like a fool."

Taking a deep breath, Michael Peters shook his head

slightly. "Derick, we've discussed this numerous times. We can't just dump the emails on the public. We have to frame the narrative that Griffin isn't a legitimate president. We have to use well-timed statements and charges. Then, just before the convention, we use the emails to prove our accusations. We're not at that point yet."

"I don't agree. We need to get it out in the open, now."

"We don't have everything in place."

"Why not?"

In the tone of a patient father answering a difficult question from a small child, Peters said, "Derick, you have to trust me on this. We're still finding witnesses and gathering emails. It takes time. We're gathering evidence, like you would as the Illinois attorney general, to prosecute a criminal case."

Thorton stopped pacing and locked his attention on Peters. He folded his arms. "Very well, just make sure I'm not embarrassed and made to look the fool."

Standing from the wingback chair in front of the AG's desk, Peters said, "Derick, I have no intention of making you look like a fool. I've run more than a few campaigns. It takes careful planning and that's exactly what we're doing."

Thorton looked at his watch. "I have to be in court at one, anything else?"

Shaking his head, Peters grabbed his briefcase and returned his attention to Thorton. "Not at this time. I'll keep you informed of our next steps." With that statement, he walked out of the office and headed toward the elevators.

***

Fifteen minutes later, he sat in a noisy café waiting on a lunch companion to join him. Michael Peters stood a shade over six feet tall. His light brown hair and blue eyes a product of the Slavic ancestry on his father's side. The lunch companion shared the same ancestry, although from a different set of parents.

Annika Belsky arrived, sat across from Peters, and smiled. "How's our attorney general doing today?"

"Thinking too much."

She chuckled. With her blonde hair tied back in a ponytail and her navy pant suit, she looked the part of the typical office dweller in this part of Chicago's downtown area. Shorter than Peters by three inches, she maintained the look of a professional businesswoman with blocky black glasses sitting in front of her sky-blue eyes. "Is he getting cold feet?"

"No, just impatient. How did your efforts in Cambridge go?"

"With all the attention on Barton's accident, no one saw me pick up the leather satchel containing his computer. The bag was over twenty feet from the body and partially hidden under a parked car. The kid had his laptop enclosed in one of those hard-shell cases cops use. It was slightly damaged after hitting the pavement, but it still works and the hard drive contains the program."

"Excellent. So, we got everything we needed?"

She nodded as a waitress approached their table.

After placing their orders, they sat in silence until she was out of sight. He said, "We now have access to the White House email server."

"Do they know this?"

"I am told by our computer friends there is no way they could."

"Michael, do not be overly confident in what our friends tell you. They have their own agenda, plus a reputation to protect. They can and do lie."

"I am aware of this, but, so far, what they have accomplished has been well worth their cost." He paused for a second, looked at the ceiling, and said, "He's asking about the money."

"So?"

"He's not stupid. He understands how campaigns work, and he can't get his head around why we have the amount we've reported to him."

"Do your job and explain it to him. The so-called *silent majority* are contributing."

"I have explained."

"And?"

"He's skeptical. But he also wants to believe he has a chance."

Annika smiled. "Keep feeding his ego. It's one of the reasons we chose him."

"Maybe we need to have a virtual fund-raising event to convince him there's support out there."

"Interesting idea. There isn't any support, but let me pose it to our sponsors. Maybe they can create an event that will satisfy his concern."

Peters frowned. "It needs to be convincing. If it's not, I'm not sure how long I can keep him engaged."

***

Derick Thorton stared out his office window at city hall, his hands clasped behind his back, thinking about his political journey so far. He had a decade in the Cook County District Attorney's office, a few years as a city councilman, then one term as Chicago's mayor and now the attorney general for the state of Illinois. Each served as a stepping stone to his ultimate goal, president of the United States. His previous plans included a run for the Senate two years in the future, but the opportunity to bounce over this phase presented itself in the guise of Michael Peters. An opportunity he jumped at.

With a law degree from the University of Chicago, Thorton's five-year stint as an assistant district attorney followed by five years as the DA for Cook County, whet his appetite for higher public office. Now in his late forties, his impatience to achieve his ultimate goal weighed heavily on his decision-making process.

Tall, at six-one, his slender frame and ruggedly handsome face, obscured the fact he knew he possessed a profound narcissistic temperament. Disguising this egocentric trait as self-confidence, his journey as a politician seemed to be on the cusp of rocketing higher.

His ruminations were interrupted by his assistant. "Mr. Thorton, Michael Peters is on line one for you."

He turned. "Thank you, Debra. Please close the door."

Sitting at his desk, he took the call. "Hello, Mike."

"Derick, I'm looking into a virtual fund-raising event. Are you interested?"

"What do you mean, virtual?"

"With the rapid growth of virtual meetings, we can get hundreds of potential donors together online throughout the country. This would give you an opportunity to outline your vision for the country's future. The cost is small, but the returns can be huge."

"When?"

"Probably a week or so. They work better on a weekday evening."

Thorton remained quiet for a few moments. "Can we introduce our findings about Griffin during this meeting?"

"Yes."

"Get it scheduled, Mike."

"Yes, sir."

CHAPTER 5

Washington, DC

JR glanced at his cell phone. "It's after nine. I thought Griggs was supposed to pick us up by now."

Kruger asked, "How many times have you been in Washington, D.C.?"

"Once, with you."

"D.C. traffic is worse than Atlanta. He'll be here as soon as he can. In fact, there he is." Kruger pointed as Jerry Griggs parked his car under the porte-cochère and waved for them to join him. Kruger slipped into the passenger-side backseat, forcing JR to sit in the front.

After the doors were shut, Griggs accelerated toward the hotel exit. "Sorry, guys. Traffic is a bitch this morning."

With a chuckle, Kruger said, "Thanks for picking us up, Jerry."

JR stared out the window.

Griggs glanced at him and then returned his attention to the road. "Have you ever been to the White House, JR?"

A shake of his head was the answer.

"Nothing to be worried about. You've met President Griffin, haven't you?"

"Yes, but he wasn't the president at the time."

"Still the same guy. He's looking forward to seeing you again."

Kruger spoke up from the back seat. "My suggestion is not to accept coffee. The last time I was in the Oval Office, all I could think about was not spilling it."

JR's frown disappeared. "Thanks, Sean. That helps."

***

Joseph Kincaid met Kruger and JR at the entrance to the West Wing and escorted them to the Oval Office. "First time here, JR?"

"Uh-huh."

"Relax, no one's going to bite you."

"Not what I'm worried about."

Kruger covered his involuntary smile with a hand as he walked behind JR who was following Joseph toward the president's office. JR pressed his lips together as he rubbed the back of his neck and stared at the closed door. Before they walked in, Kruger pulled him aside and asked, "What's wrong?"

"Sean, over the past seven years I have tried to disappear, keep a low profile, and stay out of the government's way." He gestured toward the door they were about to enter and continued. "Right now, I'm about to enter the belly of the beast, and it makes me nervous."

Placing his hand on his friend's shoulder, Kruger nodded. "Don't think of it that way. Roy is a friend. A friend who just happens to be the president of the United States, but a friend nevertheless. I doubt he even wants anyone to know we're here. From what Joseph told me before you arrived last night, no one trusts anyone in Washington right now. But the president does trust the both of us. Let's go see if we can help a friend."

Once they entered the Oval Office, President Roy Griffin smiled and walked toward Kruger and JR with his hand out. "Sean, so good to see you again."

As they shook, Kruger said, "Always good to see you, sir. You remember JR Diminski."

The president used both of his hands to grasp JR's outstretched one. "Yes, I do. I'm really glad you're here, JR."

Momentarily at a loss for words, JR mumbled, "Uh—glad to be here, too."

"Gentlemen, please have a seat." He motioned to the two sofas facing each other in front of the Resolute Desk. "Would either of you like coffee or anything?"

Kruger and JR said in unison, "No, thank you."

Glancing at Kruger, the president chuckled and sat next to Joseph on the opposite sofa. Growing serious, Griffin perched on the edge of the cushion, leaned forward, and clasped his hands. "I know Joseph briefed both of you on the current situation."

Both of the men across from him nodded.

The president said, "I've been told you are one of the country's foremost authorities on computer security, JR."

"One of them, yes, sir."

"I need you to examine the White House email server and see how bad the breach is."

"I can do that."

The president turned to Kruger. "Sean, old friend, I have to ask you to come out of retirement."

"Sir, I'm past the required retirement age for the FBI. I can't go back."

"I'm painfully aware of that." He reached into his suit coat pocket and withdrew a leather wallet. He tossed it to Kruger, who caught it.

He opened the high-gloss, black leather wallet and stared at the inside. After a few moments, he looked up at the president, then searched Joseph's face. He returned his attention to the contents of the wallet and said, "Special Investigative Agent, Office of the President? I'm not following."

Griffin sat back on the couch and stretched his arm across the backrest. "Joseph pointed out that within the Constitution of the United States, Article II, Section 3, I, as president, have the duty to make sure that laws are faithfully executed. Two of my campaign workers were murdered for unknown reasons. I think the email hack and their deaths are related. The FBI isn't interested, referring to the incident in Cambridge as a local matter. So, I'm sending you, Special Agent for POTUS Sean Kruger, to find out. Unfortunately, it only gives you jurisdiction to look into their deaths. Joseph and I are searching for an alternative, but that"—he gestured toward the badge and ID case— "will get you in the door."

"I'm flattered, sir."

"Your compensation will be comparable to a presidential counselor. As a retired FBI agent, you already have the ability to carry a concealed weapon, plus the head of my Secret Service detail will sign off on your certification as well."

"Will I have the power to arrest anyone?"

Both the president and National Security Advisor Joseph Kincaid said "Yes" at the same time. Joseph continued, "As of this moment, you will report directly to me." Joseph handed JR a similar leather card case. "As will you, JR."

Kruger took his eyes off the wallet and looked at Joseph, "How's Paul doing?"

"The chemo is working. He should be back in a few weeks."

"What about the acting director of the FBI? Is he going to get his nose out of joint about this?"

"Probably, at least until Paul gets back."

"Are they currently involved?"

With a shake of his head, Joseph said, "No, I've spoken to the police chief there. She's an old acquaintance of yours and is looking forward to your assistance."

"Who is it?"

"Marlene Hoffman."

Kruger frowned and remained quiet for several moments. "Yeah, I remember her."

"She joined the Cambridge police department sometime after she left the FBI. How did you know her?"

"We worked a case together." Kruger's muted tone told his friend he held a concern about the woman.

The president stood. "Gentlemen, I am relieved to know both of you will be involved with this matter. I'm looking forward to hearing about your success. Please excuse me. I have an appointment with the British ambassador."

Joseph, Kruger, and JR exited the president's office and retreated to the NSA's office down the hall. As soon as the door was closed, Joseph asked, "Sean, I could tell you have concerns about working with Marlene Hoffman."

"You picked up on it, huh? Concern is not really the right word. One of the reasons Hoffman left the agency was an oversized ego. She has a tendency to question the intelligence of her supervisors and her partners, particularly male ones. I worked with her once, and it didn't go well. She left the agency not too long afterward."

"Well, if she's risen to the level of chief of police in Cambridge, she must have matured some."

"We'll see."

Turning to JR, Joseph said, "Can you look at the server?"

"Yes."

"I'll get Sean hooked up with Terry Hightower, and then I'll introduce you to the White House IT staff."

***

With reluctance, the current head of the IT department allowed JR to examine the email server. His nervousness quickly disappeared after a phone call from the president. Thirty minutes later, JR thanked the man and asked Joseph for a private moment.

Back in the NSA's office, again with the door closed, JR said, "I see evidence of what we call, an APT attack."

Joseph looked over his glasses and said, "And that means?"

"It stands for *advanced persistent threats.* I won't bore you with the details, but suffice it to say, it's a long-term attack on a specific target. We're seeing this type of hack more and more in recent years. It's basically a five-stage process that starts with gaining access, establishing a presence in the system, burrowing deeper, spreading out to all the systems and then securing a position to either steal data or make changes within the system. All without the knowledge of the operators."

"Make changes?"

"Yes."

Scratching his chin, Joseph said, "Could they change emails to offer written proof of something that never happened?"

"Yes."

"Who's responsible?"

"Don't know at this point. It could be anyone."

"What do you need from the White House?"

"I need to shut down the email server, isolate it from the Internet, and basically scrub it."

"How long will that take?"

"Don't know at this point, but it could take a couple of hours to several days."

"Let me get you and the head of the IT department in front of the president."

***

"Mr. President, I am very concerned about having someone who I have little knowledge about, or their security clearance, rummaging around in our computers." Ruben Marcos stood in front of the Resolute Desk, a worried look on his face.

Griffin smiled. "Mr. Marcos, I share your concern and I assure you I would never purposely put you in that situation. When you were younger did you ever hear of a computer hacker called Zardoz?"

"Yes, sir. He was a legend when I was in grad school. There were rumors he might have been an amalgamation of several hackers. No one knew for sure."

The president gestured toward JR. "That individual, who you have characterized as *rummaging around,* is the man you heard about in grad school. He, at one time, was Zardoz. His real name is JR Diminski. He has a higher security clearance than you do and is the owner-operator of one of the nation's foremost computer security companies. He is a personal friend of mine, and I trust him explicitly." Griffin paused for effect. "And I highly suggest that you do so, as well."

Marcos stared at the man known in computer hacker lore as Zardoz. JR returned the look and just shrugged. The IT manager looked back at the president, then turned back to JR. He offered his hand and said, "I've always wanted to meet you."

As JR shook the man's hand, Griffin smiled. "Mr. Marcos, will you allow JR to shut down our mail server and find out how bad the damage is?"

"Yes, sir."

CHAPTER 6

Washington, DC

WHITE HOUSE SUGGESTS POSSIBLE EMAIL HACK
By Lauran Riley, CNN White House correspondent
June 4, - 4:00 p.m.

Washington, DC (CNN) – A White House source, who spoke on conditions of anonymity, confirmed the White House mail server was still off-line due to a possible breach in security. This is the first time the system has been completely shut down for any length of time other than routine maintenance. Our source did not know how long the computer would be unavailable to White House staff. It was taken off-line last night at 10:30 and remains in that state as of today. President Griffin indicated at a morning briefing the shutdown was a scheduled event and that it would be back up by late morning. As of this writing, the server is still not working.

Alexia Gibbs listened as JR Diminski spoke in a hushed tone from his location in the White House. "I just placed a sample of the code in our file-exchange system. Check it against our virus database. If we don't have a sample, I'll check it against Alphabet's VirusTotal database. For some reason, the structure looks familiar to me."

She said, "I'll call you back when I know."

Alexia Montreal Gibbs, JR's partner in the firm, held the same status as he, chief analyst. Her background, also as a hacker, took her on a journey ranging from her birth country, Spain, to Paris, Mexico City, and finally to the middle of the United States. Born in Spain to parents who were staunch supporters of Catalonia, they harbored deep distrust of the government in Madrid. With this background from her parents, Alexia completed her studies at the University of Barcelona and immediately left the country. Her first job took her to Paris where she worked for an ISP provider as a security analyst. During this period, she discovered a more lucrative vocation: hacking.

She called the Latin Quarter of Paris home because she felt comfortable in the bohemian atmosphere of the area. Greed got the better of her one night and drew the unwanted attention of the French General Directorate for Internal Security, the DGSI. After a hastily arranged midnight flight out of Charles de Gaulle International airport, she settled in the Mexico City district of La Condesa. There she isolated herself for nearly a decade making a semi-legal living using her hacking skills.

When a job working for a Russian oligarch went sideways, she feared her life was in mortal danger. Scared out of her mind, she reached out to a kindred spirit in the underworld hacking community. A daring daylight raid spirited her away from under the watchful eyes of her Russian nemesis by a group of FBI agents and a computer hacker called Zardoz.

Now three years after the incident, she wore her black

hair long and flowing. Her clothing emphasized her slender athletic body, which she maintained with the help of the man she married, ex-Navy SEAL Jimmie Gibbs. They swam in the lake near their home on a daily basis. In the winter, they wore wetsuits allowing both of them to keep fit and trim. She now occupied her time doting over her son and husband, while helping JR's company become one of the premier go-to computer security companies in the world.

Accessing their company's encrypted file exchange system, she found the file JR referred to. Transferring it to an isolated virtual computer they kept for testing and dissecting viruses, she watched the program execute step by step. Her concern deepened after she ran the code through a disassembler which converted the 1 and 0s of machine language to a human readable format. When she compared this to the company's virus data bank, she stopped, sat back in her chair, and said, "Ah…shit." Reaching for her cell phone, she sent a coded word via text to JR.

He called ten seconds later. "What'd you find?"

"Do you remember Dimitri Orlov?"

"Not sure how I could forget him. Is this the same code that dug into our system two years ago?"

"It's not actually the same, but it has many similarities. I would say it was developed by the same individual or group."

"We never found them, did we?"

"No, but we knew they were operating out of the Ukraine."

JR was quiet for several moments. "If I remember correctly, wasn't Vice President Pittman part of Orlov's attempt to get their guy into the White House?"

"Yes."

"They're doing it again, Alexia." He paused. "See if you can find out what happened to Orlov. I'm going to go through Pittman's emails."

***

President Roy Griffin's immediate predecessor, Richard Bryant, had been forced to take Donald Pittman as his vice-presidential candidate during the party's convention. Despite his distaste for the man, the party convinced Bryant the only way he would win the presidency was to take Pittman on as his VP. They won the election.

Pittman's background as the governor of Virginia had been uneventful both in legislative achievements and perceived scandals. Unfortunately, a dirty little secret became known after achieving the office of vice president. The majority of his campaign contributions for his run for governor were through various cutouts leading back to a questionable source. A reporter uncovered information concerning three members of an economic steering committee, chaired by Vice President Pittman, being linked to a powerful Russian oligarch. The Russian was Dimitri Orlov. After this information became public, the wheels came off of Pittman's status as VP. He eventually committed suicide in his office.

Roy Griffin was named to the vacant position of vice president by President Bryant, who later died of a massive cerebral hemorrhage, catapulting Griffin into the Presidency. The archived files of Pittman's emails were the subject of JR's search.

***

JR created a complete clone of the White House email server and then let Marcos initiate the system again. Only, this time, with a new subroutine that would monitor the activity of the malware JR discovered.

Using the server clone, JR ran numerous searches using

programs he developed over the years to seek out variances of sentence structure and grammar. The emails of every member of the White House staff were exposed to this security. No one, including Griffin, was spared this level of scrutiny. By late afternoon, JR had enough data to discuss his findings with Joseph.

When JR walked into the office of the NSA, he looked up from his desk, and said, "I've seen that look before. It's not good news, is it?"

"I'm afraid not. Got a minute?"

He pointed to a chair and said, "I'll make the time. Close the door and sit. How bad is it?"

"The good news is, I've got the bleeding stopped, and there'll be no more intrusions. I've shown Marcos what to look for and he's all over tightening the security for the server. The bad news is I found hundreds of altered emails."

"Hundreds?"

"Yeah. Most were very subtle, insignificant changes. The chances of the author realizing they hadn't written it that way would be slight. But, if taken in combination with other emails, many from the archives of VP Donald Pittman, they could be used to produce a convincing story of a conspiracy by Griffin to ascend to the presidency."

"How did you find the altered emails?"

"A couple of search engines Alexia and I have been working on."

"Okay, is that all?"

JR shook his head. "The code of the malware I found was familiar."

Closing his eyes and rubbing his forehead with one hand, Joseph said, "I was afraid of that. Russian?"

"In a way. Remember Dimitri Orlov?"

"Yes, is he back?"

"No, he disappeared immediately after he returned to Moscow and has never been seen since. Alexia is checking with some of her old contacts in Russia to see if she can confirm he's still alive. My bet is he's dead."

"So, why was it familiar?"

"It was a variant of the code they used to attack my system two years ago."

"What do you mean by variant?"

"Same guy or group of guys who attacked my computer, attacked the White House server. The only difference is that he or they are getting smarter. Their attacks are more subtle. Once into a system, it's hard to detect they're even there."

"How did you find them?"

JR smiled and shrugged. "I've been doing this for years, Joseph. No one can detect when I've been in a system. Unless you know exactly what to look for. I know. I think when my system was attacked two years ago, they discovered some of my techniques. This attack looks similar."

Staring at his friend with wide eyes, Joseph said, "JR, are you telling me someone is using your hacking techniques on the White House computer?"

"Yes."

"How am I supposed to explain that to the president?"

"Don't."

"I have to,"

"Think about it for a second."

Joseph stared at him silently for what seemed like an eternity. Then slowly, the man grew a smile and his eyes twinkled. "If you know they're in the system and they don't know you know, you can trace them back to their origin."

"Now you're thinking like a hacker. If I can find where their computer is, I can re-engineer the virus and send it back to them. If they have copies of the changed emails, and I would assume they do, I can simply encrypt the file or delete it. If someone tries to use any printed email against President Griffin, it will be simple to expose it as a fake."

"Conspiracy theorists will claim we changed the originals, JR. The media will have a field day with something like that."

"Not really. I showed Marcos a little trick I've used in the past. He's changing the email formats on current and all archived emails, plus all backups. When whoever decides to show their stolen emails to the news media, they will look subtly different, and the White House can claim them to be fakes."

"What about emails already printed for historical reasons? They'll look like the old format."

"True, so I would suggest a very thorough search for those emails. They can be printed again in the new format."

Joseph sat and tapped his finger on his desk. "When can all of this be completed?"

"It's already started."

CHAPTER 7

Cambridge, MA

Kruger stood outside the now permanently closed campaign office scrutinizing the surrounding buildings. He referred to his copy of the police report concerning the accident and turned to his left. Walking slowly, he stopped occasionally to check for signs of any security cameras not mentioned in the report he held.

When he arrived at the location where Danny Barton stepped off the curb and into the path of the oncoming truck, he stood still and studied the surrounding stores, offices, and apartment windows above the commercial spaces. On the third floor of a five-story building across from the accident location, Kruger saw what he was looking for, a Ring stick-up wireless security device. Referring back to the police report, he found no mention of this particular camera.

Checking his watch, he noticed he had thirty minutes until his meeting with Chief of Police Marlene Hoffman.

***

At exactly eleven, Kruger was escorted into her office for his appointment. As he entered the room, Marlene Hoffman neither stood nor offered to shake hands. She simply stared at Kruger until the escorting officer left the room.

"I must admit you're the last person I expected to see from the FBI."

The former FBI agent's appearance had changed since his last encounter with the woman. Her hair, which she wore short, now possessed more silver than brown. Her face, while still round, seemed fuller than her bureau days. The addition of more than a few pounds on her once-slim frame made her almost unrecognizable. But she still displayed a condescending scowl. He noticed she still ignored social niceties. From his past experience with the woman, he knew exactly how the following conversation would transpire.

He said, "I'm not with the FBI. I work for the White House."

"So, you're with the Secret Service?"

He shook his head and offered his ID. She took it and studied it for several moments. Handing it back to him, she frowned. "Since when does the president of the United States have his own private police force."

"Hard to describe it as a force, since there's only two of us. Myself and another investigator."

"Huh." She kept her gaze on Kruger and then slowly smiled. "It's nice to see you again, Kruger."

He chose not to respond.

"How can I assist the president's personal investigator?"

"I'd like to see all of the security camera videos from the Danny Barton crime scene."

"There's nothing to see. It's a simple hit-and-run."

"Have you located the truck or the driver?"

She shook her head.

"Then it's not a simple hit-and-run. It's a murder."

"We haven't determined that yet."

"Can I see the videos?"

She hesitated for a couple of seconds. Her scowl intensified as she stood. "Follow me."

***

As noted in the police report, there were seven videos from security cameras located near the accident location. Kruger used a computer in a vacant cubicle to view each of them. Five of the videos showed Danny Barton walking down the sidewalk, approaching the spot where he would attempt to cross the street. One view showed a distant view of the moving van parked, it's lights off and an obscured license plate. Kruger noticed the wavy lines immediately behind the tailpipe. Evidence of the truck idling. He made a note of which video and the time-stamp.

The seventh view showed Barton stepping off the curb and three seconds later being hit by the truck. He noted the time stamp and jotted down a question on his notepad. When finished, he thanked the attending officer and returned to Hoffman's office.

She looked up when he entered. "Find anything?"

He nodded. "What happened to Barton's computer bag?"

"What are you talking about? We didn't find a computer with the body."

"One video shows him stepping off the curb just before he is struck by the vehicle There's a leather computer satchel on his shoulder."

She stared at him for a few seconds before she picked up her phone. After punching in a few numbers, she said, "Where's Detective Bell?" She was quiet as she listened and stared at the top of her desk. Finally, she said, "Bell, did you find a computer satchel near the body of Danny Barton?" She was quiet again. "You'd better come to my office. We have a development."

***

Back at the cubicle, Detective Ginger Bell stared at the frozen video of Danny Barton stepping off the curb. The view came from the victim's left side, and Kruger pointed to a brown strap on his right shoulder.

Kruger said, "If you zoom in, you'll see the front and back of the bag. It's easy to miss without enlarging the image."

Following the request, Bell enlarged the shot and leaned over to view the screen closer. "I'll be damned."

"I take it your team didn't find the bag near the victim?"

Still staring at the image, she shook her head. "We didn't find a cell phone either."

"That wasn't in the police report."

"No, it wasn't."

"Did you pull the cell phone records of his fiancée?"

"No."

Kruger pursed his lips and took a deep breath. With a glare, he let it out slowly before he spoke. "Detective Bell, I believe it's time to see if there are any records of him calling the fiancée. If there are, then we also have a missing cell phone."

Bell cleared her throat and looked up at Kruger. "I kind of fucked this one up, didn't I?"

With a slight smile, he relaxed and said, "A little, but let's not tell Hoffman. I knew her when she was with the FBI, and you'll never hear the end of it."

Looking back at the screen, Bell nodded. "Thanks, Agent Kruger. She's not the easiest person to work for, especially for a female cop."

"I can only imagine. By the way, call me Sean."

"I'm Ginger."

***

The staircase to the fifth-floor apartment resided in the rear of the apartment building. Kruger followed Bell up and said, "Ginger, this is your case, I'm your backup. Tell me again, what this guy's name?"

She hesitated on the third-floor landing and looked at the small notebook in her hand. "The apartment manager said his name was Kenneth Deloach, and he's been renting the apartment for ten years."

Kruger looked up the stairwell, "Huh. Kind of long for this neighborhood. I wonder why?"

The fifth-floor apartment tenant, with the Ring security camera outside, also possessed a Ring doorbell next to the entrance. Bell pressed the button while Kruger stood behind her.

"Yes."

Bell held her detective badge so the camera could get an image for the nervous-sounding renter. "Detective Ginger Bell with the Cambridge PD. Can we speak to you, Mr. Deloach?"

"What's this about?"

"We think the Ring camera on your balcony might have caught an image of an accident several days ago."

"I didn't cause any accident."

"We know that, Mr. Deloach. We just need to see the video."

"How do I know you're who you say you are?"

Bell rolled her eyes and said, "Please call a number I'm going to give you, and they'll vouch for us." She recited the Cambridge PD number.

Kruger covered a smile with his hand and said, "Now we know why he has all the cameras."

A little over a minute later, they heard two security

chains being disengaged and several deadbolts being thrown. The door opened, and a tall, lean man, with thinning blond hair pulled back in a ponytail stood in the doorframe. "Can I see your IDs again, please?"

Bell opened hers and offered it to the skinny man. When Kruger showed his, the man's eyes widened. "Office of the President?"

"Yes."

"This must be something more important than just a bad accident."

Kruger nodded. "Yes, it is. Can we see the video of four days ago?"

Deloach turned out to be a work-from-home IT consultant. He transferred the Ring videos for the date in question to a desktop computer with a forty-inch screen. A total of ten separate files were available. All were short, and all showed the same sequence of events as other cameras in the neighborhood.

Disappointed, Kruger removed his half-readers. He turned to Deloach and asked, "Could you download the next six recordings?"

The man nodded and typed away on his keyboard.

With his glasses back on, Kruger scrutinized the new videos. On the fourth one, he saw something in the upper left corner of the shot. "Could you reverse this one and back it up?"

"Sure. Do you want to freeze a frame?"

"Maybe. I'll tell you if I do."

They watched the video again and Kruger said, "Stop. Upper left corner, can you zoom in on that section and play it slower?"

"No problem."

As the video progressed at half speed, Kruger pointed to a figure reaching under a parked car and retrieving the satchel that at one time had been over the shoulder of Danny Barton. "There, freeze it."

Bell leaned closer to the screen. "Damn, why didn't we see that on the other videos?"

Kruger folded his arms. "Angle. Mr. Deloach's camera is elevated versus the others at ground level."

"Did you expect that, Sean?"

Shaking his head, the new investigator for POTUS said, "No." He paused for several moments. "Mr. Deloach, would you please download this video to a link I give you?"

***

After returning to the hotel room in Cambridge, Kruger called JR. To his surprise, the call was answered on the second ring.

"We had an eventful day. How about you?"

"You first."

JR summarized his findings within the White House computer. When he was done, he said, "What did you find out?"

"I've got a video file from a security camera which may show the accident that killed Danny Barton was staged to gain access to his laptop."

"Huh." He paused. "Why? He was a campaign worker."

"I know. A cell phone is missing also. We accessed his fiancée's Verizon account and found she received a call from him about four minutes before the accident. We think the phone might have been in the satchel with the computer."

"You have a number?"

"Yes." He recited the number to JR.

"Does the video contain an image of the person's face who took the computer?"

"Not a very good one—profile only, and a long way off in dim light. I had the video downloaded to the file-share link you use."

"Good, I'll have Alexia check it. I don't have access to our facial recognition software." JR paused for a moment. "If Barton was the one they were after, why the drive-by shooting of the campaign manager."

"That, my friend, is a question I'll try to answer tomorrow."

CHAPTER 8

Cambridge, MA
The Next Day

Natalie Hart sat at a small breakfast table, sipping tea, as she answered Kruger's question. "I've never seen her before, Agent Kruger."

He held his cell phone for her to see a pixel-enhanced photo of the woman taking the computer satchel. The picture, sent to him earlier in the morning by Alexia Gibbs, showed a woman's profile as she bent over to retrieve the bag. "To be honest with you, Ms. Hart, I didn't think you would. But I had to ask. We can't identify her either at this point."

The young woman just nodded. After taking a sip of tea, she asked, "Why did someone kill Danny? He was just a data analyst."

"That's what I am trying to determine." He paused and studied the woman. She wore her light brown hair, which cascaded over a youthful, pretty face, long. Her demeanor screamed academic, and her voice so soft-spoken it tended to be difficult to understand at times. Kruger continued, "How long had Danny worked for the Griffin campaign?"

"It was a temporary gig which was only supposed to last until the election. He needed the money to help pay for his postgraduate work. The salary they offered would take care of our financial needs through next spring." She paused as tears welled in both eyes. After a deep breath and a long exhale, she continued. "He wasn't political at all. He couldn't tell you the difference between a Republican or a Democrat. He just didn't care."

"I'm sorry I have to ask these questions, Natalie. But it might help me find who's responsible."

Wiping her eyes with a tissue she continued to clutch, she nodded. "I know."

"Did Danny ever talk about his work with the campaign?"

"No, he enjoyed the process, but the information he gleaned from the data he found tedious and boring."

"How many people worked at the campaign office?"

"Well, there was Loretta Floyd. She was the campaign director for Massachusetts."

"What were her duties?"

"She coordinated all the volunteers. She and Art were the only paid staff members in the local office. Everyone else was a volunteer. Danny actually worked for the national campaign. He was the coordinator for what he liked to called the *data monkeys*."

"Excuse me. He wasn't part of the local office?"

"Not really, he just worked there because it was close to our apartment. He could have accomplished everything he needed to do here, but enjoyed the solitude of the office and needed the faster Internet."

Kruger frowned. "You just mentioned someone by the name of Art. Who's he?"

"Art Padilla."

"This is the first time I have heard his name mentioned.

What did he do for the local office?"

"I'm not sure. Danny didn't like the guy and never talked about him. The only thing he told me was he thought the guy was a creep."

"Did Danny mention why he thought that way?"

"He was always bugging Danny about the data his team put together. He wouldn't tell him anything because the data belonged to the national organization. Art had no reason to see or need for the data. At least that's what Danny told me."

"What was Art's position?"

"I'm not sure. Danny only mentioned it once. I think he was the guy in charge of soliciting donations from local corporations and small businesses. Danny really didn't care what the guy did, so he ignored him."

"Yes, you've mentioned that. Do you know how to get ahold of Art?"

Natalie shook her head. "No, sorry."

Kruger sat back in his chair. An ugly scenario started to form in the back of his mind. "Natalie, who did Loretta report to?"

"The head of the national campaign."

"Who might that be?"

She shook her head. "Sorry."

"No problem." He stood. "I'm sorry I've had to ask these questions."

She nodded and stared at her tea.

"If you remember anything you feel I should know, would you call the number on this card?" He handed her a business card with only his name and a cell-phone number. "You can reach me at that number anytime."

Taking the card in her hand, she stared at it and nodded.

He walked to the front door of the small apartment and let himself out.

***

As he sat in his rental car, Kruger folded his arms over the steering wheel and rested his chin on them. He stared at the apartment building, his mind trying to focus on the nagging suspicion he'd started to form during the interview with the grieving fiancée. *Who was Arthur Padilla? And why does the Cambridge PD have no record of interviewing the man? Do they even know about him?*

Before he started the car, he retrieved his cell phone, searched for a number from his recent calls, and pressed the send icon.

Ginger Bell answered immediately. "Detective Bell."

"Ginger, it's Sean."

"How'd your interview go this morning?"

"Does the name Art Padilla ring a bell?"

The phone went silent for several moments. "No, I can't say that it does. Why?"

"I don't remember the number of individuals you told me you spoke to at the local campaign office. How many did you interview?"

"Let me pull it up on my computer, and I can tell you exactly." She remained silent as Kruger heard the clicking of a keyboard. After a minute, he heard, "Five. But none named Padilla."

"Were all of them volunteers?"

"Yes, why?"

"Just curious. I'm done here. Are you still meeting me at Loretta Floyd's house?"

"Yes, I'm planning to leave in a few minutes."

"Good, I'll talk to you then." He ended the call as his concern about someone named Art Padilla grew. He found a frequently called number and pressed the send icon.

"Good morning, Sean."

"Joseph, who runs the national campaign for President Griffin?"

"A woman. Her name is Ruth Greer. Why?"

"Where's she located?"

"California. Again, why?"

"I'm getting conflicting information. I need confirmation on something."

"Care to share?"

"Not at the moment. It might not amount to anything. I just need to check it out."

"What do you need from me?"

"Ruth Greer's contact information."

Joseph gave it to him.

"Have someone let her know I need to speak with her."

After ending the call, he started the Mustang and followed the directions from the GPS function on his phone toward the home of Loretta Floyd.

***

Leaning against the front quarter panel of his rental, Kruger studied the driveway and the neighborhood surrounding Floyd's house. Detective Bell had yet to arrive, which gave him time to visualize what might have happened that night. Few signs of a crime being committed in the driveway were present. A six-year-old white Honda Accord could be seen parked in the driveway and a plastic tarp still covered the glass windows on the garage door.

The neighborhood appeared to be a quiet suburban locale, comprised of ranch-style homes popular from the 1950s through the 1970s. A few cars were parked on the street, but, in Kruger's experience, not as many as a typical neighborhood.

Mature red maples and northern red oaks dominated the landscape with many drooping over the street, providing shade and a homey feel.

The sharp ring of his cell phone intruded on the quiet of the locality. He answered on the third ring. "Kruger."

"Agent Kruger, this is Ruth Greer. I was told you

needed to speak to me?"

"Yes, ma'am. I take it you've been briefed of my status within the Griffin administration?"

"Yes, the president's national security adviser called and told me about your inquiry and asked me to call you. Danny Barton was a valued member of our committee. I'll help as best I can."

"Thank you. Can you give me any information on Art Padilla? I was told he was the assistant to Loretta Floyd?"

"Oh, dear, another huge loss for our campaign. Loretta and I have worked on numerous political campaigns over the last two decades."

"I'm sorry for your loss." He paused for a moment, not wanting to seem too harsh, then continued. "Did you know Art Padilla?"

"No, he was a local hire by Loretta. To me, he was just a name on a piece of paper."

Kruger frowned as the mystery surrounding Art Padilla grew. "Can you tell me how long he was with the campaign?"

"Uh—let me see." He heard the unmistakable clicking sound of fingernails on a computer keyboard. "It says here, he was hired about a month ago." She paused. "Uh-oh."

"What?"

"There's a note on his personnel file referring to an email from Loretta. Let me check that." He heard more clicking. "Oh, my. The email from Loretta was telling us she would be replacing Art Padilla due to lack of performance. In fact, his termination was dated…"

He heard a soft sob. "Ms. Greer?"

"I'm sorry, Agent. She terminated him the morning of the day she died. Do you think he did it?"

"I'm not at liberty to offer an opinion, Ms. Greer. But I assure you we'll look into it." As he finished his sentence, Detective Ginger Bell parked her department unmarked Dodge Charger. "Ma'am, I appreciate your help. One last thing. Do you have Padilla's address?

"Yes, here it is." She recited the information.

"I have to go, but if I have other questions, is it all right to call you?"

"Yes, Agent, by all means, call me if you need to."

Kruger ended the call and watched the detective walk toward him.

CHAPTER 9

Boston, MA

The JetBlue shuttle between Washington and Boston arrived ten minutes late with JR reaching the curbside pick-up area by fifteen minutes past noon. He placed his backpack and small carry-on bag in the back seat of the Mustang. After closing the passenger door, Kruger pulled away from the curb and drove toward the Logan International exit.

"What have you got us into, Sean?"

"A mess, I'm afraid." The ex-FBI profiler glanced at his friend then returned his attention to traffic. "You first, then I'll tell you where I'm at."

"Does the name Dimitri Orlov ring any bells?"

Kruger said, "Oh, no, how the heck is he involved?"

"He's not. In fact, Alexia and I have reason to believe he may not be among the living. But the group of hackers he worked with are still active. Alexia compared the malware in the White House server to our virus database and found it matched, with modest changes, the same virus that attacked my company two years ago."

"Shit."

"Yeah, that was my immediate reaction. The bad news is—"

"That was the good news?"

"Afraid so. The bad news is they learned some of my secrets and how to be stealthy after they hacked into my system. The only reason I found their malware is I know what to look for."

"How?"

"Because I wrote the code."

Kruger glanced at his friend. "You wrote it?"

"Yeah, I did."

"Who are these guys?"

JR shrugged. "Don't have a clue. Alexia is working on it. She's like me and thinks it's the same group that worked with Orlov. Which means they're probably a bunch of Russians operating out of Eastern Ukraine."

"But you don't know for sure."

"No, it's my best guess."

"Why?"

"Ukraine is a hotbed for hackers right now. These guys have been refining their skills attacking Ukrainian infrastructure, like utilities. Recently they've been branching out to other countries. Most of these breaches are designed to cause havoc."

Kruger remained quiet as he drove away from Logan International. Finally, after several minutes of silence, he said, "You've just connected a couple of dots in a pattern I'm starting to see."

"How's that?"

Summarizing what he had discovered the previous day, he concluded by saying, "My visit this morning to the home of Loretta Floyd provided additional information on someone named Art or Arthur Padilla. Ms. Floyd's sister is staying there until the family can get her affairs in order and sell the house. She let us look through a desk where we found personnel files for the campaign office. Since the CPD detective I'm working with is the lead on the drive-by shooting and the hit-and-run accident of Danny Barton, she took the files. But not before I was able to read them."

"Who's this Padilla person?"

"Someone we need to find."

"Why?"

"Because he was fired by Floyd the morning of her death. Plus, Barton's fiancée said Danny described the guy as a creep."

"Ahhh—geez."

"See what I'm getting at, JR?"

"Did you, by any chance, get a social security number?"

Kruger smiled. "I've got more than that. Detective Bell let me take a cell phone picture of the file, which included a resume."

JR nodded. "I can use the social security number to see if this guy is legit."

"He isn't. On the way over to pick you up at the airport, I drove by the guy's supposed address."

With a chuckle, JR said, "Let me guess, a vacant field?"

"No, but he does have a sense of humor. It was an assisted-living facility."

JR stared out the passenger window as Kruger drove. "So, you think someone killed Barton for his computer?"

"Before I answer that, how hard is it to hack into a VPN?"

"Depends on the encryption of the VPN client."

"Would a government VPN be hard to hack?"

"Probably."

"Then that's why they needed Barton's computer. They want access to the VPN the campaign is using."

"Then why kill Loretta Floyd?"

"To make it look like a disgruntled employee is responsible. Her death was a distraction. We need to find

Art Padilla."

***

Alexia Gibbs gathered her laptop and stainless-steel coffee mug and prepared to leave the office for the evening. With her husband, Jimmie, out of town on business, she would get an early start on her fifty-minute drive and collect their son from the care of Linda Knoll. Her plans were interrupted by a message in the bottom right corner of her desktop computer screen.

Urgent. Call J secure call only.

She sat back down and touched the space bar. The screen illuminated again, and she clicked on the VoIP icon on her screen. The call connected almost instantaneously.

"Good. I caught you before you left."

"Hello, JR. What's so urgent?"

"I need…uh, we need information on someone."

"That's a little vague. Any someone or a specific someone."

She heard a chuckle. "Sorry, I'm trying to do two things at once. A specific someone. His name is Art or Arthur Padilla."

"Spell the last name."

He did. "I have a social on him, too."

"Want me to guess?"

Her additional attempt at humor went right over his head because he recited the number without responding. When he finished, he said, "When's Jimmie back?"

"Late tonight or early tomorrow. Why?"

"Sean wants him to call."

"I'll tell him. How fast do you need the information on this Arthur Padilla?"

"Yesterday would be nice."

"Funny. When?"

"It's pretty urgent, Alexia."

"I'll do it now and call when I have something."

"Thanks."

***

JR sat back in the chair provided for the desk in his hotel room. He hated using public Wi-Fi services, particularly at a hotel. Which was the reason his company used an exceptionally secure VPN. Staring at the laptop screen, he realized this would be his third night in a hotel and he had yet to call Mia.

Without delaying another second, he made the call. She answered within a few rings.

"I was wondering when you might call."

"Sorry, Mia. I'm in Boston."

"Thought you went to DC?"

"I did, now it's Boston. Things are moving fast here. Sean had to go to Boston after we arrived and now, I'm in Cambridge with him. We're going to MIT tomorrow."

"Uh-oh. How do you feel about that?"

"Kinda looking forward to it. I doubt any of the professors I had are still there."

"You never know."

"Mia, that was over twenty years ago."

"So…"

"It really won't matter, I guess. Oh, another surprise. Sean and I are now investigators for the Office of the President."

Her laughter brought back memories of when they started dating over seven years ago. She said, "How do you feel about that?"

"It's a good thing for Sean. The president asked him personally to come out of retirement. He didn't even hesitate. I, on the other hand, am not real thrilled about it."

Another chuckle. "Why?"

"Old habits, I guess."

"Oh, JR, you have nothing to worry about. Besides, I know all about it. Unlike you, Sean called his wife last night and told her. She then called me, since she correctly assumed you wouldn't call. However, I'm used to your habits. I'm surprised you called tonight."

"Was she okay with it?"

"Okay with it? She's ecstatic. He's been moping around the house for the past six months. She told me he sounded engaged and excited, something he hasn't been for a long time. JR, you know him. He's not one to express his inner feelings. He keeps them bottled up."

"I know."

"Now, would you like to hear what's going on around here?"

Their conversation lasted another hour.

CHAPTER 10

MIT Campus

"I must admit, the place hasn't changed much since I was last here, except the students seem a lot younger."

Kruger laughed. "That's because you're a lot older." He paused and looked at the buildings. "We're supposed to check in on the first floor of Building 32. How the heck are we supposed to know which one is thirty-two?"

"I know. It's where the computer science and AI labs are. I spent most of my time in college there. In fact, I recall once spending an entire week in it without leaving." He sighed. "I miss those days of uninterrupted coding and research."

"Remind me who we're supposed to meet?"

"Danny Barton's advisor."

"I know that, what's his name?"

"Max Keller."

"That's right. Did the advisor program work well here?"

"Depended on who your advisor was. I had a good one. How about you?"

Kruger didn't answer.

JR chuckled. "That good, uh?"

"No, not really. I got my doctorate anyway." He paused for a second. "I don't even recall what the man looked like."

"If you're interested, the guy who's credited with inventing the World Wide Web is a professor here. I never had the chance to meet him, but it's kind of cool he's here. His name is Sir Timothy John Berners-Lee. He's from England and a Professorial Fellow of Computer Science at Oxford."

"Thought the Internet was invented in the US."

"It was, the Internet is a different animal. It developed over the course of a few decades starting in the 60s and 70s." JR paused and looked at Kruger. "The Defense Department awarded a contract in 1969 that eventually led to the Internet's development. Berners-Lee developed a system allowing hypertext messaging to be transferred to different computers along the first Internet prototypes."

Kruger faked a yawn.

"Sorry, didn't mean to bore you." He pointed to a building on their right. "There it is."

After entering the building, JR studied a directory while Kruger asked for directions. When he returned, he saw his friend staring at the board with a worried look. "What's wrong, JR?"

"I see a name I'm familiar with."

"Who?"

"He was a young graduate assistant when I was here. Ravi Gupta appears to have stayed and is now a full-tenured professor. I learned a lot from him. In my opinion, he was a brilliant programmer."

"Better than you?"

With a shrug, JR said, "At the time, maybe. But I've been out in the real world and all the practice that offers. I'm sure Ravi still writes excellent code, but he won't have my real-world experience." He grew quiet as they approached the elevators. "If we run into him, don't be surprised if he calls me John."

"Are you going to correct him?"

JR remained silent until the elevator door closed. "No, no one needs to know my current name."

Kruger nodded. "Got it. What do I call you?"

"Whatever you want."

"What if they ask to see your ID, what then?"

With his eyes on the floor-indicator lights, JR said, "They won't."

"But if they do?"

"Just follow my lead."

Kruger closed his eyes and shook his head as the elevator doors opened on the fourth floor.

***

The tall German with crystal-blue eyes and thinning blond hair shook the ex-FBI agent's hand. Kruger said, "I appreciate you taking the time to talk to us, Professor Keller."

Max Keller stood three inches taller than Kruger's six-foot frame. He nodded and said with a slight accent, "I am more than happy to do what I can to help. Danny was a brilliant student. His dissertation was groundbreaking." He turned to JR, "You look familiar."

"John Zachara, Professor Keller."

Keller stared at JR for a few moments as they shook hands. "The name is familiar."

"I was a student here, class of ninety-eight."

"Ahh, maybe that's it."

Kruger asked, "Professor, is there somewhere we can talk in private?"

"Of course, my office. Follow me."

The moderate-sized office contained a desk and a small

round table with four chairs. Books and mountains of paper were stacked in every available nook and corner. After they were all seated, Keller placed an inch-thick document secured with a large coil binding in the center of the table. "That is the first draft of Danny's thesis. The last time he and I met, at least three weeks ago, he asked me to critique it."

JR said, "May I?"

With a nod from Keller, JR perused the book. Keller turned to Kruger, "Your presence tells me Danny's death is not being considered an accident."

Kruger said, "No, sir. We have suspicions Danny may have been targeted because of his position within the Griffin re-election campaign."

"Why?"

"That's what we're trying to determine. We've just learned his computer is missing."

The academic furrowed his brow. "Oh dear."

"Professor, we've been told you recommended Danny for the campaign job. Did you know anything about what his duties might have been?"

A slight nod came from the academic.

"We're aware he was the lead analyst, and we will be interviewing other members of his team in the coming days. In the meantime, we'd like your perspective."

"Danny spoke to me in confidence, Agent Kruger."

"I understand, and I'm sorry we have to ask these questions, but it might help us understand why he was murdered and his computer stolen."

Keller moistened his lips and took a deep breath. "Danny's research and his work on the campaign were interrelated. His theories lead him to construct a mathematical model for predicting elections. He had tested his hypothesis on numerous local elections across a wide area of the United States and even a few locations in Europe."

While JR intently studied pages in the middle of the document, Kruger remained quiet.

Returning to his narrative, Keller said, "The results of these tests showed Danny's model yielded an almost impossible accuracy rate of 96.45 percent. This is unheard of in political predictions."

"Why was it so accurate?"

"We were trying to determine the reason. In fact, our last communication via email concerned that very topic."

JR looked up from the document and said, "His algorithms are unique. I've never seen anything like them before."

Keller stared at JR for a long time and raised an eyebrow. "You understand them, John?"

"Yes."

"I struggle to, but I would have to agree with you."

Kruger tilted his head and said, "Okay, his approach is unique. Why would someone want to steal his computer?"

Closing the documents, JR smiled ever so slightly. "Because, if you know the outcome before the elections start, you can target which precincts to manipulate the votes for your candidate to win."

Keller nodded. "It effectively makes free elections impossible to hold."

Their conversation lasted another hour. Toward the end, as JR and Kruger were preparing to leave, there was a knock on the academic's door.

The professor turned toward it. "Yes?"

A smiling man in his early forties entered. "I heard John Zachara had returned to campus." He looked at JR and spread his arms. "There he is. What a wonderful surprise."

After standing to greet his old acquaintance, JR was immediately swept into a bear hug. Kruger recognized the uncomfortable look on his friend's face as the newcomer embraced him. Pulling away, JR offered his hand. "Very nice to see you again, Ravi. You look well."

"I am, I am, my good friend."

"You must tell me what you are doing now."

With a shrug, JR said, "I'm a consultant."

Gupta folded his arms. "Nonsense, you are too good a programmer to be a consultant. Tell me what you are really doing."

"I'm a cybersecurity analyst."

"That's better. Now I believe you. How long are you in town?"

JR looked at Kruger, who offered no help in getting him out of the invitation. Turning back to the professor, he said, "Probably through tomorrow."

"Then you must be my guest for dinner tonight."

"Uh, I wouldn't want to impose—"

"Nonsense, we will go to my favorite restaurant, my treat."

JR looked at Kruger again for a way out of the invitation.

Kruger grinned. "I've got things to do tonight. Don't let me stop you."

Without an appropriate excuse, JR returned to the professor and said, "It would be an honor."

***

Dining for JR existed as a necessity to sustain life, not as a social event. His tastes were simple. But the fresh ingredients and spices of the Indian cuisine combined with the chance to interact with his old friend quickly turned into a welcome change of pace from his usual rushed meals. The early conversation with Professor Gupta brought back memories he had suppressed for years. Finally, JR's old friend said, "I have talked about myself all night, my apologies."

"None needed. I've enjoyed catching up with you."

"But I have not asked about your endeavors. Please,

John, tell me why you are helping the federal government as a consultant?"

JR took a sip of his after-dinner coffee as he tried to decide how much he wanted to reveal. "Do you remember Tony Chien and Steve Wilson?"

"Yes, but I did not know them as well as I did you."

"I wasn't aware of that." He took another sip of his coffee. "The three of us went into business together in New York City and did quite well for about a decade. Unfortunately, Tony made a bad business decision and sold his shares to a private equity company. They basically screwed him and the rest of us. I left and moved to the middle of the country to start over. Steve passed away, and I heard Tony started some kind of technology company in St. Paul." JR left out the details of his flight from New York. He also failed to mention why the FBI was after him and the reason he took on a new identity.

"I started a one-man shop helping banks deal with cybercrime. Before I knew it, the company had more clients than I could handle, so I started hiring. We now have over a hundred associates, many of whom work from their homes throughout the Western United States. We specialize in computer security and clean up the mess left by hackers."

"That is wonderful. What is the name of the company?"

"Ozark Computer Security."

"I have heard of this company."

While in the middle of taking a sip of coffee, JR struggled not to spit it out. Finally, he said, "You have?"

"Yes, wasn't it at the center of deflecting a Russian hack two years ago?"

JR nodded.

"Congratulations, we have studied this incident in one of my graduate-level classes on cybersecurity. I was under the impression the head of that company was a man named JR Diminski."

Momentarily stunned by the professor's words, JR nodded thoughtfully. Taking another sip of coffee before answering, he said, "He's involved in the company."

"I would like to meet this JR Diminski. Could you arrange it?"

"I'm sure that can be arranged."

CHAPTER 11

Chicago

Derick Thorton emerged from his office building to a throng of media cameras and shouting reporters. He stopped as the crowd enclosed around him. Determining why they were there shouting incomprehensible questions at him eluded him. Finally, he raised his hands in an attempt to quiet the mob. The commotion intensified, but he heard a question he did understand.

"Why are you challenging President Griffin in the primary, Mr. Thorton?"

"Because he has never been elected to the presidency. He was appointed. It is our duty as Americans to make sure our elections are free and fair."

Another reporter shouted, "President Griffin has the highest approval rating of any president since Franklin Roosevelt. Why do you think the American people will vote for you?"

"Because I represent fairness and an open government."

"Then why are you under investigation by the DOJ for

campaign violations?"

"Fake news. Those charges were made-up by the Griffin administration."

Realizing he was unprepared for these types of accusations, Thorton tried to backtrack into his office building. The final question he heard shook him to his core.

"Why are the Russians investing in your primary campaign, Mr. Thorton? Are you being investigated by the FBI because of ties to the Russians?"

He managed to close the door without answering the last two questions. Feeling bile rise in the back of his throat, he dashed to the restroom located on the east wall of his private office.

As soon as he emerged, he grabbed his cell phone and called Michael Peters. When the call was answered, he screamed, "Why are there reporters outside my office questioning me about being financed by Russians, Mike?"

"Derick, calm down. What reporters?"

"Just now, there were at least twenty screaming media types outside my office yelling questions at me about campaign finance violations. How can I calm down when they are accusing me of taking money from the Russians?"

"I'm sure you're overreacting, Derick. Don't respond to them, and I'll see if I can find out where this came from."

Just before he abruptly ended the call, Derick screamed, "*Figure it out, Michael.*"

***

Mikhail Petrov, known to Derick Thorton as Michael Peters, smiled as he disconnected the phone call with his so-called candidate. He turned to the woman standing next to him. "The leaked emails have reached the media."

Annika Belsky nodded. "American reporters are like sharks. If they detect the slightest amount of blood in the water, they will attack. Even if it is not real blood."

Peters chuckled. "Your suggestion to just hint at Thorton's involvement with the Russians was brilliant. When you get back to New York, give your contact the emails proving the Russians are funding his campaign."

"You think it's time?"

"Yes, let's put our dear Mr. Thorton out of his misery. Do you have the still photo of Thorton taking the computer?"

"Yes, the guy you hired did a marvelous job. It looks real."

With a nod, Peters opened a tube of Lysol Disinfecting Wipes and started cleaning the surfaces in Annika's office. "Why don't you catch the next flight to New York? My flight to Estonia leaves around eleven tonight. I'll meet you in the city when I return."

"What about Padilla? He's wants his money."

"Keep stalling him. One of my discussion points in Estonia is what to do about him."

"Good." She glanced at her phone. "I need to get to O'Hare. Be careful."

"I will. I'll be back Thursday."

She closed the door as she left.

Thirty minutes later, he closed the door for the last time and headed down the hall toward the office they leased for meetings with Derick Thorton. Having previously removed the furniture and cleaned all the surfaces containing his own fingerprints, he made sure not to disturb the surface of the remaining conference table where the district attorney sat during their meetings.

Satisfied with his handiwork, he checked to make sure Barton's computer was in his backpack. With everything in place, he exited the rented office, locked the door, and turned toward the elevators and parking garage where a rental car waited. A car he would wipe down before turning it in at the airport.

Once on the plane, he doubted he would return to

Chicago.

***

Later that evening, under cover of darkness, Derick Thorton managed to slip out of the office building without bumping into any lurking reporters. After his noon encounter, the phones had been quiet, very unusual for a week day. His staff had only engaged him occasionally with normal day-to-day business and departed the office at their regular time.

His ten-minute walk to the apartment building, where he kept a Chicago residence, also occurred without incident. Once secured inside his flat, he prepared a bourbon and water and turned-on CNN to catch up on any current developments.

The talking head on the screen summarized the day's news on the upcoming presidential primaries. Suddenly, she announced, "We have breaking news out of Chicago. Dana Hathcock is standing by." The picture cut to another reporter standing in front of the Atrium Mall, the location of his Chicago office.

He froze in mid-sip of his cocktail.

The reporter said, "Sources are telling CNN there is a developing problem with the primary challenger to President Griffin's bid for re-election." The reporter referred to the cell phone in her hand. "A sixty-second video clip has been received by numerous news outlets this afternoon where Illinois Attorney General Derick Thorton is seen discussing campaign contributions from a known associate of a Russian oligarch. CNN has not been able to confirm the source of the video clips, but we have confirmed this meeting took place on January 12th at the Hilton located on the South Loop. In the video, Thorton is heard agreeing to terms for the contribution of over ten million dollars as a down payment to get his campaign started. A spokesperson for the FBI and one for the FEC has indicated they would be discussing this incident with Thorton."

Thorton turned down the volume, stood, and retrieved his cell phone. He noticed thirty-five new emails and twenty-nine missed calls. He had forgotten to turn the phone's sound back on when he left the office. After scanning the emails, the tightness in his stomach intensified.

With hands shaking, he dialed Michael Peters and was rewarded with a message stating the number was no longer in service. The tightness in his stomach morphed into full-fledged panic as he threw the phone against a wall.

At the exact same moment, a stern knock on his apartment door was followed by a male voice announcing, "Mr. Thorton, FBI, please open the door."

***

Joseph Kincaid received a text message at 9:14 in the evening from Jerry Griggs. *Derick Thorton arrested this evening. Illinois deputy attorney general has taken over pending Thorton's indictment for election law violations. Other charges pending. Campaign manager has disappeared. Thorton's office and apartment are being searched by FBI.*

With a slight smile, he replied to the text message and then called a number he knew by heart.

"Kruger."

"Sean, it's Joseph."

"Are you still at the office?"

"No, just reading. Mary went to bed an hour ago. There's news on the Griffin campaign."

"Oh?"

"Derick Thorton is under arrest, and the campaign manager is missing."

"Huh."

"I don't have any details right now but will keep you posted. How's it going in Boston?"

"JR and I think we have a motive for Danny Barton's murder."

"Do you want to discuss it over the phone?"

"Hell no."

"When can you be back in Washington?"

"We have a flight at eight. Should be available to meet early afternoon."

"Be in my office at one. I'll have your passes at the front gate."

"See you then."

CHAPTER 12

Washington, DC

Jerry Griggs escorted Kruger and JR to Joseph's office at ten minutes after one the next day. Joseph asked, "Have any of you had lunch?"

All three men shook their heads as they sat down at a small round conference table in the national security advisor's office.

"Good. I'll have salads and sandwiches brought in."

After ordering lunch, Joseph sat next to Griggs. He clasped his hands in front of him and asked, "What'd you discover in Boston?"

Kruger looked at JR, "You understand it. Go ahead."

JR took a deep breath and let it out slowly. "Danny Barton wasn't just some campaign data cruncher. His research in Directive Analytics at MIT was apparently ground breaking. I don't think anyone in the Griffin campaign knew exactly what they had in Danny."

Joseph nodded. "After talking to the head of the campaign, I would agree with you. He was hired after a recommendation from the head of MIT's computer science department."

"He developed a remarkable series of algorithms and applied them to voter registration data in conjunction with a number of consumer behavioral indexes like A.C. Nielsen, IRI and various other measures. This system allowed him to predict the outcome of an election with a 96.45 percent accuracy. This wasn't just occasionally, it was consistent over hundreds of elections he'd measured for the past two years, both domestic and numerous ones in Europe."

Griggs and Joseph stared at JR.

JR continued, "I've studied the algorithms. I've never seen anything like them. Once I understood his hypothesis, it became clearer why they worked. The concept was brilliant."

Griggs leaned forward, "So whoever stole Barton's laptop was after his process of predicting election outcomes."

Kruger said, "If you know the outcome of specific elections in specific counties, you know where to make changes and create a different result."

Joseph raised an eyebrow. "The end of free elections as we know it."

"Basically."

"I think there's a second reason the computer was stolen." Everyone turned their attention back to JR. "The campaign team of data crunchers communicate via a VPN. VPNs are very secure pipelines for computer-to-computer communications. Hacking them can be difficult, depending on the encryption they use. I think there's a good chance they wanted his computer so they can access the campaign's VPN."

At a knock, Joseph stood and went to his office door. A Navy steward rolled in a cart with salads, various sliced meats and breads for sandwiches, and bottles of water. Joseph thanked the man, who left without saying a word.

As soon as the door closed, Joseph prepared himself a sandwich. "So, why not change the VPN?"

JR nodded. "That would seem like a good option. But whoever has possession of the computer will probably already have access to the core server. Thus, they will know when the VPN is changed."

As everyone prepared their lunch, Joseph asked, "So how do we stop this?"

JR took a sip of water. "We find the computer."

Leaning forward at the table, Griggs frowned. "How do we do that?"

"By tracking its media access control address. We can identify the computer whenever it is used. However, finding the location might be a little trickier."

"Can the NSA, do it?"

"Very efficiently." JR tilted his head and gave Griggs a sardonic smile. "But Alexia and I can do it with more stealth."

"How?"

"Trade secret."

"Gentlemen," Joseph interrupted, "my suggestion would be for JR to do what he proposes immediately." He turned to Kruger. "Sean, what are your next steps?"

After a few moments of silence, Kruger said, "I think it's time JR and I split up. I'm going to Chicago to interview Thorton. If his campaign manager has disappeared, my guess would be that individual was using the Illinois AG as a pawn. Maybe I can get a lead on who the guy is."

Nodding, Joseph said, "The stakes are too high, gentlemen, we don't have time to be using commercial flights. The president has authorized your use of Air Force assets moving forward."

"I'd like to bring Jimmie Gibbs into the investigation."

"Why?"

"He has skills we might need."

"Agreed, I'll inform the president of our decision."

"Thank you, Joseph."

***

Jerry Griggs pulled up to the all-white Air Force Gulfstream G550/C-37B parked in a discreet section of the Joint Base Andrews tarmac at four in the afternoon. Turning to Kruger, who once again claimed the back passenger seat, he said, "The pilot will drop you two off in Springfield for the evening. He'll then fly you and Jimmie to Chicago tomorrow morning. He'll remain on standby until you're done in the Windy City. Oh, by the way, he's an old friend of Jimmie's."

Directing his attention to Griggs, Kruger asked, "What if we need to stay in Chicago for a few days?"

"He'll wait. He's attached to the flight crew assigned to Air Force One, so he's at the president's disposal. When he found out Jimmie Gibbs was involved, he volunteered for the assignment."

"Is he an ex-Navy SEAL?"

"Don't know. You'll have to ask him."

"Jimmie's like Joseph, he knows everybody and if you know him, you don't forget him."

As Kruger and JR exited the car, a tall, wiry, sandy haired man stood at the top of the airstairs leading into the aircraft's cabin. As Kruger ascended the steps, the man smiled and offered his hand.

"You Sean Kruger?"

Checking the pilot's rank on his uniform, Kruger said, "Yes, Colonel."

"I'm Dale Webster, I understand you saved the boss's life."

"Another agent and I did, some years ago."

"I want to thank you for doing so."

Not knowing what to say other than, "Glad we could

help," Kruger entered the cabin and sat down on the starboard side. JR sat across from him as the pilot entered the cockpit.

"I didn't hear what he said to you?"

"He just thanked me for keeping President Griffin safe a few years ago."

"Oh, that." JR chuckled and opened his laptop.

***

With a cruising speed of 562 mph, the Gulfstream 550 took a little over two hours from wheels up to wheels down in Springfield. As the plane taxied to the KKG Solutions, LLC location on the business aviation side of the airport, Kruger saw a black Denali parked next to the hangar. A slender man with a swimmer's physique leaned on the SUV's front quarter panel with his arms folded. This was Jimmie Gibbs.

As the plane came to a halt, Gibbs smiled and pointed to the front of the plane. Apparently, the pilot and Gibbs saw each other. Less than five minutes later, Webster was on the tarmac, and the two friends were giving each other bear hugs and laughing.

Kruger and JR stood back, watching the two men poking fun at each other. JR said, "I take it they've been friends for a while."

Looking at JR, Kruger responded, "I wasn't in the military, you were. Something must have happened. One was in the Air Force and the other in the Navy."

"It will be interesting to find out."

Just then Gibbs and Webster walked over to them. Gibbs said, "Gentlemen, I want you to meet the best damn AC-130 pilot in the entire universe."

Kruger smiled. "We met on the plane. I take it you two have a history together?"

Gibbs nodded. "Dale here, saved twenty of us SEALs

one night in Afghanistan. We were surrounded in the Hindu Kush by a bunch of Taliban assholes. This guy circled the area where we were trapped. While he flew, his team blasted the hell out of them with all the firepower the gunship holds."

Webster said, "You'd have done the same for my crew if we'd crashed."

"That's not the point. We all thought we were goners until Dale showed up. With his help, we got out of there without any casualties. Needless to say, it became my mission to find him, which I did two days later. I handed him a case of beer, which we both consumed that evening. We've been buds ever since."

JR nodded. "That would do it."

"He needs to get the plane squared away. While he's doing that, I'll take you two over to your cars at the terminal parking lot. Then I'm coming back to pick him up. He's staying with Alexia and me tonight."

***

Kruger walked through the door from the garage into the kitchen, and his kids immediately surrounded him. A fast growing seven-year-old Kristin practically jumped into her father's arms with five-year-old Mikey not far behind. While he hugged the siblings, he noticed his wife, Stephanie, standing off to the side, smiling and waiting her turn.

After the kids had their fill of fatherly attention, they ran off into another part of the house. Kruger took his wife into a tight embrace, which lasted longer than normal. Finally, she pushed away and looked up at him. "When do you leave for Chicago in the morning?"

"Around nine. As soon as the kids get to bed, we can talk."

Two hours later, with the kids tucked away, Kruger lay

in bed with his hands behind his head, waiting for Stephanie to join him. She returned to their bedroom and shut the door. After slipping under the covers, she said, "They're both asleep."

"Good." He scooted over and brought her into an embrace. "Sorry I was gone so long."

She chuckled. "It's worth it seeing you have a purpose again."

"Was it that obvious?"

She rose up on one elbow, smiled, and locked her eyes on him. "Mr. Kruger, you do not take well to not having anything to do."

Returning the smile, he said, "I know."

She lay back down and put her arm over his chest. "How long is this project for the president going to last?"

"Not sure, but I don't think I'll be in Chicago very long. It'll depend on how much I can learn from Derick Thorton about why he launched a primary challenge to Griffin. The nice thing is we have a plane at our disposal for the time being, and Jimmie's involved." He paused for a moment and hugged her tighter. "I'm still not comfortable staying in hotels without you."

"That's nice to hear. But don't let it stop you from doing what you love to do."

He leaned over and kissed her. They finally got to sleep an hour later.

***

After helping Mia with dinner and getting Joey to bed, JR retired to his home office and stared at the computer screen on his desk. Various methods of finding more about Derick Thorton were available to him, so he chose a simple search first.

Using the Chicago Tribune website, he searched for articles about the disgraced attorney general. Newer articles recapped the man's arrest and lamented the continued seedier side of Chicago politics.

About fifteen minutes into his search, he came upon a photograph of Thorton posing with a man and woman during a political rally three months earlier. The man was identified as Thorton's campaign manager with the woman unidentified.

JR started another search. Only, this time he did not utilize the Chicago Tribune website.

CHAPTER 13

Chicago

The Cook County Jail sits on a tract of land in South Lawndale, Chicago, Illinois, about five miles from the shores of Lake Michigan. Operated by the sheriff of Cook County, it is the third-largest jail system in the United States, following Los Angeles County and New York City.

Kruger and Gibbs were escorted by a deputy to an interrogation room where Derick Thorton and his attorney, a man named Sedgwick Trombino, waited. After showing their IDs to the attorney, the man looked concerned. "Gentlemen, my client will not be answering questions concerning the false allegations being made against him. Particularly by investigators from the office of the man he sought to replace."

Nodding, Kruger said, "Wise advice, Mr. Trombino. However, we believe your client was being duped and coerced by a foreign government in an attempt to subvert the election in the fall."

"So, you believe my client is innocent?"

"I didn't say that. What I said was, we believe him to be the unwitting victim of a conspiracy to suppress our democratic elections. A scheme perpetrated by a foreign government."

Trombino stared at Kruger for several moments and then leaned over to whisper in Thorton's ear.

As the soon-to-be ex-attorney general of Illinois listened, he kept a neutral expression and then nodded once. "Ask your questions, Agent Kruger. If the answers do not incriminate me, I'll answer the best I can."

"Thank you, Mr. Thorton." He paused and locked eyes with the accused man. "Tell me about your campaign manager."

"His name is Mike Peters."

"Have you spoken to him since your arrest?"

"No."

"Have you tried to contact him?"

Thorton looked at his attorney, who nodded once."

"Yes. He hasn't responded to any of my calls."

Taking a folded piece of paper from the breast pocket of his sport coat, Kruger opened and turned it so Thorton could see. The photograph resembled a typical passport or military ID picture. The unsmiling, stern face stared straight at the camera. "This photo came into my possession earlier this morning. Do you recognize this man?"

Looking at the picture carefully, Thorton nodded and then looked at Kruger. "That's a younger picture of Mike Peters."

Tapping the picture, the new investigator for the Office of the President, said, "His real name is Mikhail Petrov. The picture is about ten years old, from his days as a Russian Foreign Intelligence Service agent for the agency currently known by the initials SVR. The FBI had him under surveillance up until about two years ago. They believed he was recalled to Moscow. Apparently, he wasn't. When did you first encounter this man, Mr. Thorton?"

"About a year ago. I attended a function for a charity my wife supports and he approached me during the event. He was curious about my political ambitions."

"What did you tell him?"

"Only that I was thinking about running for governor."

"What was his response?"

"He talked to me about possibly running for the US Senate. I told him the earliest opportunity for me to run for a US Senate seat in Illinois would be in four years. My professional goals required a shorter timeline."

Kruger and Gibbs did not respond.

"That was when he suggested possibly running for president. I laughed at him."

Gibbs asked, "What did he do then?"

"He gave me his card and said if I changed my mind to call him."

Tilting his head, Kruger asked, "Didn't that seem a little strange to you? A man you've never met before asked you if you want to run for president?"

"Actually, no. My ego was bigger than my brain at the time, and I started thinking about it. I called him back after a month."

"And?"

"We met two days later."

"What did he tell you?"

"He posed the scenario about Griffin being an illegitimate president and that he had evidence to back up the proposition."

"Did he show you the evidence?"

"No." When Kruger did not comment, he continued. "I know. How could I have been foolish enough to believe him. Well, like I said, my ego and ambitions were thinking for me. I took his word for it."

"Okay, what did he tell you next?"

"He told me there were plenty of donors ready to back a qualified candidate to challenge Griffin for the party's nomination."

"Did he say who these donors were?"

"No, he just called them well-heeled party supporters."

"And you didn't ask for names?"

Thorton just shook his head.

"How much was in the campaign coffer?"

"I'm ashamed to say we started off with a war-chest of ten million, plus more coming in every day. He showed me the numbers, which convinced me to get on the primary ballots. We were only able to do it in a few states."

"Did you ever see any of the advertising?"

"To be honest with you, I only saw them on social media. I helped produce a number of TV spots and recorded the endorsement statement for the end of commercials, but I never saw any of them on local or national TV."

"Did this make you suspicious?"

Thorton shook his head. "Not until after Super Tuesday."

"What happened then?"

"For all the money they reported to have spent, I received less than 1 percent of the vote."

"Did you make any personal appearances?"

He shook his head.

Gibbs pursed his lips. "Mr. Thorton, didn't you find that a little strange?"

"Thinking back on it, I do now. But Peters told me it wasn't necessary until closer to the convention when we would expose the information on Griffin's illegitimacy." He paused for a second. "I was caught up in the moment and not thinking straight."

Leaning forward, Kruger asked, "Mr. Thorton, do you have any idea why they chose you?"

The man clasped his hands in front of him and stared at

them. "I didn't at the time, but unfortunately, I do now."

"Please explain."

"A more seasoned candidate would have seen through Peters' BS pretty quickly. I've never run a nationwide campaign. And I didn't really have to campaign that hard to get the attorney general's position because my opponent wasn't that competent. I think Peters saw a patsy in me, and now I'm paying the price for being gullible."

Both Kruger and Gibbs stood. Kruger said, "Thank you for answering our questions, Mr. Thorton."

Looking up, Thorton furrowed his brow and asked, "Do you have any idea what he was trying to accomplish?"

Kruger nodded.

"Can you tell me?"

"The Russians are trying a new way to subvert our elections."

***

Standing outside the Cook County Jail, Kruger turned to Gibbs and asked, "Do you believe him?"

Looking back at the building, Gibbs said, "I couldn't get my head around why they involved him in the first place. It seems counterproductive to get someone like him involved. He has zero national exposure, and he's a little naïve. After talking to him, I understand. He's not the sharpest knife in the drawer and was easily manipulated. So, to answer your question, yeah, I believe him."

"So do I."

"Where did you get the picture?"

Kruger pulled a different image out of his sport coat pocket. "JR found this one of Thorton and Peters together at a campaign rally on the Chicago Tribune website. He acted on a hunch and ran Peters' photo through his facial recognition software. With his newfound status as a cyber investigator for POTUS, he was granted access to the FBI database. It matched an FBI surveillance snapshot of the man from 2013." He pulled the military picture out and stared at it for a few moments. "With a little more digging, he found this one."

Gibbs chuckled. "Since when did not having official access to the FBI database stop JR?"

"Never. But it's nice to know he has it."

"Who's the woman to Peters' left?"

"We don't know her name, but JR confirmed she's the person who took Danny Barton's computer the night of the accident." Kruger put both pieces of paper away. "If Peters was posing as a certified campaign manager, my bet is he would also have had an office in Chicago. We need to find it."

"I'm on it." Gibbs pulled his cell phone out and called his wife.

***

Afternoon – Same Day

The Uber driver dropped them off in front of the west entrance to the President's Plaza complex. Ten minutes later, after showing their IDs to the complex manager, she asked them to follow her. A strikingly beautiful woman in her mid-thirties, she was tall and slender in build with the air of a highly paid model. Kirstin Seaton, ushered them into her office, and they all sat around a small conference table in the corner of her professionally decorated space.

She asked, "What can I do for you gentlemen today?"

Kruger started. "We have reason to believe a man named Michael Peters leased an office here. Can you confirm that?"

She opened a small Microsoft Surface Pro and entered the name. She studied the screen and nodded. "Yes, he leased 1200 square feet last fall with a twelve-month contract. He paid the full year in advance, which is a bit unusual. Why?"

"We have reason to believe, Ms. Seaton, that Michael Peters is a fictitious name and he was utilizing the space to commit a crime."

She stared at Kruger with a slight frown and pursed lips. "Are you sure, Agent?"

"Like I said, we have evidence pointing in that direction."

"I can assure you, we run extensive background checks on all of our tenants. It would be almost impossible for us to miss something like that. What sort of crime did this Mr. Peters commit?"

"We're not at liberty to discuss the charges against him at the moment. But I can assure you, Ms. Seaton, it has to do with the security of our country."

She consulted her computer again and then looked up. "His certificate of organization checked out with the state of Illinois, and his bank references were excellent."

"I'm sure they were."

"What are you saying, Agent Kruger?"

"Can we see the office?"

"I'm going to need a subpoena before—"

Kruger leaned forward. "You and your company are not in jeopardy, Ms. Seaton. Agent Gibbs and I just need to see if he is still utilizing the office."

She blinked twice and then nodded.

Ten minutes later, Gibbs and Kruger were standing in the middle of an empty office. Each room looked freshly cleaned. There were four separate areas, all empty except one where a large conference table remained. It did not appear as clean. Dust and smudges were visible on one side. Kirsten Seaton walked through the space opening doors and appearing more and more stressed as she moved from office to office. She said, "This is most unusual. I don't understand. It appears no one has been here for months."

"No, the only evidence of it being occupied is the conference table."

At that same moment, Kruger heard noise coming from the reception area.

CHAPTER 14

Southwest Missouri

On the southwest side of Springfield, north of a busy four lane highway, sits a multiuse commercial center with restaurants, professional offices, banks, retail and numerous other businesses. Located in the middle of this busy section of town, is a nondescript buff-brick two-story building. No sign adorns the front of the structure. The only identification on the building are the numbers announcing the physical address. Inside this non-descript location is one of the premier cybersecurity companies in the world.

On the second floor, in the corner of a massive cubicle farm, sits a soundproof conference room that serves as the heart and soul of the operation. No one in the company, regardless of position or seniority, is offered a private office. If someone needs to have a confidential meeting with a client, they reserve the conference room. Otherwise, it remains empty.

JR entered the soundproof room holding a laptop computer. His personal cubicle, just outside the conference room door, did not allow the privacy he required for a meeting with Alexia Gibbs. As he sat down, she entered, closed the door and sat across from him at the long table in the middle of the room. When she gained access to the company's VPN, she said, "Jimmie called a little while ago from Chicago."

JR looked up from his position at the table. "What about?"

"They needed the location of Michael Peters' office."

"Where was it?"

"Are you familiar with the President's Plaza complex?"

"No."

"It's close to O'Hare and a rather exclusive business address."

"Huh." He paused a moment. "Did they have their interview with Thorton?"

She nodded.

"And?"

"Jimmie called him a naïve stooge."

With a frown, JR asked, "Why would he say that?"

She summarized the interview as described by her husband. "Jimmie was having a hard time believing this guy considered himself a viable candidate for president."

JR remained quiet for a few moments. Finally, he said, "That helps with a puzzle I've been trying to figure out since Sean and I were at MIT."

"What's that, JR?"

"After talking to Danny Barton's advisor at the university, I can't help but think there might be a sinister reason to kill Barton and steal his computer. One that involves more than just the next presidential election."

"Interesting. Like what?"

"I haven't discussed it with Sean yet, but—" JR started typing furiously on his laptop while Alexia watched him. After several minutes, he stopped, studied the screen and then turned back to her. "I need to call Ravi Gupta at MIT."

She stood preparing to leave when he said, "Stay, I want you to hear this. But I need something from my desk. I'll be right back."

He left the conference room, rummaged around the top middle drawer of his cubicle desk, and quickly returned to the conference room, closing the door behind him. He consulted a business card and dialed a number on his laptop, which instantly transferred to the Polycom conference phone in the middle of the table.

Before the call rang, Alexia said, "There are more modern conference phones, JR."

"I know. I like this one."

They both remained quiet as the sound of a phone ringing could be heard.

"Hello, this is Ravi Gupta."

JR smiled. "Professor, this is John Zachara."

Alexia furrowed her brow as she stared at JR. He held his hand up and whispered, "I'll explain later."

"John, what a wonderful surprise. I told several of my colleagues about your visit. They would have enjoyed meeting you." He paused for a moment. "What can I do for you?"

"The last we spoke, you indicated you would like to meet JR Diminski?"

"Yes, yes, I would." He chuckled. "Is he there?"

"He is extending an invitation for you to tour his company. He would like for you to fly out with all expenses paid. There would also be an honorarium for you. In addition to the tour, we would like to confer with you on a particularly troublesome problem."

"I am honored. When?"

"As soon as possible."

"Will you be there, John?"

"Yes, I can assure you, I will be there."

They heard another chuckle. "How about the end of next week?"

"I'll send you an email with the details."

When the connection ended, Alexia folded her arms and said, "What was that all about?"

"Ravi Gupta is an old friend at MIT who is brilliant concerning Internet communications protocols. He's written several books on the subject." He paused, "He only knows me as John Zachara."

"That was obvious."

"I had dinner with him the night we were in Cambridge. He knew of our company and about the computer hack by the Russians. Apparently, one of his upper-level graduate courses uses it as a case study. He asked me if I knew JR Diminski. I told him I did, which is not a lie. He then asked me to introduce him to JR."

She smiled. "Why didn't you just tell him what happened?"

"I don't know. I should have, but I also didn't think he'd believe me. So, I went along. Once he's here and we explain the problem, it will be a professional challenge for him."

"Do you think he can help?"

"You and I are two of the best hackers around, which makes us excellent security geeks. Neither one of us is as attuned to locating a specific network card on the Internet as Ravi is."

"Why would we need to find a specific network card?"

"Because that's the way we're going to find Danny Barton's computer."

She smiled. "I didn't think of that. What happens when we find it?"

"Ever hear of Stuxnet?"

"Wasn't that the malware designed to attack and destroy the Iranian nuclear centrifuges in 2010?"

JR nodded. "It only attacked a specific industrial controller module made by Siemens. Those controllers were used to manage the cascade of centrifuges owned by

Iran. The malware was harmless when it infected another computer, but once it migrated to the controllers used by Iran, it caused the controllers to malfunction. The concept of the attack was brilliant and had a devastating effect on the Iranian nuclear program."

Alexia's eyebrows rose. "What are you planning, JR?"

"If we can find Danny Barton's computer and I emphasize the word, *if*, I'm thinking of infecting it with our own version of Stuxnet."

"Where do we start?"

"We need access to the Griffin Campaign's VPN."

With a slight smile, she said, "Joseph?"

JR nodded. "Joseph."

***

Joseph Kincaid stood in the doorframe leading to Griffin's private office in a hallway just off the Oval Office. The president looked up and Joseph asked, "Got a second?"

Looking at a clock on his desk, he nodded. "Any news from our new investigators?"

"A lot."

Griffin pressed the intercom button on his desk phone.

Robert Short, President Griffin's chief of staff answered. "Yes, Mr. President."

"Bob, I need you to postpone my appointment with the House speaker."

"For how long, sir?"

"Give me at least an hour."

"Yes, sir. I'll take care of it."

Griffin motioned for Joseph to enter. "Close the door." As soon as the national security adviser sat in one of the two wingback chairs across from the desk, the president said, "What've they found?"

Joseph summarized the events so far and then waited for

any comment from Griffin.

"What do you think, Joseph?"

"After speaking to Sean and then JR this morning, I have to agree with them. There's more to this than just trying to manipulate one election."

"And that is?"

"Multiple possibilities. All of them bad."

"So, what do we do?"

"JR has asked for access to the VPN being used by your campaign."

Griffin smiled. "JR's asking permission?"

"Yes, sir."

"Why doesn't he just hack in?"

"He already has, but wants it to be official for what he needs to do next."

The president laughed. "And that is?"

"He plans to pose as one of the campaign number crunchers."

"Not following you."

"JR's theory is that Barton's computer was taken to gain access to the VPN. Those on the network will be targets, and he wants them to attack his computer."

"Why?"

Joseph smiled. "So, he can plant a virus."

CHAPTER 15

Chicago

Kristin Seaton followed Kruger back toward the deserted office's reception area. When they arrived, three men and two women, all in dark suits, were standing in the area. As Kruger emerged from the hallway, a tall agent approached him.

"Sean Kruger, what the hell are you doing here?"

Kruger took a few moments to assess the agent and determine why he looked familiar. Finally, it dawned on him. The last time Kruger encountered Frank Reed, the man standing in front of him, was in Freemont County, Wyoming. Their meeting had not gone well for the younger agent. In fact, he had been demoted from his position as a special agent in charge back to agent. Apparently, he was stationed in Chicago and working his way back up the ladder.

"I might ask you the same thing, Agent Reed."

"This is an FBI investigation, my investigation. As I recall, you retired. Now, why are you here?"

Withdrawing his ID case from his sport coat pocket, Kruger opened it and held it so Reed could see the contents. "I work for President Griffin."

Reed reached for the badge, but Kruger withdrew it beyond his reach.

"I have no knowledge of your authority to be involved, Kruger. You and the individuals with you need to extract yourselves from this office. I'm declaring it a crime scene, and you are destroying evidence." He paused for a second and glared at Kruger. "You don't want to be accused of destroying evidence do you, Kruger?"

Tilting his head, Kruger narrowed his eyes and was about to respond when Kristin Seaton walked up and said, "This is private property. You need to—"

Kruger raised his hand. "Ms. Seaton, Agent Reed is correct. We need to leave and let them do their job."

Kristin stared at Kruger, her mouth agape. After several seconds, she relaxed and then nodded.

Kruger looked back at Gibbs and motioned with his head for him to follow. As they walked out of the office, the door closed abruptly. The three walked silently down the hall to the bank of elevators. Gibbs asked, "What was that all about?"

When Kruger raised his hand and extended his index finger, Gibbs realized his friend did not want to discuss the situation just yet.

The elevator door opened, and they all filed in. As soon as the door closed, Kruger said, "We now have a turf war on our hands, Jimmie." He turned to Kristin, "Sorry, Ms. Seaton, but your company's leasing an office to Mike Peters is going to raise questions you'll need a lawyer to answer."

***

Washington, DC

Acting Director of the FBI, Todd Perkins, read the memo for the second time. His anger intensified with each sentence. A stickler for demanding all internal-agency communication to be in hard copy, he placed the sheet of paper on his desk and pinched the bridge of his nose. Perkins held a strong belief Director Paul Stumpf would announce his retirement soon due to a recent cancer diagnosis. Once this occurred, his status as acting director, would immediately jettison the word *acting* in his title.

An unapologetic traditionalist, he demanded suit coats to be worn at all times by agents in the field and while at the Hoover Building. In Perkins' mind, Stumpf was too lax with the rules. He, on the other hand, demanded discipline. The FBI was a professional organization, and Perkins saw it as his mission to reinstate the standards originally envisioned by J. Edgar Hoover.

He picked up the handset of his desk phone and pressed the intercom button to his assistant. He heard, "Yes, sir."

"Bob, get me the attorney general on the phone."

"Yes, sir."

Perkins replaced the handset and read the memo one more time while he waited. When the intercom buzzed, he picked it up. "Yes."

"Sir, you're on hold for the attorney general."

"Thank you, Bob."

The hand set went silent as he waited. After thirty seconds, Attorney General Dale Delgado said, "Good afternoon, Todd. What can I do for you?"

"Thank you for taking my call, Dale. What do you know about the president having his own private investigators?"

Delgado remained silent for a few moments. "I'm not aware of any program like that. Why do you ask?"

"Because I just received a memo from the Chicago Field Office that a retired FBI agent by the name of Sean Kruger is flashing an ID around claiming to work for the Office of the President."

"Really. Then he must be under the auspices of the Secret Service."

"The field agent who filed the complaint knows what those badges look like. This was different."

"Well, send me the details via email and I will ask the president."

"When?"

"When I have the opportunity. I'm not going to make a special request for something like this."

The acting director of the FBI took a deep breath and let it out slowly. "Sir, I believe it is of sufficient importance to make an immediate inquiry."

"So noted, Mr. Perkins. Now if you don't mind, I have a few other concerns on my desk."

The call ended.

Perkins closed his eyes. He knew one day he would push the wrong person too far. But until then, he had an agency to run.

***

Washington DC

The attorney general replaced the handset harsher than normal. He would be glad when Paul Stumpf returned from medical leave. Perkins was starting to wear on his nerves. Tapping his finger on his desk, he picked up the phone and dialed a number. The call was answered on the fourth ring.

"National Security Advisor."

"Joseph, it's Delgado."

"Good afternoon, Dale."

"What do you know about the president having a private investigator?"

"The president has a lot of investigators. You know that."

"I'm talking about someone working directly for him."

"What brought this on?"

"FBI Acting Director Perkins has his nose out of joint about an agent in the Chicago Field Office complaining about an agent flashing a badge around saying he works for the president."

"Did he say who this someone was?"

"Yes, someone you and I both know. He claims it was Sean Kruger."

Joseph chuckled. "Yes, Sean is looking into the death of Griffin's campaign workers for him. But I seriously doubt he is flashing a badge around."

"Kind of what I thought, too. Is Kruger working for DHS?"

"No, he's working directly for the president."

"Oh, boy—"

"It's legal, Dale. He cleared it with White House Counsel."

"Why wasn't I informed about it."

"I'll have the president brief you personally on the matter."

"That didn't answer my question."

"I know."

"Dammit, Kincaid, I need to know about these kinds of matters."

"Like I said, I'll speak to him."

"Griffin pulled me out of retirement for this job, I can just as easily retire again."

"Dale, you and I both know President Griffin's life was saved by Sean Kruger. He trusts him. Plus, he wanted the inquiry into the campaign members' deaths looked at discreetly. He has a reason for not getting the DOJ or DHS involved. You'll have to trust him on this one."

"When is Director Stumpf due back?"

"Soon."

"It can't be soon enough. I'll take care of Perkins."

"Thank, you Dale."

***

Joseph retrieved his personal cell phone out of his desk drawer and dialed a number.

"Kruger."

"Who did you piss off at the FBI?"

"That was fast."

With a chuckle, Joseph asked, "When did it happen?"

"This morning."

"Want to fill me in?"

"We found the office of Thorton's campaign manager. It appears to have never been occupied. While we were there, the Chicago FBI showed up."

"Let me guess, you failed to display your famous charm."

"Actually, I did. Remember Frank Reed, the SAC I ran into last year in Wyoming?"

"You're kidding."

"Nope, he was there. I didn't recognize him at first, but it was him."

"What did you say that pissed him off?"

"Not sure, although it might have been when he asked me why I was there."

"And you told him?"

"I work for the president."

With a note of sarcasm Joseph said, "I'm sure that satisfied his question."

Kruger continued, "Not in the slightest. He immediately became rude with the building manager and that's when we took our leave. He didn't seem too pleased about running into me."

"No, from the conversation I just had with the attorney

general, that's a reasonable assessment."

"What'd Reed do? Whine to the acting director?"

"Apparently." He paused for a second. "Where are you on this?"

"First we're looking for a man hired by Loretta Floyd who goes by the name Art Padilla."

"Never heard of him. You say Loretta Floyd hired him?"

"That's correct. He was responsible for corporate contributions for the Boston area. Due to lack of performance, he was fired by her the morning of Barton's accident. Now he's disappeared."

"That's not good." Joseph paused. "Do you suspect he's responsible for Loretta's death?"

"I think that's what we are supposed to believe. I'm not buying it." Kruger was silent for several seconds. "The personal information about Padilla didn't check out, and he is nowhere to be found. That makes two men who've been involved with this mess who've disappeared."

"Two?"

"Mike Peters is the second one. He was the campaign manager for the man planning to challenge the president at the convention. His office is where we ran into Frank Reed. The building office manager told us Peters signed a lease for twelve months, paid in advance. Jimmie and I saw the suite this morning, it didn't appear to have been used or occupied for months. The home address Peters used on the lease agreement turned out to be an upscale apartment complex. Jimmie and I spoke to the management company. Just like the office, it appears no one's ever lived in the apartment. We found no food in the refrigerator, zero furniture and no personal items. The lease was signed on the apartment a month before the lease on the office space. The one-year lease on the apartment was also paid for in advance."

"Someone was setting up a legend, weren't they?"

"That's my guess."

"Okay, keep me posted."

"As soon as I know something, I will."

CHAPTER 16

Tallinn, Estonia

As a former satellite of the now defunct Union of Soviet Socialist Republics, Estonia declared its independence on August 20, 1991. The capital of the small nation is Tallinn, located on the coast of the Baltic Sea in the northeastern section of the country. Its location puts it directly across the Gulf of Finland from Helsinki. Estonia possesses a high-income economy and the fastest-growing one in the EU, which it joined in 2004. Technology companies have thrived in this environment of free enterprise over the past two decades.

Tallinn Airport, also known as Lennart Meri Tallinn Airport, is the largest airport in Estonia. Located five kilometers southeast of the center of Tallinn, it serves as a hub for both international and domestic flights.

Mikhail Petrov walked through the concourse of this airport after leaving O'Hare International Airport on a Lufthansa Airlines direct flight to Tallinn. The overnight flight left him with a mild case of jetlag, but after several espressos toward the end of the flight, he felt ready for his midday meeting.

Tomas Pavlovich, the man Petrov would be meeting, was a Russian ex-pat who stayed in Estonia after independence. Ten years after Estonia's liberation and right before the country joined the EU, Pavlovich became a billionaire. His fortune only grew after creating a holding company for buying startups and existing companies. Within these multiple subsidiaries, one company stood out as a shining star, Odin Analytica. Classified as an information technology and consulting firm, its real purpose was far more sinister. The money behind the origin of the establishment came from an oligarch located in the largest land mass country on the planet, directly to Estonia's east.

Petrov carried the object Annika Belsky obtained in the orchestrated accident on the streets of Cambridge, Massachusetts in a leather satchel attached to a long leather strap over his shoulder. When he arrived at the airport's passenger pickup area, he noticed a black Porsche Cayenne with dark-tinted windows parked in a restricted area. A man in a dark suit stood on the passenger side of the vehicle, his hand on the door handle leading to the rear seat.

Checking his cell phone, he reread a text message sent during his flight. This was his ride. Without a word he approached the vehicle and the man opened the door. He slipped into the back seat, as the driver shut the door and hustled around to the driver's seat.

As they sped away toward the airport exit, the driver said, "I trust your flight was uneventful."

Petrov said in his non-accented English, "Yes, thank you for making the arrangements."

The driver nodded and remained silent for the rest of the trip. Forty minutes later, they stopped in front of a modern skyscraper near the city center. Before Petrov stepped out of the Porsche the driver said, "Reply to the text I sent earlier when you are ready to return to the airport."

"Thank you, Darius."

As the Cayenne sped away, Mikhail Petrov walked with purpose toward the front entrance of Odin Analytica.

***

Tomas Pavlovich smiled as he sipped coffee and stared at the laptop computer sitting in the middle of the conference room table. His English had a slight London accent. "The text message I received from Annika said it was damaged."

Petrov shook his head. "That was our first thought. We had difficulty getting through the passcode, once we did, we found the hard drive intact. Barton had it in a military-grade protective case which helped secure the unit's solid-state hard drive. We also discovered his login information for websites and VPNs were in a password manager app. It was a little disappointing to have someone of his intellect use an off-the-shelf password app."

The Russian raised his eyebrows, "You said we, who else helped you?"

"Sir, only Annika and I worked on the laptop, I cracked the passcode."

"Good, so, we have access to everything?"

"Correct."

Pavlovich paused for a brief moment. "I need to bring you up-to-date on the latest developments here."

"Thank you."

"As you know, we have been developing our social media database. One of our associates in the US obtained a data dump on almost 110 million users, of whom most are US citizens. The associate has shared this information with us." He pointed to the computer. "I am being told the data Barton worked on can be cross-referenced with the social media file."

"Good, I'm glad we were able to supply the computer."

"I am told the program our associates have developed would be, as it stands now without the Barton algorithms, fairly successful in disrupting any election we chose. However, with the Barton application, our system will basically bring the US to its knees. We believe we can pick and choose who we want to win any election in the US all the way down to local municipalities."

"I didn't realize this system was that important."

"My dear, Mikhail, it is beyond important. It was the final crucial key to our plans."

Petrov smiled but stayed quiet.

"The last time we spoke I asked you about Art Padilla."

"What about him?"

"Is he going to be a problem?"

"Maybe."

"What does that mean?"

"He's a greedy son of a bitch."

The Estonian entrepreneur took another sip of coffee. "How so?"

"He keeps asking how much and when he'll be paid for helping acquire the laptop. I've told him to be patient. His compensation would depend on how useful the data on the drive might be. Apparently, he didn't like that answer, because he won't shut up about it."

"Unfortunate. Is he a threat to our project?"

"Possibly, he hasn't threatened to inform the FBI yet, but I don't think it will be too long before he does."

"He must not be allowed to speak to the FBI. How much does he think he needs in compensation?"

"That's the problem—he won't tell us. All he will say is, if it's not enough, he'll let us know."

"Hmmm—" Pavlovich stood and walked over to his large oak desk. The top was clear of any paperwork, the only objects present a keyboard and a forty-inch flat-screen monitor. He opened a drawer and withdrew a business card. He then returned to the conference table. Sitting again, he offered it to Petrov. "If the situation with Padilla gets out of hand, simply call this number and leave this message: *It is time*. The person who picks it up will know what they need to do."

The man known as Mike Peters slipped the card into his inside sport coat pocket and stood. "Is that all you needed from me today, sir?"

"Yes. When are you heading back?"

Petrov glanced at his watch. "If I leave now, I can catch a flight back to New York tonight."

Standing, Pavlovich offered his hand. "Safe trip. Keep me appraised."

"I will, sir."

***

As the door to Pavlovich's office closed, a door on the opposite wall opened, and a man entered the inner sanctum of Odin Analytica. His round face exhibited a frown.

Pavlovich looked at him and asked, "What do you think?"

"Padilla is a loose end we do not need." The newcomer's English-accented Russian contrasted sharply with the fluent Russian from Pavlovich.

"Agreed." He paused and stared at the door Petrov exited.

"Do you wish for me to handle it?"

"Dah."

"Good. Now that you have the computer, when will you start?"

"Soon. Since we now have the original data, our programing team will evaluate the algorithms and give us a timeline for when we can proceed."

A nod came from the newcomer. "I am told the FBI

agent who uncovered our project in Montana last year has retired from the agency. So, he will no longer be a problem."

Pavlovich frowned. "My dear Kreso, never assume something like that. He will have left case notes about his investigation, and they will be available for whoever takes his place."

Kreso Markovic, known to Sean Kruger as Kevin Marks, stared at the CEO of Odin Analytica for a long moment. "Possibly. But it gives me a little more freedom to get this new project off and running."

"Have you made a contact yet?"

Markovic nodded. "Yes, she is the administrative assistant for the divisional director in Montreal."

"How close are you two?"

"Gentlemen do not tell tales, Tomas. But suffice it to say when we are ready to plant the virus, I will have access to PEC's software."

"Just be careful."

"What about our diversion?"

A smile came to the Russian sitting at the desk. "It is ready and will be implemented shortly. Your idea was brilliant. Force the Americans to look in another direction while we sneak in the back door."

"Save your praise, my friend, the Americans have always been known for being able to do two things at the same time."

***

The Next Morning
New York City

Annika Belsky merged into morning traffic after leaving JFK International. She glanced at her passenger. "You look tired."

"I'm okay, just a little jetlag."

"I'll take you back to our hotel room, and you can catch a nap there."

He nodded and then paused for a few seconds. "How much do you trust Padilla?"

She muttered something to herself and then said out loud, "Not at all."

"Me neither."

Petrov pulled out the business card from his sport coat with a telephone number embossed on it. He stared at it for a moment and then put it back in the pocket. He turned to look at Annika. "I may have a solution for us."

"Good, because he's starting to get on my nerves."

"Where is he?"

"I've no idea, and I don't care to know."

"Is he still calling on a daily basis?"

"It's up to three times a day."

"You're kidding."

She shook her head. "He did the day you left and again yesterday. He's starting to sound desperate."

Petrov furrowed his brow. "Desperate?"

"Yeah, almost whining."

"Is he still threatening to tell the feds where we are?"

"No, not like he did last week. Are you going to pay him?"

Shaking his head, Petrov said, "No. I think we need to eliminate the possibility he might talk as soon as possible. Can you call him?"

"No, he's using a different cell phone each time."

"Okay, next time he calls, tell him I need to talk to him."

CHAPTER 17

Southwest Missouri

Ravi Gupta's flight from Cambridge connected in Charlotte, North Carolina and landed in Springfield just before two in the afternoon. JR waited in the cell phone lot for his friend to call and let him know he was ready to be picked up.

With the professor in the car, JR asked, "Professor, at one time you expressed your interest in returning to India to teach. What happened?"

With a smile, Gupta said, "Money."

"Money? I'm not following you."

With a chuckle, the professor nodded. "In America, as a starting assistant professor, I would make four times what I would be allowed to make in India. As a full-time professor in the United States at a prestigious university, such as MIT, my salary would be five times that of a similar position in my home country. So, yes, money helped with my decision to stay."

JR glanced at the man sitting in his passenger seat. "I

was not aware of the difference."

"You should consider taking a sabbatical from your duties and join us at MIT as a guest lecturer for a semester."

Shaking his head, JR said, "I hate public speaking."

Gupta shook his head. "There's another reason for your reluctance, isn't there?"

"I enjoy what I do, and I excel at it. Not sure I know how to relay information to others."

To JR's surprise, Gupta laughed out loud. "None of us do at first, my friend. I was referring to you hiding your true identity from the world."

JR shot a worried glance at Gupta before returning his attention to the road. "Uh, I'm not following you, Ravi."

"I do not know the reason you changed your name, but this alter ego of yours has been known to me for a while. You and JR Diminski are one and the same person. However, you will always be John Zachara to me."

Silence filled the car as JR drove toward his company's building.

"My friend, you have attended Black Hat before, have you not?"

A nod was the professor's answer.

"I saw you and a lovely woman I assumed to be your wife at Black Hat four years ago. I wasn't sure it was you, so I asked one of the concierges if they could tell me if John Zachara was registered for the conference. When they told me no, I got nosey and learned the man I saw was named JR Diminski. When I returned to Cambridge later in the week, I did a little research to satisfy my curiosity. After numerous searches on the Internet, I found a reference to a JR Diminski in the local Springfield newspaper. The person in the picture was, of course, you. You were receiving an award from the local school system for your donation of funds to standardize the purchasing of computers for every student in the system."

JR remained silent for a few moments then said, "You should have seen the hodgepodge of computers they had. I figured the students were struggling to learn anything on them, so I made the offer."

"That's what the article quoted you as saying. When I read that, I knew John Zachara was, in fact, JR Diminski. Now, the only question I have is, why?"

JR shot a quick glance at his friend then said, "Long story. I'll tell you tonight when it's my turn for you to be my dinner guest."

"I look forward to the conversation."

***

After a tour of the building, JR, Alexia and the professor sat in the sound proof conference room. Gupta asked, "Very impressive. I take it you have offsite backup?"

Alexia nodded. "After the cyberattack on our system two years ago, we located the site in a town south of here. The dedicated connection is reminiscent of the old T1 lines. Only ours is much faster and only connects during randomly scheduled backup periods."

"Excellent." He paused for a moment. "Now that you have demonstrated your real-world skills are far greater than anything I have experienced, how in the world do you expect me to help?"

JR said, "What is your expertise, Ravi?"

"Internet connectivity."

"Exactly. How would you propose to find the location of one specific computer on the web?"

The professor blinked several times and then said, "I would suggest using the network card address, why?"

"Alexia and I have very little experience tracing something like that. You, on the other hand, have written several books on the topic. We need to find one specific computer. And we need to find that computer quickly."

Gupta looked over his reading glasses at JR and then at Alexia. "Why the big rush?"

"Professor, Danny Barton's computer was stolen the night he died. I've studied his algorithms and can tell you we need to find that computer."

Now chewing on the temple tips of his glasses, Gupta stared at the conference tabletop. "I heard rumors of his work—something to do with combining voter registration and consumer data."

"Yes. His method would give any political campaign or party an edge on where to target their advertising."

"Why are you involved, John?"

"Let's just say I'm a consultant for someone in government."

Folding his arms, Gupta wrinkled his nose. "Government? I never thought of you as someone who cared about politics."

With a slight smile, JR said, "I don't. But I do care about my country. If Danny Barton's algorithms get into the wrong hands, and we think they already have, this country could be in danger."

"Just who in government are you consulting with?"

"Have you heard of a man named Joseph Kincaid?"

"Yes, isn't he the national security advisor to the president of the United States?"

"One and the same."

"Uh—that means…"

"Yes." JR pulled out his new ID and showed it to Gupta. "I'm currently working for the president. And we need your help."

Gupta remained perfectly still. His mouth was slightly open as he stared at JR. After a long silence, he smiled. "Before I can begin the search, I will need to know the net card address."

Both JR and Alexia nodded.

"Was it his computer, or was he using one from the

university."

Alexia said, "We've been told he was working for the campaign with the blessing and suggestion of his advisor."

The professor tapped an index finger on his lips. "We don't pay our graduate assistants squat. My guess would be it's a loaner from the department. Therefore, there should be a record somewhere of the particulars of that specific computer."

With a nod, JR said, "That's our assumption as well. However, we can't let anyone know we're looking for it via the network card."

"Why, John?"

"We don't know who we can trust within the university. From what I've been told, Danny's work was unknown outside the walls of his department. How would someone on the outside be aware of the importance of this work?"

"I didn't think of that." He remained quiet for a moment. "Yes, indeed, how did they? But I still need to know the address before we can search for it."

Both Alexia and JR smiled. She said, "You have access to the department computer system, correct?"

"Yes, but I don't have access to those types of records."

"Doesn't matter. If you can get us inside the university computer system, JR and I can find the records we need."

"I can't do tha—" He stopped in mid-word, and a slight smile appeared on his lips. "I need to stop thinking we would be stealing something, don't I?"

JR nodded. "Yes, Ravi you do. We're searching for stolen property with the intention of returning it."

The professor's eyes grew as wide as his smile. "Jolly good. Let's break into MIT's computer system. I've always wanted to be a hacker."

JR closed his eyes and slowly shook his head.

***

A vacant desk on the other side of JR's cubicle became Ravi Gupta's designated spot. After showing Alexia how to access the MIT system, he left her alone, not wanting to know what she would do while inside the university computer.

JR followed her progress from his cubicle, while Ravi wandered around the second floor introducing himself to associates not currently on the phone helping clients. When he saw an instant message appear in the lower right corner of his middle screen, he stood and hurried to the north wall.

The cubicle Alexia occupied stood in the northwest corner of the second-floor cubicle farm. When he arrived, she motioned for him to look at her screen. "What does that look like, JR?"

Bending over, he adjusted his rimless glasses as he stared at the left screen on her desk. He straightened and scanned the room for the location of Gupta. He said, "The professor is talking to Virginia. I'll go get him."

When the two returned to Alexia's station, JR asked the professor, "Who designed the firewall at MIT?"

"I haven't the slightest idea. Why?"

He pointed to Alexia's screen. "Because it's absolutely worthless. It has more holes in it than a slice of Swiss cheese."

Bending over, he studied Alexia's screen. "Oh dear. That's not good, is it?"

JR said, "Not at all."

"I have to report this."

Alexia looked up at the professor. "Not if we fix it."

"What do you mean?"

JR folded his arms. "Ravi, this company does it all the time. We've seen it before, in fact, it's the same worm we found on our system two years ago. If you report the problem, then whoever hacked the system will know we know."

Gupta removed his glasses. "Who attacked your

system?"

"We've always assumed it was Russia."

The professor looked at the screen and then back at JR. "Oh dear. They need to know."

"I agree. But not till we know exactly who is behind the hack."

CHAPTER 18

Southwest Missouri
The Next Day

Kruger ascended the stairs to the second floor of JR's building two at a time. With his trip to Chicago producing more questions than answers, he needed to get JR's opinion concerning the three individuals his investigation had identified so far. When he arrived at the top of the stairs, the normal low-pitch murmur of multiple one-sided conversations did not exist. In its place, he heard an excited cacophony of voices. He noticed JR, in the far corner, talking into a phone, his hands waving in animated gestures. Alexia held a stack of files as she walked rapidly toward JR's position. Next to JR stood a man Kruger recognized from their trip to MIT.

After surveying the room, Kruger noticed JR adamantly waving for him to join them. Navigating around the outside wall, he watched his friend listen to whoever was on the other end of the call. JR pointed to the conference room, which Kruger entered immediately. Alexia joined him and closed the door once they were inside.

"What is all the commotion about?"

"We stirred up a hornet's nest this morning."

"Apparently, what happened?"

"Professor Gupta gave us access to the MIT computer system yesterday, and we found it compromised. I'm not sure if compromised is the correct word, but in Spanish we would say, *enormemente jodido.*"

"That bad?"

She nodded.

"Whose JR talking to?"

"He's arguing with MIT's IT manager."

"Who's winning the argument?"

She grinned. "JR."

"When did Gupta get here?"

"Yesterday." She chuckled. "He already knew about JR's change in identity. They had dinner last night, and JR explained the whole thing. The professor laughed the entire time JR told the story."

"He looks concerned."

"Who, JR?"

"No, the professor."

"He is. They think a lot of the computer science department's research data from the past two years has been copied and stolen. There is also a concern that many of the papers they are about to publish have corrupted data. The professor thinks it will mean a complete reevaluation of every research project currently underway or recently published."

"What about finding the computer?"

"Ravi believes he may have found it."

"Where?"

"Estonia."

Kruger frowned. "Estonia? What's in Estonia?"

Alexia put the files she carried on the conference table.

She tapped the stack. "JR vaguely remembers a client whose computer was hacked in a similar fashion to the MIT computer. These are hard copies of client solution files from the past five years. Each folder contains a single page summary of what the client's problems were and our solution. The answer to where in Estonia may be hidden in them."

"I didn't think JR kept paper files."

"He doesn't. I printed these out so more than one person could sort through them at one time. Now that you're here…"

JR entered the room, followed by Gupta. The professor approached Kruger and offered his hand. "It is good to see you again, Agent Kruger."

"Nice to see you as well, Professor." He turned to JR. "Did you win the argument with the IT manager?"

"I'm surprised the man has a job at MIT."

Gupta said, "If the damage is as bad as we think, he won't have one very long."

Placing his cell phone in his pocket, JR nodded. "It's a mess."

"I understand someone found Barton's computer."

Pointing to the professor, JR said, "He did. Alexia and I just watched, but we learned a lot in the process."

Tilting his head slightly, Kruger asked, "Where is it?"

"Estonia."

"Alexia already told me that. Where in Estonia?"

"That, my friend, is the question we will answer by going through these files."

Kruger frowned. "Why not just do a system inquiry?"

With a sly smile, JR said, "We don't keep these types of files on our server. I keep them on a flash drive so if anyone hacks our system again, these files will not be accessible. So, to make the search faster, we printed them out. Now that you're here, you can help."

***

Two hours later, Kruger stared at a sheet of paper with the words Odin Analytica buried in the third paragraph. He asked, "What is Odin Analytica?"

Without saying a word, Alexia started typing on her laptop.

JR raised his head and reached for his coffee. "Never heard of it. What's the context?"

"It says here they're located in Tallinn, Estonia."

Gupta slapped his head with the palm of his hand. "Of course, now I remember. Estonia has a highly developed technology sector. One of the best in Europe. Odin Analytica is the country's leading data analysis company. Four years ago, one of my graduate students, who was from Estonia, returned to the country to work for them. He told me he would be moving to Tallinn. Since I had never heard of them, I checked them out. Very aggressive and forward-looking company."

Alexia looked up from her laptop. "Odin Analytica is owned by a man named Tomas Pavlovich. His holding company bought Odin three years ago and has transformed it into a political consulting company for Western European democracies."

JR stared at her for several seconds. He then turned to Kruger. "Let me see the page referring to Odin, Sean."

Once he held the sheet, he scanned it quickly. "This is the incident I remembered. It was right after the attack we experienced, Alexia. Do you remember the community college in Florida?"

"Oh dear, yes I do."

Kruger frowned. "Want to enlighten Ravi and me?"

JR stood and walked out of the conference room and went straight to the coffee service. He returned and said, "Now that I think about it, the community college was probably a test run for them before they went after bigger fish, like MIT."

Gupta clasped his hands in front of him. "I'm not following you, John."

Looking at the professor, JR said, "Russian hackers like to test their malware on similar destinations before they attack their main target." He held up the one sheet Kruger found and continued. "This college contacted us after one of their assistant professors noticed test scores for his finals in the colleges main computer did not match his hard-copy records. After checking test scores for the entire semester, they found every member of the student body's grades were corrupt. That's when they called us."

"What did you find?"

"The hackers took advantage of a zero-day vulnerability within the college's grading software."

Kruger tilted his head. "What's a zero-day vulnerability?"

Gupta turned to Kruger. "Basically, it is a vulnerability a hacker or a group of hackers discovers in a software program. If the vulnerability is exploited by a hacker before a patch can be made, it is called a zero-day attack. Which means any computer with that specific software is vulnerable to a hack. Once the software company is made aware of the error, they have to hurry and fix the problem. That is why you get software updates at random times."

Looking at JR, Kruger said, "I take it you guys found the problem and fixed it."

After taking a sip of coffee, JR shook his head. "No, we contacted the company that developed the software and told them about the error. They patched it and provided the update to all their clients who used the software. More than a dozen colleges had the same problem. When we found the malware the hackers downloaded, we compared it to our library of viruses."

"And?"

"It bore the signature of the same virus that hit our

system. And, I'll make a bet the one that hit the MIT computer resembles it as..." He stopped and stared at his coffee."

"As what, JR?"

Alexia's eyes widened. "JR, are you thinking the same thing I'm thinking?"

With a nod, JR walked over to the white board on the one wall of the room not made of glass. After setting his coffee cup on the conference table, he took a marker from the shelf beneath the board and drew four dots, each as the corner of a square. He turned back to face the room and said, "Let's label each of these dots as one of the hacks we know about." He wrote on the top left dot, *WH*, then one on the top right, *MIT*, bottom right, he wrote *CC FL,* and finally, on the lower left he marked it, *Ozark Computer*. He turned again. "What do each of these hacks have in common?"

Alexia smiled, Kruger rested his chin on his palm, and Gupta adjusted his glasses.

JR turned again and wrote *Estonia – OA* in the center of the square. He then drew a line from the *CC FL* dot to the center. "We know the college in Florida was connected to Odin. We know the virus used in that attack was similar to the one used to attack our company." He drew a straight line from the *CC FL* to *Ozark Computer*. He then drew a line to the *WH* and then to *MIT*. When the square was complete, he connected the dots in the four corners to the center.

"They are all connected with a common style of malware."

Kruger straightened and crossed his arms. "JR, what's the bottom line to all of this?"

"Sean, the bottom line is we always assumed Russians hacked our system. Now that we know the same type of attack was made on the community college and MIT, I think we have to assume the hacks originated in Estonia with Odin Analytica." He tapped the spot in the center of the square.

Kruger raised a hand and tapped his lips with an index finger. "Estonia was in the Soviet sphere until the early 90s, JR. That's almost three decades without Russian influence."

"I know. What do the Russians do better than most countries?"

Nodding slowly, Kruger said, "Long-term planning."

"Exactly. I'm not saying it actually happened this way, but what if the Soviets left behind numerous young believers within Estonia, and those young believers are now in control of key government and corporate positions?"

"You would have a de facto Russian influence in the country."

JR nodded.

Kruger turned to Alexia. "Can you prove Odin Analytica did any of the three hacks?"

She said, "The community college one we can. The signatures of the White House email hack and the other two viruses are the same, which gives me reason to believe Odin is involved."

"Wouldn't that lead a good investigator to believe Odin Analytica is a so-called entity of interest in the death of Danny Barton and Loretta Floyd?"

"Yes, it would, JR." Kruger paused. "Now how do we prove it?"

Gupta smiled. "We pinpoint the location of Danny's computer."

Alexia and JR turned their attention to the professor. They said in unison, "How?"

"Since we believe Odin may be involved in the MIT attack, we can assume that is how they learned of Danny's research."

Kruger held up his index finger. "If we assume they had

access to the MIT computer, we also have to assume they would have access to Danny's research. Why kill him?"

With a shake of his head, Gupta said, "They wouldn't necessarily have access to it. If he kept it off the server, they would only know what his research was about. Danny would have kept his actual files separate from the university."

Kruger did not answer right away. Finally, he said, "But they would know who he was. It would be simple to locate him from there to get his student records and figure out where he lived."

The professor nodded. "I agree, Sean. If they are responsible, all we have to do now is gain access to Odin's ISP provider. Once we have it, we can look for the stolen computer's network card address."

JR stared at Gupta for several seconds, then stood and exited the conference room. He immediately sat in his cubicle and started typing on his computer's keyboard.

CHAPTER 19

Washington, DC

Joseph knocked on the doorframe of the president's private office. When Griffin looked up, Joseph said, "Got a minute?"

"For you, yes."

As was his habit, he sat in the wing back chair immediately across from the president's desk. "Todd Perkins is making noise about Sean. He's leaked the information to a particular senator on the Judiciary Committee."

"Let me guess, Krista Brock?"

"One and the same."

"Is she going to cause us trouble?"

"As you know, she is one of your more vocal critics."

"Yes, I'm aware of that." Griffin frowned and tapped his finger on the desk. "Joseph, my instinct tells me we need to make this a permanent position for Sean and JR. Not this temporary status we fabricated. Can we place Kruger and JR inside the Secret Service?"

"You can JR, but the Secret Service abides by the same rule as the FBI: an agent must retire at fifty-seven."

"What about Stumpf? When's he due back?"

"He's had a minor setback. According to his wife, his doctor is being overcautious."

"What kind of setback?"

"She wouldn't say."

"I hope he's okay."

Joseph nodded. "Me, too."

"In the meantime, what do we do about Perkins? Can I replace him?"

"You can, but the optics would be bad."

"Optics are the least of my concern, I'm concerned about the welfare of this country, the deaths of the campaign workers, and a possible computer breach at the White House. You obviously have a solution, Joseph, or you wouldn't have brought this to me."

"Yes, sir."

"Tell me."

"The last communication from Sean indicated they'd found links between the White House email hack, the death of the campaign workers, and a foreign entity."

Griffin remained quiet as he listened.

"The foreign country in question is Estonia. Under the executive order you signed, neither Sean or JR would have the authority to go overseas in their current position. However—"

Catching on to where Joseph was headed, he blurted out, "Defense Intelligence Agency."

"Exactly. Even though it is a part of the Defense Department, it operates independently from the DOD. Also, you as the president, can make an exception for agents until they are sixty."

"Why didn't we think of this before now?"

"Too much going on. I apologize, sir."

Griffin smiled. "Apology accepted." He stared out the

window behind Joseph. "Would this solve the problem I mentioned earlier about allowing Sean to continue to help us out on other projects?"

"Yes, sir. There is an added bonus."

"And that is?"

"Your ability to reorganize a department without congressional authority. Once Kruger is sixty, you can appoint him as a director of a new department within the DIA. That keeps him around even after he reaches mandatory retirement. If he wants to."

The president remained quiet as he thought through Joseph's proposal. "Will this resolve our problem with Perkins and Senator Brock?"

Joseph shrugged. "I doubt it. But it will short-circuit Perkins' ability to do anything to stop Kruger's inquiry."

"Ask DIA Director Santos to join us today."

"Already did. He'll be here around noon."

"Good. He can be our guest for lunch."

With a smile, Joseph nodded.

***

Director of DIA Bert Santos shook Joseph's hand. "I take it this is a friendly meeting since we're in your office."

"When have we ever had an unfriendly meeting, Bert?"

"Well, there's always a first time."

"It's friendly. Very friendly."

"Good. What's on your mind?"

"You've heard of a retired FBI agent named Sean Kruger, haven't you?"

"Who hasn't. He's one of the agents who saved the president and his wife from an assassin in San Francisco before Griffin became a senator."

"One and the same. He's doing a favor for the president right now."

"Good for him."

"Bert, it involves the death of two campaign workers in Cambridge."

Santos tilted his head. "Thought they both died in accidents."

Joseph shook his head. "That was the story given to the news media. Their deaths were not accidents."

"Okay, you have my attention."

"Danny Burton worked as a researcher for the campaign. He was also a promising grad student at MIT in the computer science department. His specialty was data analysis and number theory."

"I'm not going to like what's next, am I?"

"Probably not. Danny's computer was stolen the night he died. In fact, we believe he was killed specifically to steal his computer. Sean Kruger is looking into his murder."

Santos remained silent.

"Sean and his team have determined the computer was stolen to gain access to MIT's VPN."

"Is that a danger to the US government?"

"Not directly. But—"

"There's always a however, isn't there?"

"In this case yes. One of Sean's team is a cybersecurity expert. He believes whoever stole the computer is using it to get the Barton kid's research."

"Spit it out, Joseph."

"His algorithms."

"What kind of algorithms?"

"The kind that can predict an election with a 96 percent accuracy rate."

"In the wrong hands, that could be exceedingly dangerous."

"Sean and his team think there's a foreign country involved."

"Joseph, you've been dancing around the reason I'm here since I arrived. What is it?"

"The president would like to make Sean and his team DIA agents."

Santos chuckled. "Is that all?"

"He also wants them to be independent."

"Hmmm. If I say no?"

"You know the president. He does not like to micromanage. You were chosen for your current position because you don't need adult supervision."

With a smile, Santos took the comment as it was meant. Supportive. "Why not put him back under the FBI?"

"Personnel issue."

"Ahh—Perkins?"

"Correct."

"What about Secret Service?"

"We need the broader scope of DIA for this to work."

"Have any of his team been in the military?"

Joseph nodded. "One's an ex-Navy SEAL, and the other was in the original cyberwarfare command."

"What about Kruger?"

"No. He has a PhD in psychology and over twenty-five years with the FBI."

Santos laughed, "Good enough, 50 percent of the individuals working for DIA don't have military experience. Will they need assistance?"

"We haven't thought it through that far. We just need his team sanctioned by a government agency with international reach."

"Why?"

"They've followed the computer to the town of Tallinn, Estonia."

With raised eyebrows, Santos said, "They can find the exact physical location of one specific computer even if it is being hidden?"

Joseph nodded.

"Will they share that information when this is over?"

"I'll make sure they do."

"Tell them, welcome to the DIA."

"Good. Do you have time for lunch with the president?"

***

"Joseph, I really don't have time to fly to Washington, DC right now. We're making progress and—"

Joseph cut him off. "We need you, JR, and Jimmie in DC tonight, Sean."

Holding the cell phone tight against his ear, Kruger closed his eyes and blew out a breath. "Why?"

"As of noon today, the three of you became special agents with the DIA."

"We're what?"

"Defense Intelligence Agency. Being agents for the DIA gives all of you the authority to travel overseas if necessary. It also gets you out from under the FBI's shadow."

"What did Perkins do?"

"Complained to a Senator."

"Figures."

"One other benefit."

"What's that."

"Under an exception signed by the president, you can remain an agent until you are sixty. You might want to actually retire then. Who knows?"

"Okay. I like that. How are we getting there?"

"DIA Gulfstream. It will pick everyone up at two."

Glancing at his watch, Kruger said, "That doesn't give us much time to pack a bag."

"Figure it out."

"I'll tell JR."

***

JR sat across from his friend with Jimmie Gibbs directly

behind him in the passenger compartment of the small Gulfstream as it slipped through the sky toward Joint Base Andrews. Turning toward Kruger, JR said, "Too bad we don't get frequent-flyer miles on these things."

Smiling, Kruger nodded and then turned serious. "Do you have any idea where the three individuals we know about are located?"

"Unfortunately, no. But Alexia thinks she has a lead on Art Padilla."

"Where?"

"She checked the references given when he applied for the campaign assistant director's job. He provided an address in Plymouth as his permanent residence. It was vetted and, at the time, he did live there. However, that's not the case now. She found a change of address listing within the USPS computer."

Kruger smiled. "You're kidding? Where?"

"New York City."

"Huh." He turned to stare out the window next to his seat. Clouds passed beneath the aircraft in slow motion as the jet flew east. "Do you know where in the city?"

"Yeah."

"Did you bring a duffel?"

With a nod, JR said, "I know better than to come to one of these meetings without a change of clothes."

With a chuckle, Kruger turned to look back at Gibbs. "You up for a detour to New York City after our meeting in DC?"

"Always. What or who's there?"

"Your wife may have found one of our suspects."

"Remind me never to hide from her."

Kruger smiled and retrieved his cell phone from his sport coat pocket to make a call.

CHAPTER 20

Cambridge, MA

Ginger Bell answered the phone on her desk as she noted the time on its LED screen. "Detective Bell. How may I help you?"

"You the cop looking into Danny Barton's death?"

Sitting straighter, she grabbed a pen and found a scratch pad to write on. "Yes, who's calling?"

"He was murdered, you know. All those talking heads on TV don't know shit. He was killed."

"Yes, sir. May I ask who's calling, please?"

"Not important. I have a video of the bitch who stole his satchel. She didn't care about Danny. All she cared about was stealing what was in that bag."

"Sir, what do you mean you have a video?"

"My security camera caught the whole thing. She was the one who pointed to Danny as the truck pulled away from the curb and ran him over. Later, I saw her pick up the bag and walk away as Danny lay there dying."

"Does your video show Danny being struck?"

"No, just the bitch. It does have a good shot of the truck's license plate."

Bell started to get excited but remembered she did not have the man's name. "Sir, is there a way you could get me a copy of this video so we can take a look at it?"

"I can't get involved."

"Why not?"

The caller did not answer.

"Did you know Danny, sir?"

"Yeah."

"Can you tell me how you know him?"

"I could, but I don't want to. You'd be able to identify me, and I can't let that happen."

"Sir, the courts won't let us use undocumented evidence. Now, tell me your name and when we can get a copy of the video."

"I've posted it to YouTube. Here's the link." He told her and then repeated it. "Go get it, I'll wait. Once you have it, I'll delete it."

"Please, stay on the line, sir."

"You've got five minutes. Any longer than that, and I hang up."

Bell typed in the address the man gave her, but she reversed two numbers, which caused the link to fail. After checking her work against what the man told her, she repeated it and found the video clip. The clip lasted thirty seconds and showed a clear picture of the woman's face as she stood by the cab of the truck. Bell could easily read the front license plate. She took the call off hold and said, "Are you still there, sir?"

"Yeah. Did you get it?"

"This is a very helpful video. But for it to be used in a court of law, I will need your name and address."

"Sorry. Use it the best you can." The call ended, and Bell stared at the now silent handset.

She pressed the end call button on the phone and dialed

zero. An operator came on the line. "Can I help you, detective?"

"Can you tell me the phone number of the call you just patched through?"

"Yes." She read it off.

"Thanks, Sheryl."

Bell turned to her desk computer and accessed a reverse directory program the department maintained for just such situations. After entering the number, the results came back within seconds as *Ginger Bell.*

She quickly searched her purse for her phone and found it in a side pocket. Curious as to how someone could fake a number, she dialed the number for the cybercrime division.

"Mannford."

"Bobby, this is Ginger."

"Hey, Ginger, what's up?"

"Is it possible to fake a cell phone call?"

"Sure, through spoofing."

"Say again?"

"It's called spoofing. It's usually done with a computer and VoIP calling software."

"English, Bobby."

He chuckled. "VoIP is Voice over Internet Protocol and is a phone call using the Internet. The ability to spoof a number is easy with numerous open-code software programs. Scam artists use it all the time. In fact, I have a whole stack of complaints on my desk concerning those types of calls."

"Is there a way to trace the call?"

"Way above my paygrade, Ginger."

"Okay, thanks, Bobby." She ended the call and retrieved a thick business card holder from her right-hand top desk drawer. She opened it and found the card she needed. Once the number was dialed, she waited.

***

Kruger glanced at the caller ID and quickly answered the call. "Kruger."

"Agent, this is Detective Ginger Bell."

"Yes, Detective, what can I do for you?"

"I just had a strange phone call about the death of Danny Barton."

Raising his eyebrows, he said, "What do you mean by strange?"

"The caller wouldn't identify himself, but he did supply us with a security camera shot of the woman and the truck." She summarized her call with the man. "When I checked the caller's number, it turned out to be my cell phone number. How is that possible? Do you know anyone who would understand how the guy made the phone call?"

"I do. In fact, both he and I are in DC preparing to leave for New York City. Do you mind if we divert to your location first?"

"Not at all. Let me know when you are arriving, and I'll pick you up."

"I'll call you back with the details."

***

While, JR worked on his laptop in the back seat of the detective's vehicle, Kruger and Jimmie Gibbs used a screen shot from the video to determine the location of the security camera responsible for the video. After an hour of checking angles, they located the camera above the front door of a small pharmacy on the opposite side of the street from the now-closed campaign office.

The young detective said, "No wonder we didn't check this camera. It's facing the wrong direction from where Danny was killed."

Bell's statement caused Gibbs to furrow his brow and Kruger to roll his eyes and slowly shake his head.

With Jimmie standing in the same spot as the woman in the video, the now retired FBI agent checked the angle of his friend's position versus the printout. He glanced up and waved for Gibbs to join him. He then turned to the detective. "Have you located the truck?"

She nodded. "They located it at a U-Haul rental place in Boston. Our forensics team is going over it with a fine-tooth comb."

"Good. If they find anything, let me know."

Bell nodded.

Staring intently at the image of the woman, Kruger had the strange feeling he'd seen her before. When Gibbs arrived at the pharmacy, Kruger showed the picture of the woman to him. "Does she look familiar?"

Gibbs took the photo and studied it for a few moments. "Yeah, she does. I can't remember…" He stopped suddenly and looked at Kruger. "The picture JR found of Thorton and Peters at the campaign rally. There was a woman standing to the left of Peters. JR has a copy of it on his laptop, doesn't he?"

"I believe he does."

Back at Bell's car, JR pulled up the image on his computer. Gibbs smiled and folded his arms. Kruger concentrated on the still image of the security camera and then compared it to the woman standing next to Peters. "How about that? You're right." He looked up at the ex-SEAL. "This is starting to look like a conspiracy, doesn't it?"

"It sure does."

***

An hour later, Gibbs and Kruger were standing behind the computer wizard in his hotel room as he worked on his laptop.

JR said, "Alexia has cross-referenced the woman's

picture against the FBI and Interpol's database. So far, she's coming up empty."

Kruger started to pace. "It's not a coincidence she's in the campaign rally photo—they know each other." He stopped pacing and snapped his fingers. "Kristin Seaton."

Gibbs snapped his fingers. You're right. She might recognize her."

JR looked up. "Who?"

"She manages the office building where Peters leased an office he only used to meet with Thorton." Kruger accessed his phone and started searching numbers he recently called. "Here it is." He pressed the send icon on the only number in his list with a Chicago area code. She answered on the fourth ring.

"President's Tower Leasing, this is Kristin."

"Kristin, Sean Kruger. We met with you last week?"

"Yes, Agent, how are you?"

"Did you get any grief from the FBI agents?"

"I didn't. They interviewed my boss for a couple of hours. He later told me it was a big waste of time."

"Good. I'm glad you didn't have to get involved. Do you remember anyone else in your dealings with Mike Peters?"

"No, I only dealt with him. Why?"

"We've identified another individual we suspect may have been involved with him."

"He was the only individual I dealt with. Sorry."

"If we send you a picture, would you at least look at it?"

"I'd be happy to. But remember, there just wasn't anyone else involved with the transaction."

"I understand that. But I need to cover all my bases."

"Very well."

"We're going to send it to you via email. Where do you want it sent?"

She recited the address and said, "Are you going to wait?"

"I have to. It's pretty important."

"Very well. I'll put you on speaker so I can use the computer."

"Thank you."

After JR sent the picture, Kruger waited as he heard the woman's fingernails clicking on the keyboard. After several minutes, he heard in the background, "Oh dear, she does look familiar." More typing and another lengthy pause.

Finally, she picked up the phone and took it off speaker. "Agent, I have to apologize. I do recognize her."

Kruger smiled. "Who is she?"

"She leases a similar-size office down the hall from the one Mike Peters occupied. I haven't seen her since she signed the paperwork four months ago. Our files include a copy of her driver's license."

"Could you send a copy of the picture to the email address we just used?"

"Sure, just a second."

He heard more typing and then Kristin said, "Her name is Annika Belsky. The lease agreement paperwork claims she runs a consulting firm."

"Is that information in the file you're sending?"

"I can include it."

"Good. Thanks, Kristin."

The email showed up two minutes after the call ended. Kruger stared at the photo of the driver's license on JR's laptop screen. The image was the same woman in the security camera video and the photograph from the campaign rally in the newspaper.

Folding his arms, he said, "Well, well, gentlemen, now comes the hard part. Finding her."

CHAPTER 21

Washington, DC

**WHITE HOUSE MUM ON ILLINOIS ATTORNEY
GENERAL THORTON BEING CHARGED WITH
MURDER AND POSSIBLE ESPIONAGE**
By Lauran Riley, CNN White House correspondent
Updated 1 hour ago, June 9

Washington, DC (CNN) – White House Press Secretary
Sara Woolworth said in a statement this afternoon, the
president will have no comments on a developing story
concerning Illinois Attorney General Derick Thorton. The
man is being charged with orchestrating the murder of a
Griffin campaign worker in Cambridge, MA. Considered
an unfortunate accident at first, Daniel Barton died in a hit-
and-run incident ten days ago. A security camera video of
Thorton stealing Barton's laptop while the young man lay
dying in the street has been obtained by CNN. In the video,
Thorton can be seen retrieving a satchel from beneath a
parked car twenty yards from where the young grad student

was struck by a large truck. The Cambridge Police Department has recovered the truck and found evidence it is the vehicle that struck Barton on the night of May 29. A federal court in Chicago filed charges of murder and conspiracy today against Thorton.

Thorton was challenging President Roy Griffin in a failed primary fight to unseat the popular president in his first presidential contest. Griffin was appointed vice president by then President Bryant after the suicide of Vice President Pittman. When Bryant died two weeks later of a massive brain aneurysm, Griffin became president.

CNN will update this story as events unfold.

***

Kruger frowned as he read the CNN story on his cell phone. The story contained a grainy picture of Thorton bending over and holding the leather briefcase by the strap. He showed it to JR and said, "Does that picture look familiar?"

Pushing his glasses up his nose, JR studied the image and nodded. "Same photo we have, only it's Annika Belsky bending over. Excellent Photoshop techniques, I might add. Hard to tell it's fake."

Taking his cell phone back, Kruger tilted his head. "Whoever did this had access to the security camera video. How?"

"Simple, Sean. They either got a copy before it was given to the Cambridge PD, or there's a leak within the department."

"Yeah, those were my thoughts. I hope the latter isn't the case."

"It should be easy to find out. Check with Ginger Bell to make sure the Cambridge PD still has the original. If they do, the fake one would be easy to disprove. But—"

"Yeah, but if they don't, we know there's a leak."

"Exactly."

Kruger pulled out his cell phone and searched for the number. He pressed send and waited.

"Homicide, this is Detective Parker."

"Detective, is Ginger Bell available?"

There was silence on the phone for several moments. "Who's calling?"

"Special Agent Sean Kruger with the DIA."

"Uh—Agent, when was your last contact with Detective Bell?"

The question gave Kruger pause, as he considered the implications of the statement. "Detective Parker, what's happened to Ginger?"

"I need to know when you last spoke to her."

"Yesterday morning. Again, Detective, what's happened?"

"She didn't show up for her shift this morning. We sent a patrol car to her apartment. They found it ransacked and no trace of her. Her department laptop is missing as well."

Kruger remained quiet for a moment. Finally, he asked, "Can you connect me to your chief of police, Detective?"

"I'll see if she's available."

An instrumental version of the iconic Beatles song, "Let It Be" could be heard as he waited for the call to be transferred. Kruger wrinkled his nose as he listened, hoping the horrendous version would not stick in his head for the rest of the day.

Thankfully, the wait was short. When the call connected, Marlene Hoffman screamed, *What the hell did you get Ginger Bell involved in, Kruger?*

Shutting his eyes, Kruger debated about ending the call, but concern about the missing detective overcame his distaste for Hoffman. He said, "If I remember correctly, this investigation started on your watch, Hoffman. I came in after the fact. The question should be what do you know about Ginger's disappearance?"

There was silence on the call as he heard rapid breathing. He finally heard, "At this stage, not much. When did you last speak with her?"

"Yesterday morning, she called me about a new security camera video she received from a caller who would not identify himself."

"That information is not in her case notes. What did the video show?"

"It showed a clear picture of a woman, we have identified as Annika Belsky, pointing out Barton to the driver of the truck. We have photographic evidence that same female later retrieved Barton's computer."

Hoffman was quiet for an unusual long length of time. "What do you mean you have evidence the woman retrieved Barton's computer?"

"One of the early discovered security tapes from the neighborhood shows a woman recovering the computer bag Barton carried from underneath a parked car shortly after the accident. Detective Bell placed a copy of that video in your department's evidence locker."

"The video in our possession shows a man taking the computer."

Kruger grew quiet and stared at JR who stood across the room listening. Finally, he asked Hoffman, "Is it the same video being circulated by CNN?"

"What do you mean being circulated by CNN? We haven't released a video, I just viewed it this afternoon after we learned Detective Bell was missing."

"Someone has altered the original security video. I believe you have another problem on your hands in addition to a missing detective."

The only sound on the call suddenly became the chief of police breathing rapidly. Finally, he heard, "I'll have to get back to you, Kruger."

Ending the call, Kruger asked, "You still have the original copy of the security camera video we got from the computer guy in Cambridge, don't you?"

JR nodded. "Is Detective Bell missing?"

"Unfortunately, she is. Can you prove the one you have is the original?"

"It's a direct transfer from the security camera, remember?"

"Hoffman claims she didn't know about the CNN video but said the one she watched in the evidence room this afternoon showed Thorton taking the bag."

"Not possible, Sean."

"I understand it's not possible. So, who switched the videos?"

JR took his glasses off and cleaned them with a tissue. "Probably the same person who gave the video to CNN."

"Can you tell if a security camera video has been altered?"

"Yes. There will be pixel disparities."

Kruger started pacing. JR sat on the arm of a sofa.

"What are you thinking?"

"JR, how easy is it to determine a photo has been altered?"

"Fairly easy with the right software."

"Would most police departments have the capability?"

"My guess is most metro police departments would. Why?"

"Would CNN?"

"Most definitely."

"What if the video hasn't been altered but was staged?"

Frowning, JR asked, "What do you mean staged?"

"What we saw on CNN tonight was a typical security camera long shot, correct?"

JR nodded.

"The guy looked like Thorton, correct?"

"Don't know. I didn't go to Chicago."

"Trust me, he resembled the man."

Kruger stopped pacing and checked his watch. "Get

your computer. We're going to visit the man whose camera captured the video shot."

***

Kruger stood in the exact same spot where Danny Barton stepped off the curb ten days previous. As he had during his first trip to Cambridge, he looked at the third-floor of a five-story building where he had spotted the Ring security camera on his previous visit. He frowned as he pointed toward it. "JR, see the window with the closed blinds on the third floor?"

"Yeah."

"There was a Ring camera on the outside eight days ago. It's not there anymore."

"That's not good."

"Nope." Kruger glanced both ways before he led JR across the street.

Five minutes later, they stood at the door to the apartment occupied by Deloach. He pounded on the door three times and received the same response three times. Silence from within.

A tall young man with blond hair tied back in a ponytail walked past them toward another apartment door. As he passed, he said, "I haven't seen Kenny in about a week."

Kruger turned to him. "Do you see him often?"

The man nodded. "Yeah, I usually see him every day. I'm normally headed for work when he's coming back from getting coffee at the shop next door."

"Did he move?"

"Who's asking?"

JR and Kruger showed their DIA identifications.

"Wow, I always thought Kenny was just paranoid about the feds being after him."

"We're not after him. We just need to ask him a few questions. Now, did he move?"

The man shook his head. "Are you kidding? He's got too much shit in there to move. It'd take days just to unhook all the electronics."

"Thanks, that's good information."

"No problem. Maybe he's just out."

When the man disappeared inside his apartment, Kruger looked at JR. "I'm calling Marlene. We need a wellness check."

***

Two hours later, Cambridge EMTs removed the body of Kenneth Deloach from his apartment for a trip to the coroner's office and an autopsy. Numerous detectives searched rooms as the Cambridge police chief spoke to Kruger. "Is this where the original video was found?"

"Yes. The camera used to take the shot is gone."

"How do you know?"

"It was outside that window." He pointed to the wall to their left where the blinds hid the night scene beyond the apartment. "The reason we checked on Deloach was I noticed the camera missing."

JR sat on the couch looking through Deloach's laptop. Marlene glared at him. "What the hell is he doing? He's destroying evidence." Her tone grew harsher as she directed her comments toward JR. "Get away from that—"

Kruger moved in between Hoffman and JR. "He's not destroying evidence. The computer was wiped clean before we got here. There weren't any fingerprints left on it." Kruger turned to his friend. "Find anything?"

JR scrolled through photos on the computer screen and then looked up. "Want to see a picture of the person who killed Deloach?"

CHAPTER 22

New York City

The taxi stopped and deposited Arthur Padilla at the corner of 5th Avenue and E. 96th Street on the eastern side of Central Park. The instructions received from Mike Peters requested they meet on at the East 96th Street playground. With lots of pedestrian traffic, it would be a safe place to conduct business without drawing too much attention.

Padilla arrived sixty minutes before the appointed time. This would give him ample time to scout out the location and determine appropriate routes for escape should he be double-crossed.

By nine a.m., Padilla stood behind a large maple tree across from the playground. This position provided a perfect spot to watch bicycle riders and pedestrian traffic traveling beside the playground. If things got dicey, he could slip into the brush and over the knoll, allowing him to disappear into Central Park without being spotted by anyone standing near the playground.

Peters' delay in paying him for his role in obtaining the

computer diminished his faith in the man. Not that he ever trusted him in the first place.

At 9:12 he noticed Peters approaching the playground from the south on the sidewalk next to the park. Keeping in the shadows, Padilla searched for anyone following or paying too much attention to Peters. He saw no one.

Stepping out from behind the tree, he looked both ways on East Drive and hurried across the street. Peters noticed and stopped walking as Padilla approached.

"Do you have my money?"

"Arthur, we've had this discussion before. Until we can determine the value of the information on the computer, we can't offer you top dollar. You don't want to cheat yourself, do you?"

Padilla tilted his head and pursed his lips. "How do I know you won't stiff me by telling me the info on it was worthless?"

"Seems we have to trust each other, doesn't it?"

"Something I am less inclined to do each day."

"Really, Arthur, you have no reason to distrust me."

"Danny wasn't supposed to be killed."

Peters shrugged. "Shit happens."

"He was a good kid. A little naïve, but a good kid."

"Like I said…"

Padilla narrowed his eyes and appraised the man standing three feet from him. "Here's the deal—no more in-person meetings. Money is to be deposited into my account by Friday. Or—"

With a snarl, Peters said, "Or what, Arthur? You'll go to the police? I think not."

At this moment, Padilla noticed two men converging on his location: one from the north and another from the south. Without saying a word, he dashed back across the street and up the brushy knoll. The two men rushed to catch up, but when they got to the top of the knoll, they stopped. The vegetation and brush were so thick, they could not determine which way the fugitive had traveled.

The taller of the two turned, looked at Peters, and shook his head.

***

Padilla's preplanned escape route worked better than he had anticipated. Within five minutes he determined no one followed. He slowed his pace and blended into the midmorning occupants of Central Park. By eleven, he found himself back at the extended-stay hotel. He packed the few personal items he'd brought with him and exited the building without advising the front desk of his departure.

After a short taxi ride, paid for with cash, he found himself at Moynihan Train Hall buying an Amtrak ticket. The twenty-three-hour trip would get him out of New York City to Chicago, where he would make contact with Derick Thorton. He and the ex-attorney general of Illinois could collaborate on the story Padilla was prepared to tell the media.

***

Chicago
The Next Day

Derick Thorton appeared behind the glass in the visitors' section of the Cook County Jail and stared in surprise at the man waiting for him. He picked up the handset and waited for the visitor to do the same.

"Who the hell are you?"

Arthur Padilla said, "Your ticket out of here."

Thorton laughed. "Right. I'm not buying what you're selling." He started to hang up the intercom.

Padilla held his hand up and pointed to the handset.

When Thorton could hear again, the visitor said, "I can give your attorney proof the video was altered."

Raising his eyebrows, the prisoner said, "I'm listening."

"Who was your campaign manager?"

"A scumbag named Michael Peters, why?"

"His real name is Mikhail Petrov. He set you up to draw attention away from their real plan. He then had your image substituted in the security video so you would be accused of the murder. You apparently don't have an alibi for that night, am I right?"

Thorton stared hard at the man, "Yes."

"I didn't think so. They played you. You were with a woman no one can find?"

"How'd you know?"

"Do I have your attention now, Derick?"

"Yes."

"I was privy to their planning for a while."

"You know these people?"

"Yeah, I worked for them and they screwed me. Time to get payback."

"Who are you?"

Padilla proceeded to tell him.

***

Michael Peters listened quietly as he learned Arthur Padilla had vanished. When the caller stopped talking, he asked, "You're sure he's left the hotel?"

"Yes. He didn't check out, but all of his clothes and personal items are gone."

"Did anyone see him leave?"

"Not that we can find. There are a lot of exits, and the front desk isn't manned all the time."

"This is the second time you've lost him, Dimitri."

The man on the other end of the call did not respond.

"Keep looking for him."

The call ended, and Peters walked to the window of the apartment he shared with Annika. Sound came from the front door, and he turned to see her enter.

"Have they found Padilla?"

He shook his head and returned his attention to the view out the window. "He's gone."

She frowned. "How much does he know?"

"Enough."

"Where do you think he'll go?"

He whirled around and growled. "If I knew that, I'd go find him."

"Zip it, Mikhail." She folded her arms. "Bringing Padilla into our confidence was your idea. So far, it has not been one of your best."

Taking a deep breath, he said, "I know." He walked over to the TV and used the remote to change the channel to CNN. "Have you seen the video, yet?"

She shook her head. "No. Does it look convincing?"

"I believe it does." He threw the remote onto the sofa and stared at the TV for a few moments. "They repeat the story every five minutes, even though they don't have any additional new information about it."

When the video started again, she concentrated on it and then nodded. "Yes, it was well staged." She glanced at him, "At least you did this right." It was said with a slight smile.

He walked over to her and unbuttoned her blouse. She, in return, unbuckled his belt.

CHAPTER 23

Cambridge, MA

The late Kenneth Deloach's paranoia manifested itself in motion-activated cameras throughout the small apartment. After viewing the video found by JR, Kruger determined the location of the hidden camera used to record the apartment tenant's death. After his discovery, an extremely agitated Marlene Hoffman started barking orders for her detectives to determine any other camera's location and to secure them. Afterward, she stepped out of the apartment.

While the detectives scurried around the interior space, Kruger said, "Let me see it again."

JR nodded and activated the recording.

Kruger stood with his arms folded as he watched. One index finger tapped his lips. "When Ginger Bell and I were here the night we interviewed Deloach, he was extremely cautious about letting anyone into his apartment. In fact, it took us almost twenty minutes to gain his confidence."

"Looks like he opened the door right after looking through the peephole."

"I know, JR. What does that tell you?"

"He knew the person."

"Exactly." Kruger grew quiet for several minutes as he watched the scene captured in the hidden camera. "Play it again." The same scene repeated itself. At the time stamp of 1:22, when the door to the apartment opened, Kruger said, "Freeze." He pointed to Deloach's face. "That is not the face of someone who fears for his safety. The killer is someone he's familiar with, not a stranger."

Hoffman walked back into the apartment and hurried over to where Kruger and JR watched the recording. "What'd you find?"

"Deloach knew his killer. Play it again. JR. Stop when the door opens."

JR started the video again and stopped it at the spot Kruger indicated.

Hoffman said, "So?"

"The night Detective Bell and I were here, Deloach took twenty minutes checking us out before he would open the door. Look at his face. He knows the man entering the apartment."

She stood watching with a scowl on her face. As the events unfolded, she bent over to look at the screen closer. "How did you see that?"

JR smiled but kept quiet, while Kruger just shrugged.

The video continued as they watched Deloach turn his back to the visitor and move back into the apartment. The visitor raised a suppressed pistol, which jerked twice, and Deloach fell forward.

"My guess is the coroner will find he was shot with subsonic .22 rounds. With the suppressor, no one in the building would have heard the shots." Kruger stopped and returned his attention to his friend. "Wait a minute. JR, did you find any software on his laptop that could alter videos?"

"I didn't look, Sean. Why?"

"Check and see if you can find one." He paused and started pacing. "Why would someone kill Deloach?"

"No idea."

"Because Detective Bell and I weren't supposed to find the guy. He was hired to make the original video and then edit it to make the video CNN is showing."

JR frowned. "Then why did he give you the original?"

"Because he panicked."

"What do you mean, he panicked?"

"He was told the police wouldn't find him. When we did, he panicked and gave us the original video."

Hoffman stared hard at Kruger. "You think Bell's involved, don't you Kruger?"

"Until I know different, the answer is, no. But we need to locate her as soon as possible."

"She's either abandoned her duties, which means she's fired, or she's dead and we just haven't found her body yet."

He narrowed his eyes and returned Hoffman's glare. "The glass is always half empty with you, isn't it, Marlene? Until I know different, I'll assume she has a good reason for disappearing."

***

Ginger Bell sat in the spare bedroom of her parent's modest home in Monroeville, Pennsylvania, trying to decide how to explain her sudden departure from Cambridge. The phone call, threatening to kill her parents, seemed, at first, to be a prank. But as the caller described their house, the location, and her mother's daily habits, she panicked and drove the 560 miles to their home. Only to find them perfectly safe and unaware of any threats against them.

The fact she had not notified her supervisor about her decision to check on her parents seemed to confirm a decision she had been contemplating for some time. It was time to find another work environment. The one managed by Marlene Hoffman was toxic, especially for a black female cop.

As she prepared to call and offer her resignation, she noticed a missed call from Sean Kruger. After checking her phone, she discovered she had inadvertently silenced it. She pressed the return-call icon.

"Kruger."

"Agent Kruger, this is Ginger Bell. I just noticed I missed a call from you."

"Where the hell are you?"

The tone, and the question, gave her pause. "I'm at my parents' house. I received a threatening phone call about them and drove to Pennsylvania to make sure they were safe."

There was silence on the call for a few moments. "Hang on just a minute, I need to get to a place where I can talk."

The call went silent again as she waited. A minute later, she heard, "Ginger, there have been a few developments here."

"What kind of developments?"

"Well, for starters, you disappeared without a trace, your apartment was ransacked, and there's a BOLO out on you. Second, Kenneth Deloach was found murdered. One of the videos he gave us has been altered and is now all over CNN."

"Wait—what? My apartment was ransacked?"

"Yes. When did you leave?"

"Last night a little after eleven. The call I got was way too specific. The caller knew things a prankster wouldn't."

"Do you have your laptop with you?"

"Yes, I was going to check in with my supervisor, but, well—I just didn't."

"Okay, not a good decision, but it may work out for the best."

"Did I hear you right, Deloach is dead? Do you know what happened to him?"

"Yes, someone shot him. Someone he knew because he immediately opened the door and invited the individual in." He paused. "Ginger, at this point, I think it best if you just stay at your parents' house. It's safer."

"I don't understand, Sean. What's going on?"

"There's a video showing a man taking Barton's computer. The video you and I received showed a woman. I have possession of the original, but the one in the department evidence room has been altered exactly like the one on CNN."

"Am I under suspicion?"

Kruger did not answer immediately. "Should you be?"

"No—I didn't switch anything. Geez."

"At this point, you could be implicated, but I'm working to make sure you aren't. I think it wise for you to stay there. Give me the phone number that called you about your parents. I have a way of checking on it."

She checked her phone and recited the number. She asked, "Who's suspecting me?"

"Hoffman. Do you have a history with her?"

"Not that I'm aware of, but then, she's always treated me like shit."

"That's a personality flaw. She's been like that for decades. There has to be something else."

Ginger Bell fell silent as she thought back on the last ten days. "Sean, she's been acting different for the past two weeks. Check around the department. I'm not the only one who noticed it."

"Okay, I will. But in the meantime, stay where you are and protect yourself and your family. I'll call you. Got it?"

"Yes, sir."

"Ginger, I'm being serious. I'm not sure who you or I can trust right now."

She ended the call and closed her eyes as the tightness in

her stomach intensified.

***

Kruger stood outside the apartment building and looked up at the window where the Ring camera had been ten days ago. The call from Ginger Bell, while relieving his concern about her, only raised more questions about the death of Danny Barton.

JR exited the building and walked over to his position. "Who was on the phone?"

"Ginger Bell."

"I take it she's okay."

"Yes. She got a menacing call about her parents. The caller knew too much about them so she freaked out."

"Uh-oh."

"Yeah, she drove to Pennsylvania immediately. Everything was fine."

"Then, who ransacked her apartment?"

"That, JR, is another piece of the puzzle. She gave me the number that called about her parents."

"Good. I'll send it to Alexia."

"Tell her to hurry."

Kruger gave him the number and watched his friend send a text message to his assistant.

When JR finished the task, he asked, "What's going on here, Sean?"

"JR, I really don't know. I'm not sure if we can trust the Cambridge PD right now. The video they and CNN have is a fake, but we seem to be the only individuals who know that. Did CPD give it to CNN, or was there a separate source? If Thorton is the man in the video, why is he being indicted in Chicago and not extradited back here?" He paused and looked back up at the window. "None of the dots are connecting right now. And I'm tired of it."

JR chuckled. "Not our first rodeo."

The comment caused Kruger to smile and relax a bit. "No, it certainly isn't. But we're not getting anywhere standing around like this."

"Hoffman makes me nervous. Does she you?'

Kruger nodded.

"How did she get promoted to chief of police with her attitude?"

"It was worse when she was with the FBI." He looked up at the third-floor window. "Something isn't right in her department, so, as far as I'm concerned, we're done dealing with her."

JR's phone vibrated. He glanced at the screen and answered. "What'd ya find, Alexia?"

Kruger watched JR as he listened, his face a blank mask.

"Got it. Thanks for the quick response." He pressed the end icon and looked at his friend. "Guess who the phone number belongs to?"

"Not in the mood, just tell me, JR."

"It's a burner phone."

"Figured."

"However, it was purchased with a debit card belonging to Marlene Hoffman."

"You're kidding. She can't be that stupid."

"Apparently, she is. The phone made a call from this area thirty minutes ago."

Kruger frowned. "Didn't she step out of the apartment around that time?"

JR nodded. "She called a number in New York City."

CHAPTER 24

Cambridge, MA

Back in his hotel room, JR watched the video of Deloach's death again. His curiosity about something noticed in an earlier viewing rewarded him with a discovery. He closed the laptop, left, and walked down the hall to Kruger's room.

His knock produced a response within a few seconds as Kruger opened the door, his cell phone pressed against his ear. "I gotta go, Steph. I'll call you back in a few minutes." He ended the call. "What?"

"Found something on the video of Deloach's assassination."

Wrinkling his nose, Kruger said, "When you say it that way, it sounds ominous."

"It is ominous." He opened the laptop and pressed the space bar. The computer came to life, and he used the touchpad to move the screen arrow to a large triangle. "Watch this. Pay particular attention to the hand holding the gun."

As Kruger watched, the hand gripping the pistol rose. JR froze the picture and pointed to the joint between the thumb and the forefinger. "What does that look like?"

Walking to a nightstand, the retired FBI agent retrieved his reading glasses and put them on. "Play it again."

JR did and stopped it on the same image as before.

Kruger stared at the screen for a few moments. "Huh."

"Yeah, that's what I said."

"That's a pretty distinctive scar, isn't it?"

"I would say if we find the man with that scar, you'll have your killer."

Straightening, Kruger folded his arms. "The CPD has these videos, too, don't they?"

"Maybe."

"What do you mean, maybe?"

"Well…"

"What did you do, JR?"

"Marlene Hoffman was being such a pain in the ass, I might have forgot to include this video in the initial download from Deloach's server."

"Then, how did you get it to your computer?"

"Uh…trade secret."

"JR, she saw this one, she's going to know it's missing."

"She saw a lot of videos today, I bet she doesn't notice it."

"Is it still on Deloach's server?"

"No."

"So, they can't prove it ever really existed, can they?"

"Nope."

"So, we have the only evidence that can specifically identify the man who shot Deloach?"

JR nodded.

"And, there isn't a clear shot of his face in any of the videos you found."

"That's correct. This is the only one that shows a distinct-and-clear image of his hand."

"Why this one and this one only?"

"I had a hunch when I first saw it, so I kind of hid it."

Kruger smiled. "I'm sure glad you're on my team."

JR returned the smile.

***

Chicago, IL

Sent to Chicago by Kruger after receiving their DIA credentials, Jimmie Gibbs watched as an unexpected bonus for his trip walked out of the Cook County Detention Center and crossed South California Boulevard toward the complex's parking lot. Following at a discreet distance, the ex-Navy SEAL observed the make, model, and license plate number of the car Arthur Padilla entered. A cell phone picture of the automobile made its way to his wife, Alexia.

During the process of his request to interview Derick Thorton, his status as a DIA special agent prompted a Cook County deputy to reveal Thorton currently had a visitor. His cell phone vibrated as he watched Padilla drive off.

"Gibbs."

"Jimmie, it's Sean. Sorry I missed your call."

"Arthur Padilla just left the Cook County Jail after speaking to Thorton."

"Interesting."

"I've sent a picture of the car and license plate to Alexia. If it's a rental, maybe she can tell me how long he's staying in Chicago."

"Good. JR and I are heading back this afternoon. Do you want us to meet you there?"

"I'm not sure at this point. Let me see what Alexia discovers, and I'll let you know.

"Got it. Have you talked to Thorton?"

"Not yet."

"When you do, we need you to ask him if he can identify an image JR will be sending you momentarily."

"What is it?"

"The image of a hand with a distinct scar. The hand is holding the gun that killed a possible witness."

"How distinct?"

"You'll see when you get the image."

"Got it." Gibbs felt his phone vibrate and looked at the ID. "Hey, Sean, Alexia is on the other line. I'll call you back."

He immediately accepted the waiting call. "That was fast."

"Only for you, my love."

"That's my girl. What'd you find?"

"The car was rented to Arthur Padilla by Budget at their location near Union Station yesterday. The reservation is for seven days. The same American Express card paid for a room at the Marriot east of the airport. I have the address." She gave it to him and then said, "Be careful with this guy, Jimmie."

This comment gave Jimmie Gibbs pause. Alexia seldom said anything like this to him. "What's wrong, Alexia?"

"Nothing I can pinpoint at this time. But this particular Arthur Padilla didn't exist until five years ago."

"Do Sean and JR know?"

"I sent JR a message just before I called you."

"Huh."

"Just be careful."

"I will."

***

As Padilla exited the Cook County Jail parking lot, a gray Toyota Camry pulled out of a parking slot one row over and started to follow him at a discreet distance. The female driver kept several car lengths behind. Once Padilla arrived at his hotel, she pressed the send icon on her cell phone.

***

Derick Thorton frowned as he sat down across from Gibbs in the visitor's area. The plexiglass shield between them was dirty with finger prints and other odd smudges. Thorton frowned and said, "You again."

"Yeah, me again."

"What do you want?"

"Who's Arthur Padilla?"

"Never heard of him."

"Then who just visited you?"

"My attorney."

"Careful, Mr. ex-Attorney General, you don't want to add lying to a federal agent to the growing list of charges being filed against you."

Thorton blinked a few times and said, "Who it was, is none of your business."

"True, but if it was a man named Arthur Padilla, you might be wise to ignore any advice he gives you."

"And why is that, Agent Gibbs?"

With a shrug, the Ex-Navy SEAL smiled. "What did you discuss?"

"Since you won't answer my question, I don't have to answer yours."

Gibbs nodded. "No, you don't." He reached for his phone in his back jeans pocket and laid it on the bench in front of him. "I thought I might mention a man connected to the security camera video showing you taking Danny Barton's computer, the night he died, was shot in cold blood yesterday."

Thorton's expression remained neutral as he said, "I have an alibi, Agent Gibbs. I was here."

"We know. That's why I'm here. We want you to look at a picture and see if you recognize anything."

Folding his arms, Thorton leaned back in his chair. "I'll look. But if it's going to incriminate me, don't expect an answer."

"That's fair." Gibbs found the picture of the hand holding the gun and turned the phone to show Thorton. "Anything familiar in this picture, Derick?"

As Thorton studied the picture, a worried expression spread across his face. "Uh—what am I looking at, Agent?"

"It's the right hand of a person cleaning up loose ends associated with the death of Danny Barton."

"Loose ends? I'm not following you."

"The loose end here is a man named Deloach, whose security camera recorded someone stealing Barton's computer the night he died. We believe Deloach is the one who manipulated the image of you in the video. The original image is that of a woman. Care to see the original video?"

Thorton stayed quiet while Gibbs showed him the original security video. The prisoner's eyes widened as he stared at the image.

Gibbs put his phone away. "Know who she is?"

A nod was his answer.

"Care to tell me?"

"Her name is Annika Belsky, she works for Michael Peters, my so-called campaign manager."

"What about the hand, Derick? Anything familiar about it?"

"Yeah, something's familiar."

"What?"

"The scar."

"Who does it belong to?"

"Arthur Padilla."

***

"He seems ready to cooperate with us, Sean."

"Good, I'm flying into O'Hare with a DOJ attorney this afternoon. JR is heading back home to work with Alexia."

"Do I need to pick you up?"

"Yes. I'll call you just before we take off."

"What about Thorton?"

"That's why I'll have someone from the DOJ with me. They want to discuss this with the Cook County prosecutor and then offer Thorton a deal."

"If it will get him out of jail, he'll jump at it."

"It will, but he will need to resign from his office as the Illinois attorney general. He'll probably lose his law license, as well."

"That's kind of steep, isn't it?"

"No. DOJ is investigating him for other incidents, like dismissing charges against high-profile individuals for political gains. But charges in the death of Danny Barton are being dropped."

"Any leads on this Annika Belsky and Michael Peters?"

"No, and that's another reason JR is heading back. He has a few ideas and needs to be at his office. As he told me, he needs a bulldozer, and all he has with him is a hand shovel."

"Let me know when you need to be picked up at the airport."

CHAPTER 25

Southwest Missouri

The majority of the building's second-floor lights were extinguished since only JR Diminski occupied the floor. Alarm systems were set and controlled by him as he worked late into the night.

JR Diminski's arrival in Springfield from his trip to Cambridge and Washington DC occurred in the midafternoon. After a quick stop at his home to explain to his wife why he would be working late at the office, he departed with her blessing.

At ten minutes to ten he sat back in his chair and stared at the middle of three screens on his desk. He clicked an icon at the bottom and a small box appeared in the lower right corner. He used the ten-key pad on his keyboard and punched in a ten-digit code. The sound of a dial tone and then the ringing of a phone could be heard over the computer speakers.

"This is Joseph."

"It's JR."

"I will assume you are not calling from Hanaraku's Floral Shop in Nagasaki, Japan."

"Correct. Hope it's not too late to ask a question."

"For you, JR, it's never too late."

"How important do you think it would be if an election in Suffolk County England, where a Conservative party member has held the House of Commons seat for the past century, suddenly went to a member of the Labor Party?"

"That depends. Was the seat vacant?"

"No."

"Was the Labor Party candidate well-liked?"

"Don't know. He didn't even campaign. He's as shocked by the outcome as everyone else in Suffolk County."

"What are your thoughts, JR?"

"I think we are seeing a preliminary test by whoever stole Danny Barton's algorithms."

There was silence on the phone for several moments. Joseph finally said, "Let me make a phone call to someone who might have more insight into the matter."

"I would appreciate that."

"It will be tomorrow morning, JR. Go home and get some sleep."

"I will, but I have a few more elections to check first."

***

The call from Joseph came as JR sat down at his desk the next morning, a fresh mug of coffee in his hand. "That was fast."

"My call this morning was met with questions of how did I know."

JR chuckled. "How'd you handle that?"

"With my normal charm and wit."

"You called Jonathan Chapman, didn't you?"

"How'd you guess?"

"What did he say?"

"He wanted to know where I got my information. I told him a little bird told me, and he proceeded to inform me that was not an answer."

"Did they know about it?"

"They knew about the election but had not put two and two together. Now there's a full-blown investigation underway."

"You'll need to call him back. There were five more county elections hacked across England on the same day. The one in Suffolk County was the most obvious."

"Interesting. Can you give me more details?"

"I'll send a summary when we're through."

"So, you believe these to be tests?"

"It's an assumption at the moment. Russian hackers have a tendency to test their systems before they move on to their real target."

"How are they doing it?"

"I'm still working on it. But after studying Barton's system, I'd say they look at the polling data and then literally hack the voting computer systems to change the results."

"JR, using the Barton system seems like an extra step. Why do they need the polling data if they plan to change the results?

"Like I said, I'm still working on it. There has to be a reason for stealing Barton's computer."

"Have you located it yet?"

"Yes, but since then, whoever has it, has not accessed the Internet with the computer."

"Keep me posted."

"I will."

After disconnecting the call, JR sipped his coffee and then stood to see if Alexia had arrived. Looking in the direction of her cubicle, he saw the top of her head.

***

Chicago, IL

Dereck Thorton sat at his kitchen table dressed in jeans and an old Loyola Rambler's Basketball long-sleeve T-shirt. He sat with his hands clasped in front of him and studied the three individuals sitting across from him. DIA agents Sean Kruger and Jimmie Gibbs. The third person opened a file in front of her and looked up at Thorton.

Department of Justice Attorney Hannah Martin said, "Mr. Thorton, are you sure you don't want legal representation for these meetings?"

Thorton looked at the DOJ lawyer. "Ms. Martin, I'm an attorney, or at least I used to be. I believe I know what not to say."

She glanced at Kruger, who nodded slightly. She said, "Very well. Let's start with the basics. When and how did you meet Michael Peters?"

"It was about three years ago. I was attending the Illinois chapter of the Association for Prosecuting Attorneys' annual meeting here in Chicago. I was a keynote speaker that year discussing the ethics of running for higher office while handling your duties as a DA." He paused for a brief moment. "Yes, I know. Ironic, isn't it?"

No one said a word. They just kept their gaze on the man in front of them.

"It was later that afternoon during a social hour, Peters introduced himself. He was congenial and congratulated me on a concise-and-to-the-point presentation. I thanked him, and he wandered off to speak to other members. I totally forgot about it. Two weeks later, he called and asked if I could meet for dinner on the Loop at The Gage. At first, I declined and then he reminded me of our brief conversation at the meeting. Since The Gage is one of my favorite restaurants, I agreed."

Kruger said, "So, at this time, he had not mentioned why he wanted to meet with you, is that correct, Derick?"

"No, not a word. In fact, at the time, I didn't know what he did for a living. I assumed he was another attorney."

Hannah asked, "This was during the time you were Cook County DA, right?"

"Yes."

She continued. "Go on about the dinner."

"Anyway, we had a few cocktails, and I got a little talkative. I mentioned one of my long-term goals was to become the attorney general for Illinois and then one day a Senator." He stood and went to the refrigerator and pulled out a bottle of water. "Anyone else like one?"

All three of the remaining people sitting at the table shook their heads.

He returned and took a sip. "That's when he gave me a business card. He explained he was a political consultant and felt I had the qualifications and personality to run for Illinois attorney general. We talked during dinner and well past. I told him I would consider it and call him back with my decision later in the week."

The DOJ attorney asked, "I take it you accepted his offer?"

"Not really. I was going through a divorce at the time and needed to make other decisions. A month after the divorce was finalized, I called him back and told him I was ready to start a campaign." He paused again and sipped some water. "This was when he really got me hooked into the scheme. He told me since he had not heard back from me, he had written me off and was working with another candidate."

Gibbs asked, "Was he?"

Thorton shook his head. "No, it was another ploy to suck me in. It worked. I pleaded with him to take me as a client, and I won the election in the fall."

Hannah asked, "When did he start talking about running for president?"

"Almost immediately."

Kruger tilted his head and said, "So they've been planning this for over three years?"

A slow nod of Thorton's head was his answer.

"Why do you think they chose you, Derick?" Kruger leaned forward as he asked the question.

With a slow shake of his head, Thorton stared at the bottle of water he grasped with both hands. He finally looked up and said, "Because I'm a selfish, ambitious, greedy prick. That's why I'm a divorced selfish prick. Plus, and I'm not proud of this, I wanted to make sure my ex-wife would be sorry she divorced me."

Kruger smiled. "Obviously, you had an epiphany while in jail."

"Amazing how a two-by-four between the eyes changes your perspective."

Hannah Martin tapped a pencil on the notepad in front of her. "Mr. Thorton, how serious were the efforts by Peters to get you involved with all the primaries?"

"I should have seen the signs then, but I was too caught up in the idea of being president. To answer your question, I was kept out of the loop. He continued to tell me not to worry, he had everything under control. It's when I started questioning where the money was coming from that he pushed back. That's when the whole scam fell apart. He had his patsy, and it was me."

"When did Annika Belsky get involved?"

Thorton grew quiet and did not answer right away. He looked at Kruger and said, "She showed up at a so-called fund raiser one night." He looked at the ceiling and kept his gaze there for half a minute. "I drank too much, and she was so attentive…" He took a deep breath. "We ended up in bed."

Gibbs smiled. "Did they blackmail you to keep going

with the primary challenge?"

"Yeah, the next day I called Peters and told him I was embarrassed with the lack of turnout at the fund raiser. He proceeded to tell me that was how it went in the early stages of making a presidential challenge. When I insisted, I did not want to continue, he reminded me of sleeping with a campaign worker. Not a good image for the attorney general of Illinois to have."

"Did they have pictures?"

Thorton nodded.

Kruger asked, "Did you sleep with her again?"

"No."

Silence prevailed over the meeting as Hannah finished making notes. Kruger's eyes never left those of Thorton, who looked away and refused to meet the newly installed DIA agent's gaze. After a minute of the visual standoff, Kruger asked, "Tell us about the scar on Padilla's hand."

Thorton straightened in his chair and took on an air of lawyerly superiority. "Are you referring to the scar I observed on the man's right hand?"

"Yes."

"Very well. He has a particularly unique mark on his right hand. It's in the shape of a Z, reminiscent of the signature of the fictional character, Zorro. Whether the hand in the video picture is the same as the one on Padilla's hand would be—"

Gibbs cleared his throat. "Actually, the character Zorro is based on the actions of a man named Joaquin Murrieta during the mid-1800's in the western most section of the United States. He became known as the Robin Hood of California even though historical documents confirming his existence are scarce."

Kruger tried to cover a smile as Gibbs delivered his soliloquy knowing full well the reason for the interruption.

Thorton stared with confusion at Gibbs. He said, "Excuse me?"

"I was just pointing out that most historical legends are usually based on the actions of someone in history." He paused and then continued, "Would you agree the scar you've observed on Padilla's right hand matches the one on the hand of the individual shooting Deloach?"

No reply came from the ex-Attorney General.

With his smile now repressed, Kruger asked, "Derick, you realize if Padilla is cleaning up witnesses that can associate him with the death of Danny Barton, you would be on that list."

Thorton grew silent as his gaze shifted from Kruger to Gibbs. Finally, he just nodded.

Hannah closed her notepad. "I believe we have enough for now, Mr. Thorton. I remind you that you are under house arrest and are prohibited from leaving your apartment."

"I know."

She looked at Kruger and Gibbs. "I have all I need for the moment."

CHAPTER 26

Chicago, IL

Arthur Padilla sat on the edge of the hotel room bed leaning closer to the television set as he watched the throng of reporters shouting questions at Derick Thorton. Two Cook County deputies guided the handcuffed man to an awaiting dark SUV. The disgraced former Illinois attorney general stared straight ahead, ignoring the inquiries from the media. As soon as the scene on the TV switched back to the local Chicago station announcer, he began packing. The faster he left his room the better the chances he would beat the arrival of any law-enforcement agents knocking on his door.

Less than five minutes later, he walked with purpose toward the elevators, pulling his rolling suitcase behind him. The trip to the lobby went without incident. As he walked out of the hotel entrance, he exhaled, having held his breath during the long trek across the open lobby.

A shadowy figure emerged from behind a column of the porte cochère and followed Padilla to his rental car.

The man with the scar on his right hand reached his destination and placed the suitcase inside the truck. After closing the lid, he felt a hard object against his spine.

"Leaving so soon, Arthur?"

The voice was instantly recognizable. "What do you want, Peters?"

"You left New York City without saying goodbye."

Padilla did not respond.

"Get in the car. We're going to see Thorton."

"He's been released into the custody of the federal authorities."

It was Peters' turn to be silent. Finally, he said, "Unfortunate. I hope you were judicious in what you told him."

"I told him nothing."

"For your sake, I hope so." Peters paused a second. "So, where were you going?"

"I hadn't decided yet."

"You were leaving without fulfilling your obligation to make sure Thorton didn't talk?"

"You haven't paid me for the other so-called obligations. Why should I continue?"

"As I told you, Arthur, we're still evaluating the value of the laptop."

"Bullshit."

"A negative attitude is not in your best interest."

"Tough."

"You need to finish what you started, making sure Mr. Thorton does not spill his guts about me and my associates."

"You don't get it do you, Peters? Since I haven't gotten paid, I don't feel the need to do what you tell me."

A gray Toyota Camry pulled up behind Peters and without hesitation, he pulled the trigger on the suppressed

Ruger Silent-SR. The hollow point subsonic bullet left the barrel with no more noise than the opening of a wine bottle. The impact pushed Padilla forward, his spine shattered and the left ventricle of his heart mangled.

The impact pushed Padilla onto the sheet metal of the trunk. At the same moment, Peters slid into the passenger seat of the car and Annika Belsky accelerated away from the incident. Without the support of his legs, Padilla slid down the smooth surface and crumpled onto the parking lot pavement. Unable to move, he blinked several times and gasped for air as his lungs filled with blood. Before anyone could call 911, he took his last breath.

***

Kruger, Gibbs and Hannah Martin arrived at the Marriott five minutes after Padilla died in the parking lot. An ambulance and several police cars surrounded the spot. With their rental car parked under the porte cochère, Kruger turned to Gibbs in the passenger seat. "You two find out if Padilla is still checked in. I'll go see if my suspicions about the police and ambulance are correct."

The two exited the car and Gibbs followed Hannah into the hotel.

Walking up to a police officer, Kruger showed his DIA ID and asked, "Excuse me, Officer, but can you tell me if the man on the ground is Arthur Padilla?"

The policeman stared at Kruger and then at his badge and ID. "Why would the Defense Intelligence Agency be interested in Arthur Padilla?"

"I take it that's him?"

"Let me get my sergeant." The man whose name badge read Lomar turned his head and yelled, "Hey, Sarge, can you come over here?"

A tall slender uniformed man with three stripes on his sleeve approached. "What's the problem here?"

Kruger showed his badge and ID to the new arrival and said, "If the man on the ground over there is Arthur Padilla, he's a person of interest in a series of murders in Cambridge, Massachusetts."

"Thought that would fall under the FBI."

Kruger's mouth twitched. "It normally would, but because of who was murdered, it got bumped up to me."

The sergeant offered his hand. "Bob Boone, Chicago PD."

Shaking the officer's hand, he said, "Sean Kruger."

Boone tilted his head. "Where you from, Kruger?"

"Missouri, why?"

"My brother is Allen Boone. He's mentioned your name several times. Thought you were with the FBI?"

"Allen Boone's brother?" Kruger gave the officer a smile. "It's a small world, Sergeant."

"It can be sometimes."

"I'm retired from the FBI and was asked to help with this problem. How is Allen?"

"Good, I guess. Haven't talked to him since Memorial Day." He paused and folded his arms. "Want to try again about this Padilla person and why you're involved?"

With a grin, Kruger said, "Just like your brother, you don't let much get past you. Let me show you a picture." Taking the photo with the hand holding the gun from Deloach's security camera out of his sport coat, he showed it to Boone. "This scar will be on"— he pointed to the body on the ground— "his right hand."

Boone motioned for Kruger to follow and bent down next to the body. He placed a latex glove on his own right hand and then lifted the right arm of the body. The Z-shaped scar stood out plainly on the dead man's hand. Boone looked up, "Okay, you have my attention."

The sergeant stood and took several steps away from the spot as the paramedics brought a stretcher from the ambulance. "Who was he, Kruger?"

"That's what we were here to try and determine. According to the information we've been able to find on him, this particular Arthur Padilla didn't exist five years ago."

The two men were interrupted by Officer Lomar. "Hey, Sarge, we found a couple who saw the whole incident."

***

Looking frail and scared, Oscar and Vera Fitzgerald were escorted to a conference room in the hotel and offered coffee or bottles of water. Both declined. Having introduced Sergeant Boone to both Jimmie Gibbs and Hannah Martin, Kruger followed the elderly couple into the room.

Kruger, as was his habit, included Boone in every aspect of questioning the Fitzgeralds.

"Mister Fitzgerald, my name is Sean Kruger, I am a federal agent with the Defense Intelligence Agency. Next to me is Sergeant Robert Boone with the Chicago Police Department. Next to him is one of my fellow agents, James Gibbs. This is Hannah Martin, an attorney with the Department of Justice. She's here to help you understand your rights as witnesses. I want you and your wife to understand neither of you are in trouble. We appreciate your cooperation and any information you can provide. Is it all right if we call you Oscar?"

The older man nodded. "We'll do our best."

"Thank you. Sergeant Boone, do you want to start?"

Boone smiled and said, "Oscar, tell us what you saw in the parking lot."

"My wife and I were getting ready to board the shuttle to O'Hare when we saw a man walk out of the hotel in—" He turned to his wife. "What did you call it, Vera, a huff?"

She nodded. "He acted like he had been holding his breath and could suddenly breathe."

Oscar continued, "Anyway, he started toward the parking lot and was walking so fast, he almost ran."

Vera said, "That's when we saw the other man throw down a cigarette. Such a nasty habit. He started walking fast, following the man who was running."

Kruger asked, "What did this man look like?"

The elder gentleman turned to Kruger. "Tall, mid-forties or early fifties, dark hair, dark glasses, so I didn't see his eyes. As he walked away from us, he pulled a pistol from his belt. It was a small caliber Ruger with a suppressor."

Boone frowned. "How could you tell it was a Ruger, Oscar?"

"I used to work for Cabela's before they were bought out by Bass Pro. I was the head buyer in their gun department."

Jimmie Gibbs offered the picture of Thorton and Peters at the campaign rally with Annika Belsky standing beside them. He showed it to the Fitzgeralds, "Is he in this picture?"

Vera gasped, and Oscar nodded. "Yes, that's him." He turned to his wife. "What's wrong, Vera?"

"She pointed at the woman in the picture. "That's the person who drove the Camry and picked up the man with the gun."

Kruger smiled. "I don't suppose you remember the license plate number, do you?"

She smiled. "I may be getting old, Agent Kruger, but my mind is perfect." She told him the number.

***

Kruger left the conference room and found a quiet alcove where he could call JR. His friend answered immediately.

"Learn anything?"

"Yeah." He summarized the interview with the

Fitzgeralds. "I need you to trace a license plate."

"Tell me."

Reciting the number, he then said, "I'll wait."

"Shouldn't take too long." JR remained quiet for close to five minutes while Kruger watched the activity in the lobby of the hotel. "Here it is."

"Tell me."

"The car was reported stolen three days ago."

"You're kidding, from where?"

"A parking garage near the Willis Building. That's the old Sears Building, by the way."

"I know. Has it been recovered yet?"

"Not according to the Chicago Police Department."

"Keep an eye on it for me."

"Will do. When you heading back?"

"Don't know yet. We know Peters and the woman were here. Where they are now is the question."

"I'll check airline manifests and get back to you."

"Thanks, JR." He ended the call and walked back to the conference room. When he entered, he motioned for Boone to join him. In a low voice, he said, "Sergeant, the Camry was stolen three days ago in downtown Chicago. Can you put the word out we need to find it?"

"You got it."

CHAPTER 27

O'Hare International Airport

Annika Belsky approached the Delta international ticket counter in Terminal five and said to the attendant. "I need two adjacent first-class tickets to Tallinn, Estonia, with an open-end return date."

The young woman smiled as she typed on her computer. After several moments, she said, "I have several options. The first is at 2:20 p.m., but I don't have two seats together."

"Anything else?"

More typing as she studied the screen. "Most do not have two seats together." She paused. "Ah, here's one, but it has two-separate layovers. One at JFK and the other in Amsterdam. It leaves in an hour. Will that work?"

"Yes, thank you."

"Passports?"

Annika handed the woman two passports, one in the name of Mikhail Petrov and the other in the name of Annika Petrov. The man known as Michael Peters stood behind her and smiled. The young woman looked at the pictures in the small booklet and compared them to the two individuals standing in front of her. With a smile, she handed them back. "That will be thirty-two hundred dollars for two first-class round-trip tickets with an open-end date of return."

Handing the woman a Gold American Express card, Annika said, "Thank you for helping us. We have a family emergency in Tallinn."

The young ticket agent smiled but did not respond as she processed the transaction.

An hour later, as the Boeing 737 climbed into the cloudless summer sky over Chicago, Mikhail Petrov leaned over to whisper in Annika's ear. "We have to change planes in New York. We'll need to keep watch around our departing gate to make sure it's safe to get on the plane."

She turned to look at him. "Why wouldn't it be?"

He patted her arm, "Just be prepared to walk out of JFK if I tell you to."

***

Kruger's cell phone signaled an incoming call at 1:12 p.m. Gibbs and Hannah Martin sat in the Marriott's restaurant across from him as they finished their lunch. Glancing at his caller ID, he immediately accepted the call. "What'd you find?"

"They're on a Delta international flight to Tallinn, Estonia."

"Shit."

"Not to worry, they have a two-and-a-half-hour layover at JFK. Their connecting flight leaves at 5:38 this afternoon for Amsterdam."

"What's the flight number."

JR told him. "They're traveling under the names Mikhail and Annika Petrov, first class seats."

"Okay, that helps. I'll call Joseph and see if he can persuade the FBI to intervene."

"I'll send him a heads up also."

"Thanks, JR. Keep in touch."

"Sean?"

"Yeah?"

"Be careful. These two don't seem averse to killing people."

"Don't worry, JR. We will."

Ending the call, Kruger looked at his two companions. "How do we get to JFK before 5:30?"

Gibbs smiled and pulled out his phone.

***

Joseph Kincaid walked down the hall to the Oval Office and stepped inside. He watched as President Griffin shook the hand of the senate majority leader and said, "Thanks, Mike, I appreciate your support. Anything I can do for you?"

"Yes, Mr. President, I have a request from several Senators to meet with you to discuss infrastructure legislation."

"Mike, I think that is an excellent idea. Get with Bob Short and put it on the schedule."

"Thank you, Mr. President."

The man turned and nodded to Joseph as he walked out of the Oval Office. Griffin motioned for his national security advisor to follow him. He then walked down a short hall and entered Griffin's private office. When both men were seated, the commander in chief asked, "Do you have an update?"

"Which federal agency would you trust to intercept two individuals at JFK?"

Griffin raised an eyebrow. "Who are they?"

"They're the ones who may have orchestrated the death

of Danny Barton."

"I'm not inclined to send the FBI at the moment."

"I know, what about US Marshals?"

"Hadn't thought of that."

"Mr. President, they have the broadest arrest authority of any federal law enforcement agency."

"Then do it, Joseph." The president paused for a few moments. "Should we have put Sean and his team under the US Marshal authority?"

"It's a thought, sir. The US Marshals do have authority to operate overseas under cooperation agreements with other countries."

"Huh, didn't know that." He paused for a second. "Can Sean and his team get to JFK in time?"

Joseph shook his head, "Not in time to make the arrest. They'll need assistance."

"Okay, write up the writ, and I'll sign it."

"Thank you, Mr. President."

"And, Joseph, let's explore the US Marshal option."

Joseph smiled and said, "Yes, sir."

***

Attorney General Dale Delgado accepted Joseph Kincaid's call. "Good afternoon, Joseph. What can I do for you today?"

"Thanks for taking my call, Dale. How fast could you get US Marshals to JFK for the interception of two individuals of interest in the Griffin campaign workers' incident in Cambridge?"

"Pretty fast. Give me the details."

Joseph proceeded to summarize what he knew and then waited for Delgado to respond.

"Joseph, why did you and the president want Kruger to be in the DIA? We would be better served with him under the US Marshals service."

"The president and I agree. How would we do that?"

"Let me get agents on their way to JFK, and I'll call you back."

Delgado kept the phone receiver in his hand and called the director of the US Marshals.

Director Adrian Watson answered.

"Adrian, how quick can you get agents to JFK?"

"An hour or less, why?"

The attorney general explained. When he finished, he asked, "Adrian, are you familiar with a retired FBI agent named Sean Kruger?"

"Yes, very. Why?"

"How would you like for him to be a Deputy US Marshal?"

"Isn't he over the age of retirement?"

"Yes, but the president is prepared to issue an executive order to keep him around for a while."

"Interesting. Isn't he out of Missouri?"

"Yes. He lives in the southwest corner."

"Hell, I've got a marshal retiring in the Western District of Missouri. Kruger would be perfect."

"Good, get your best people to JFK and call me back."

"Will do."

***

JFK International Airport

Sitting in a coffee shop in the airport concourse, Mikhail and Annika sipped tea and watched the gate where their 5:38 p.m. flight would depart for Amsterdam. It was nearing four and, so far, they did not detect anyone paying too much attention to the area. At 4:13, that all changed as a man and woman, both dressed in business casual attire, were hustled through the gate entrance to the plane without having their boarding passes checked. Petrov sat a little straighter as he casually glanced around the area surrounding the café.

Annika said in a low whisper, "There is a man about thirty meters behind you leaning on a column surveying the passengers in the gate area. He arrived just before the man and woman were allowed through the door toward the plane."

"What does he look like?"

"Jeans, untucked blue Oxford shirt, dark glasses, and a backpack."

"Hair?"

"Semi-long, swept back behind the ears."

"Not FBI."

"No. They keep their hair shorter."

"Could he just be a passenger?"

"He could, darling, but he has a military presence about him."

Petrov stopped talking as he observed a woman in her mid-thirties glancing at him and then looking back at a cell phone. She did this twice and then placed the phone to her ear.

He stood. "There is a woman behind you paying way too much attention to us. Time to leave, separately. Find a cab and go to our agreed-upon location."

She nodded and sipped her tea as he stood. Without another word, he turned and walked toward the airport exit at the other end of the concourse. She watched the man leaning against the column follow Petrov with his gaze. As soon as Petrov walked past him, the man raised a cell phone and glanced at the screen. Pushing off the column, he hitched his backpack onto his shoulder and followed. As he departed, another man sitting in the gate area stood and proceeded to trail them.

As quickly as possible, she typed a text message on her cell phone and hit send. As she stood to leave, she felt the presence of two people directly behind her. Then a strong hand pushed her back into the seat. "Annika Belsky?"

She looked up at the barrel-chested man behind her. The woman she suspected Mikhail spotted stood next to the large man. "I'm sorry, you have me mistaken for someone else."

The man said, "I don't think so. Please stand with your hands behind your back."

"What is this about?"

"US Marshals, we have a warrant for your arrest."

Annika resisted slightly and turned to them. "You can't arrest me. I haven't been read my Miranda Rights."

"We aren't asking questions. We're just placing you under arrest. Now, please come quietly."

***

Petrov walked rapidly through the crowded concourse as he read the brief message on his cell phone from Annika. *Two men following you.*

Cursing under his breath, he started searching for ways to elude his pursuers. As he approached the air-tram entrance, he discovered he was in luck. The tram door was just starting to close when he ran to catch it. He entered just in time for the door to close behind him, and he turned as the two US Marshals arrived and tried to open the door Petrov entered. He watched as one of the marshals ran his fingers through his hair as the other pulled out a cell phone. Petrov smiled and waved to them as the tram sped away.

CHAPTER 28

New York City

Kruger listened as US Marshal Paulette Valdez summarized the arrest of Annika Belsky. "We got the call at 2:55 p.m. to proceed to Gate 190 at JFK. The photos you sent were invaluable in identifying them."

"Glad it helped. What about the man?"

"We think they became aware of our presence when two of our agents were escorted through the gate."

Kruger nodded as he stared at Annika on a video monitor at the Queens Central Booking Center.

Paulette continued. "The man stood, said something to her, and hurried down the concourse to the airport terminal. When he passed two of our agents, they followed him. We then observed the woman send a text message. When we checked her cell phone, we saw a number which we believe is her accomplice's. It spooked him, and he picked up his pace. Our team followed him to a tram station. He got lucky and entered a tram just as the doors were closing. We checked with airport security. There is a security camera shot of him getting off at the fourth stop. He is last seen entering the taxi queue area."

"Any security camera views of him entering a cab?"

She shook her head.

"It happens. Has she said anything?"

"Only when we arrested her. She wanted her Miranda Rights read. Marshal Burman told her we were only arresting her, not questioning her."

With a chuckle, Kruger said, "I'll have to remember that one. Has she asked for an attorney?"

"No."

He turned to her. "Marshal Valdez, would you accompany me into the interrogation room?"

"I'd be honored, Agent Kruger."

He frowned and looked at her.

"Your reputation as an FBI agent proceeds you."

"Don't believe anything you've heard, Marshal."

"I'm still looking forward to accompanying you."

With a smile, he said, "Let's go."

They entered the interrogation room with Valdez standing near the door and Kruger sitting across from the prisoner. Annika said, "I want my Miranda Rights and an attorney, in that order."

Kruger smiled and asked, "Why? You haven't been charged with anything. Are you guilty of something?"

"If that's the case, why am I under arrest?"

Kruger pulled out the campaign rally picture of Derick Thorton and Michael Peters with Annika standing behind Thorton. "You are under arrest because of your association with Derick Thorton and the other man in this picture. We are trying to locate the other man who we have identified as Michael Peters, also known as Mikhail Petrov. You were sitting with him at a restaurant in JFK International Airport with a ticket to Estonia with a lay-over in Amsterdam."

"I've never seen the man before."

With a smile, Kruger said, "You might want to re-think

that statement. First, you are in the picture, which was taken in Chicago. Second, your seat assignment was adjacent to the man on the flight from Chicago and also on the next leg to Amsterdam. Third, you texted him from your cell phone after he left the café. And fourth, your tickets are in the name of Mikhail and Annika Petrov. So, Ms. Belsky, want to try again?"

"I want my Miranda Rights and a lawyer."

Kruger stood. "Very well." He turned to Paulette. "Marshal Valdez, as the arresting officer, would you inform her of her rights?"

***

Mikhail Petrov waited in the small café across from the hotel where Annika and he agreed to meet if separated. The time approached nine in the evening and Annika remained absent. At exactly nine, he stood, placed a five-dollar bill on the check for his coffee and walked out of the shop.

Standing in the café entrance alcove, he looked up and down the street and saw nothing suspicious. He waited until he saw a taxi pull to the front of the hotel and let a passenger out. He hurried across the street and slipped into the back seat of the taxi just as the other passenger exited.

"I'm off duty, sorry."

Petrov handed the man a hundred-dollar bill and said, "Will this get you back on duty?"

The cabbie licked his lips and said, "Where to?"

"La Guardia."

"No problem."

Fifteen minutes later, the cab dropped him off in the passenger unloading zone. He watched it drive off and then headed into the terminal. Once inside, he followed directions to the Red Shuttle Bus area for the trip to Terminal A where the car rental agencies kept their pickup desks.

At 10:15 p.m. he drove the rental car out of the parking area and headed west toward New Jersey and Highway 87. This route would take him north toward Canada with his final destination of Montreal. The fact he was leaving Annika behind only bothered him for a few moments. After he thought about it for a while, he shrugged and concentrated on his driving.

***

Kruger stared out the window of the New York to Washington DC shuttle. Going on twenty-four hours without sleep, he closed his eyes and leaned the seat back. When he heard the person behind him grumble, he said, "Sorry," and returned it to an upright position. With a sigh, he leaned his head against the bulkhead and closed his eyes. The next thing he knew, the plane touched down at Dulles International Airport. The whirlwind flights from Springfield to Washington, then to Chicago and the quick flight to New York all within the last thirty-six hours were starting to wear on him. In his early FBI career, these types of back-and-forth trips were common place. But after almost a year of not stepping onto a plane, he felt out of practice.

He grabbed his carry-on, deplaned, and waited in the gate area for Jimmie Gibbs to emerge. When he did, Kruger said, "You look about like I feel."

"When I was in the military, I thought riding in a C-5 Galaxy was uncomfortable. Flying commercial these days is worse."

Kruger chuckled as they headed toward the passenger pickup area. "I just sent a text to Jerry Griggs. He's in the cell-phone lot and will pick us up." He glanced at his watch. "Didn't know it was a quarter after midnight."

"I didn't either. Where're we going?"

"I was told a hotel, but which one, I have not a clue."

"As long as it has a bed, I really don't care."

With a smile, Kruger shook his head. "This town does not believe in downtime. I honestly don't know why Joseph is still working for the president."

Gibbs said, "I do."

"Enlighten me."

"Joseph's an action junkie; at least he has been since I've known him. He always has to be in the middle of things. That's why half the world knows him."

Laughing out loud, Kruger nodded. "I never thought of it that way. But you're right."

Arriving at the passenger pickup area outside the terminal, Kruger saw Griggs' Ford Explorer waiting for them. After throwing their carry-ons into the back of the SUV, Kruger sat up front with Griggs with the ex-Navy SEAL in the rear passenger seat.

As he closed the door, he said, "Thanks for picking us up. Where're we going?"

"I was supposed to drop you off at the Hampton near the White House, but there's been a change in plans."

With a frown, Kruger said, "What kind of a change in plans?"

"You two are staying at the White House tonight for an early morning meeting and then a Gulfstream will be taking you both to Lyon, France for an emergency meeting with Interpol."

Jimmie Gibbs shook his head as Kruger stared at Griggs. "Interpol? What the hell for?"

"Apparently, there's an international uproar about the fact that elections in England were hacked using Danny Barton's algorithms. Your team will be the representative from the US at an Interpol conference."

"That means we'll need JR."

"He's already at the White House."

The only reaction Kruger could give his driver was a silent stare.

***

White House
Early Morning

After a short night in very comfortable beds, Kruger, JR, and Gibbs were escorted to the Oval Office at seven a.m. for a meeting with President Griffin, Joseph Kincaid, Attorney General Dale Delgado, DOJ Attorney Hannah Martin, who appeared to be extremely uncomfortable in her environment, and a gentleman Kruger did not know.

During introductions, the stranger was identified as Adrian Watson, Director of the US Marshals Service. As he shook Kruger's hand, he said, "Your reputation proceeds you, Agent Kruger. It is a pleasure to finally meet you."

"It is nice to meet you, too, Director Watson."

The man's smile revealed he knew something the others did not.

Griffin cleared his throat. "I apologize for the early hour of this meeting, but a rapidly developing situation in Europe is causing us to accelerate our plans for your team, Sean."

"What plans, sir?"

"Your team is being transferred to a permanent assignment in the US Marshals Service."

"Uh—may I ask why?"

Griffin turned to Delgado. "Dale, would you explain, please?"

"Yes, Mr. President." He addressed Kruger. "Interpol is more comfortable working with the Marshals Service versus the Defense Intelligence Agency. It's a political consideration we did not take into account when we formed your team, Sean. In addition, under the US Marshals, you will have broader authority to arrest fugitives both inside the US and internationally, should you need to."

"Okay, that makes sense. What about the others on my team?"

"All covered, Marshal Kruger."

With a smile, Griffin said, "I signed an executive order yesterday evening extending your service to your country until your sixtieth birthday." He turned his attention to Watson and said, "You have something to add, don't you, Adrian?"

Watson turned to Kruger and handed him a badge wallet. "Your status is now officially a US Marshal in a newly created district. When this is over, we can discuss you taking over the Western District of Missouri as marshal. In addition, JR Diminski and Jimmie Gibbs are officially Deputy US Marshals within your new district."

Gibbs raised an eyebrow and JR closed his eyes and shook his head, muttering, "Oh, wonderful."

Kruger tilted his head and looked at Delgado, "Mr. Attorney General, is that all it takes?"

President Griffin, Joseph and Delgado nodded in unison. Joseph said, "There's some paperwork all of you need to sign, but that's it. Sean, your posting is permanent. After this episode is over, JR and Jimmie can determine what they wish to do."

After looking back and forth between Delgado and the president, Kruger smiled. "Okay—what's the situation in Europe?"

CHAPTER 29

Lyon, France

For the third time in twenty-four hours, Sean Kruger sat on a plane. This time eastbound across the Atlantic. Joining him were Jimmie Gibbs, JR Diminski, and DOJ Attorney Hannah Martin.

The swearing-in ceremony for his new position as a US Marshal and the newly installed Deputy US Marshals, Gibbs and Diminski, took place five minutes before they were whisked away in a Black Chevy Suburban to Joint Base Andrews. There, after boarding a Gulfstream G650ER, one of the fastest and longest-range private jets, they were ferried at 85 percent the speed of sound toward Interpol's headquarters in Lyon, France.

With a trip lasting roughly six-and-a-half hours, and Lyon six hours ahead of Washington, D.C., the team would lose roughly half a day. Time Kruger did not feel they had the luxury to lose.

As was his custom on private jets, JR sat across from Kruger. He leaned over and said, "What is so important that we have to get to France so fast, Sean?"

"At this point, you know as much about it as I do, JR. I received a text message from Sergey just before we took off."

Looking at his friend, JR said, "Really? Are we going to work with him on this?"

"Apparently, he's scheduled to pick us up at the airport. Have you ever been to Lyon, JR?"

"No. When I was in the military, I was in Marseille for a while, but we never got up to Lyon."

"I've never been there either. When Steph and I stayed in Paris, we toured some of the wine regions but didn't get that far south."

"Speaking of Stephanie, how's she doing with you being gone so much lately?"

"Better than I'm doing with it. I haven't had this much jet lag in years. What about Mia? You're never gone."

JR chuckled. "I think she's actually enjoying my absence. When I'm home, my hours can be a bit erratic, depending on what's going on at the office. To her, this is kind of a vacation."

The two friends settled into a comfortable silence as the Atlantic Ocean slipped rapidly beneath them.

Ten minutes later, Kruger broke the quiet. "JR, how confident are you Danny Barton's computer is in Tallin, Estonia?"

"One hundred percent."

"Can you pinpoint its exact location?"

"If it ever accesses the Internet again, we might. But my guess is it won't. They've more than likely downloaded his programs and algorithms and have them on a new system. His computer's probably been destroyed."

"So, how are we going to find it?"

JR leaned his head back against the seat and closed his eyes. "As you are fond of saying, I'm still working on it."

***

Sergey Brutka shook Sean Kruger's hand and laughed. "It is good to see you again, my friend. I am so glad it is my chance to return the hospitality you showed me in your wonderful city of Springfield."

Smiling, Kruger looked at his friend as a massive callused hand released his. Brutka was a large man. Even though they stood at eye level with each other, the Ukrainian's bulk was twice that of Kruger's. The Interpol detective's attire remained the same as the last time Kruger saw him. Levi jeans, a beige cable knit turtleneck sweater and an oversized corduroy sport coat. With disheveled dark-brown hair and an untrimmed drooping mustache, he was a throwback to fashion of the early 1980s. When he spoke, his bushy eyebrows danced with delight.

"Thank you for meeting us at the airport, Sergey. You look well, my friend."

"Nonsense, I am older and just as fat." He narrowed his eyes, "Word is you are no longer an FBI agent."

"My age required retirement from the FBI. But, for some reason, my government thought it wise to make me a US Marshal."

Brutka threw his head back and laughed with gusto. "A wise decision by your government. I have worked with many of your US Marshal brethren and found them to be extremely competent. You will find yourself in good company."

Kruger folded his arms and stared at the large man. "Can you tell me the reason for this sudden meeting here in Lyon?"

Brutka nodded. "There has been a rash of cyberattacks on Western European governments of late. Interpol has requested representatives from various members' countries to form a task force to find the perpetrators and bring them to a halt. I was most pleased to learn you would be one of the representatives from the US."

"How many attacks, Sergey?"

"I have heard of as many as twenty in the last week. Each more brazen then the last."

"Where are they coming from?"

"That, my friend, has not been divulged to me."

Kruger paused and stared at his old friend. With a nod, he said, "Let me introduce you to my team."

"JR, I know, but not the others."

***

After the introductions, Brutka ferried the four individuals from the airport to the hotel where he was staying near Interpol's headquarters. Due to the lateness of the hour, all five retired to their rooms.

Later, as he lay in bed, hands behind his head and staring at the ceiling, he had the urge to call Stephanie. As he picked up his cell phone, he realized she would still be in the middle of her last class of the day. He chose to postpone the call. The time difference and his severe jet lag gave him pause about his decision to rejoin a federal law enforcement agency.

After thirty minutes of lying-in bed and feeling sorry for himself, he got up and put on a pair of running shoes and shorts plus a University of Oklahoma T-shirt. He checked through the amenities of the hotel and found it possessed an exercise room. When he got there, he found Jimmie Gibbs occupying one of the two treadmills. As he climbed onto the unoccupied machine, he said, "You too?"

"When I was a SEAL, I could fall asleep anywhere and at any time. Not tonight."

"Yeah, I almost called Stephanie until I realized she was still at work."

Chuckling, Gibbs said, "I did call. Alexia is jealous I'm in France, but not so much about my being in Lyon."

"Did she say why?"

"No, but I think it's because this is where Interpol is located. She didn't have the best relationship with them when she lived in Paris."

"Ah—that would make sense."

The two friends fell into a silence as they exerted themselves on the treadmills. The spirited competition between them grew too much for Kruger. Being more than a decade older than the ex-SEAL, he ended his routine after thirty minutes and stood off to the side watching Jimmie finish his.

When Gibbs stepped off, Kruger said, "How long can you go like that?"

The younger man smiled. "I'm a swimmer, Sean. That was nothing."

Rolling his eyes, the newly installed US Marshal bid his friend good night and retired to his room.

***

By nine the next morning, the lead member of the United States delegation to the Interpol gathering sipped coffee as he waited for the meeting to start. Kruger looked around the reception area, hearing numerous foreign languages being spoken all at once. He noticed Jimmie Gibbs keeping track of a pair of gentlemen conversing in Russian to Kruger's right. He wandered over to Gibbs and asked, "What are they talking about?"

"Believe it or not, they're speculating on Russia's chances of winning the next World Cup."

"Good, don't let them know you speak their language."

"Got it. Do you think Russia is behind the hacks?"

"I'm not sure. JR is starting to question his original assumption it was the Russians."

"Really? Where is he, by the way?"

"Last I knew, he was on the phone with Mia. He will use

any excuse available to stay out of crowds."

Gibbs waved at Hannah Martin as she entered the reception area. She joined them and asked, "Have I missed anything yet?"

Kruger shook his head as he kept an eye on the Russians. "No, just a bunch of old guys talking about sports."

JR arrived at exactly 9:15, just as the doors to the conference room opened and the delegates filtered in to find their seats. Auditorium seating filled the room with a podium on the lowest level facing the crowd. JR made sure he sat next to Kruger and, as they sat down, he whispered, "Did you know Sergey is now a big shot with Interpol?"

"No, he didn't mention anything last night."

"Well, he is. In fact, he's in charge of this operation and specifically asked for you and me to be involved."

Kruger studied his friend for a moment, "How would he…" He stopped talking as Sergey Brutka approached the podium. This morning he was dressed in a navy suit, a white silk shirt with a red and gold-striped tie. His normally disheveled hair neatly brushed.

"Good morning, everyone. Thank you for taking the time to travel for this most important conference."

CHAPTER 30

Montreal, Canada

Premier Election Concepts, Inc. commonly referred to as PEC, a major supplier of voting machine equipment and services in North America, grew to its current employee count after two companies of similar size and mission statements merged in the second decade of the new century. With field office locations in over thirty states in the US and four in Canada, its location in Montreal buzzed with activity on this particular Saturday morning. The reason for the frantic pace centered around preparing for the largest security update to their election software in the company's history.

The company's Montreal Divisional Director, Tim Goodman, finished a rare Saturday conference call with his fellow company executives at ten a.m. The software updates the firm would be pushing out to clients on Tuesday of the following week came with a bit of trepidation to Goodman. The last major update went out in 2018 and helped deliver a growth spurt of over one hundred county and municipal government clients switching to their voting equipment and counting processes. His growing status within the company and the potential of being promoted to their St. Paul, Minnesota home office made the release of this update all the more important for him.

He looked up from his desk as his administrative assistant, Lydia McDonald, entered his office with a mug of steaming coffee in her hand. As she set it down on his desk, she said, "I know you don't like me doing this, but you've been on the phone for an hour, and your coffee has to be cold."

Goodman smiled and handed her his cold, half-finished mug. "Not part of your job description, but I appreciate you thinking about it."

She returned the smile. "Is everything ready for Tuesday?"

"I believe so. Not sure why this one makes me nervous."

"It's probably due to all the recent media attention on the security of elections."

He took a sip of his fresh coffee. "Maybe." He paused and stared at the steam coming off the dark liquid in the mug. "Are you planning on taking your laptop home with you this weekend?"

"I wasn't, but I can. Why?"

"Just in case there are any last-minute changes to the official announcement. I want to make sure I have someone available to put another set of eyes on it before I send it out."

This was one of the traits she admired about Goodman; he wanted those around him to feel they were part of his team, not just employees. "Not a problem, happy to help."

***

Lydia McDonald's status as a divorced and childless woman in her early thirties occurred after a disastrous five-year marriage. In order to forge a new life for herself, she moved to Montreal after accepting the job with PEC. She kept trim by stopping at a women-only fitness center for a daily regimen of yoga and cardio-workouts. While she did not consider herself beautiful, she was comfortable with her appearance and wore professional conservative clothing. Her current boyfriend, a gentleman ten years or so older and a sales executive with a Fortune 500 clothing manufacturer, apparently liked the way she looked because they were still dating after eleven months. While the subject of marriage had never been discussed, she was undecided on how she would respond should he ever ask. After the last marriage, she seldom thought about committing herself to anyone.

She did enjoy her job. Working for Tim Goodman was one of the reasons. She knew he was destined to be transferred to St. Paul at some point in the next year or so. The company liked to promote from within, and no one in the Montreal office knew his job as well as she did. When he was out of town either on business or vacation, she filled in and handled the day-to-day activities for him. While the promotion had never been discussed or promised, Tim hinted on numerous occasions she was in line for his position. Another reason she did not feel the need to commit herself to a relationship at the moment.

On this particular Saturday, she arrived home a little after five looking forward to an evening out with Kevin. As she prepared to take a shower, her doorbell rang, and she glanced at the clock on her nightstand. It was too early for him to arrive, so, dressed in a bathrobe, she checked who it was before opening the door. It was Kevin.

As she let him in, she said, "You're early."

Kevin Marks smiled and stepped into her apartment. "Couldn't wait to see you." A congenial man, he appeared to be in his late forties, aided by professional hair coloring, a trim waist, and sturdy shoulders. She was unaware of his true age. He possessed an oval face, thick dark-brown hair and bushy eyebrows that danced when he told one of his stories. His chocolate-colored eyes peered through rimless glasses and rested on a long, slender nose.

Their embrace lasted a few moments and, when they disengaged, he opened her robe just a bit and smiled at what he saw. "Little early for this, don't you think?"

She returned the smile and closed her robe. "Way too early. You caught me before I could take a shower. Now, make yourself at home while I get ready."

"Yes, ma'am."

***

When he heard the small click of the bathroom door being locked and the sound of running water, he turned to the dining area table where she kept her laptop. As was her habit, she had placed the machine in sleep mode. When he touched the enter key, the screen came on and asked for her security pin. Over the time they had been dating, he had stealthily discovered her pin.

Knowing she would be in the shower at least another fifteen minutes, he placed a flash drive into one of the computer's USB ports. He left it there while the small device did what it was designed to do.

When the computer told him the specifically designed subroutine had completed its installation, he ejected the flash drive and placed it in his pants pocket. He then put the computer back to sleep and went to her refrigerator for a beer tucked away in the back waiting for him.

***

The next morning, Lydia McDonald opened her laptop to check if Tim Goodman had sent an email during the previous twelve hours. Of the twelve new emails, one came from Tim asking her to review the wording of a memo. She corrected a few typos and suggested a way to make a particular sentence less cumbersome.

Unknown to her, as she replied to the message, the subroutine installed the previous night by her so-called boyfriend, attached itself to any email ending in the @PEC.org domain

Tim Goodman opened the email from Lydia McDonald at 9:05 a.m. Sunday morning. He made note of the typos and rewording suggestions. Agreeing with all of them, he corrected the master copy and proceeded to send the memo via emails to various fellow PEC employees at his level of management. He also copied the CEO and owner of PEC, Tony Chien. With this accomplished, he then sent an email to the director of IT requesting any revisions needed in the timeline for the upcoming software update. By noon on Sunday, Goodman completed his to-do-list, shut the computer down, and spent the rest of the day with his family.

With each email sent, ending in the @PEC.org domain, a simple set of computer instructions, known to the common man as a virus, attached itself to the message. The malicious code would then install itself in the recipient computer and repeat the process. When the company finally released the software update in the coming days, a small piece of malware would be placed on every computer receiving the update. With the flurry of emails on this Sunday prior to the software distribution, the virus now lay dormant on nearly 76 percent of PEC, Inc. computers and deep within the company server.

With the stage set for a devastating attack on the very pillar of American democracy, Odin Analytica's long-range planning would soon bear fruit as free elections in North America became a thing of the past.

CHAPTER 31

Lyon, France

Sergey Brutka shed his navy suit for his normal attire when he met Kruger and JR in the hotel bar after the day's conference. He started the conversation after beers were served. "So, what did you think of our conference today?"

Kruger took a sip of beer and shrugged. "The same way I think about most conferences."

Brutka let out one of his hearty laughs. "Yes, I agree. A total waste of time."

"I didn't say that. But I was thinking it." With a tilt of his head, Kruger locked eyes with his Ukrainian friend. "JR, Jimmie, and I have zero reason for being here, Sergey. Why did you ask for us?"

Turning to JR, Brutka asked, "Have you ever heard of SolarWinds?"

"Of course."

"Do you use them?"

"They're a cybersecurity company. Why would I need to?"

"You, my friend would not need to, but you know what happened?"

JR nodded and took a pull on his beer.

Kruger asked, "Care to enlighten me, JR?"

"SolarWinds is a company based in Austin, Texas that develops software for businesses to manage their computer networks, systems, and information technology infrastructure. I'm talking large companies, with huge computer systems. I'm also talking government systems. It's more complicated than that, but it gives you an idea."

"Okay, what about them?"

"Somehow they got hacked and a nasty piece of malware found its way into their system. When SolarWinds sent out a software update, they basically gave the malware a free ticket into a whole bunch of government computer systems."

"Who did it?"

JR looked at Brutka. "You want to answer that one?"

"Sure. Everyone is pointing their fingers at our old friends the Russians."

With a smile, Kruger said, "But you don't think so, do you, Sergey?"

"I think they wrote the malware, but I have another suspect in mind that accomplished the original hack into SolarWinds' system."

With a frown, JR said, "Not following you, Sergey."

"No one can explain how the Russians hacked into SolarWinds in the first place. That information is being concealed."

"That makes sense, no reason to upset the stock holders about trivial matters."

With a chuckle Brutka said, "You are correct, JR. They are making sure they don't reveal the true nature of their breach. But I think I know who might have helped the Russians get access to their systems."

"Who?"

"A company out of Estonia called Odin Analytica."

Kruger and JR shot quick glances at each other and then turned back to Brutka.

The big man smiled. "Ah, you have heard of them, yes?"

JR nodded. "Yes, we have. What do you know about them?"

"It is one of the reasons for my promotion within Interpol."

Kruger leaned over the table. "You never told us about that, Sergey."

"Very embarrassing, my American friend. Very embarrassing."

"Somehow I doubt it. What happened?"

"I stumbled upon it by accident, not by utilizing my sources and solid police work."

"Sometimes it's better to be lucky than good. Do you want to explain?"

"It was right after I returned from working with you in the United States. If you remember properly, I stayed in Paris for a few months watching Dimitri Orlov. After his demise, I was called here to Lyon for a new assignment. The assignment was to look into the activities of a man named Tomas Pavlovich."

After a sip of beer, Kruger asked, "Who is he?"

"That is part of the tale. I'll explain. We have to start with Estonia. The country has a long history of being controlled by foreign powers through much of its history. This past century saw multiple years of dominance by both the Soviet Union and Nazi Germany. On June 17, 1940, Soviet troops occupied the Republic of Estonia, and they installed a communist government in August of that year. That did not last long as the country was invaded by Nazi Germany in 1941, and it remained under their influence until 1944 when the Soviets liberated the country.

"Most governments of the world did not recognize the Soviets' incorporation of Estonia after World War II. So, by world standards, it was considered an independent state under occupation from 1940 through 1991. The country was renamed the Republic of Estonia on May 8, 1990 and then, after the attempted Soviet Union coup d'état in Moscow on August 20th of 1991, Estonia declared its independence from the disintegrating USSR."

JR took a sip of beer. "Nice recap of history, but what does that have to do with Tomas Pavlovich?"

"I am getting there. Tomas was a young KGB officer working undercover in the Estonian capital of Tallinn on November 6th, 1991. Do either of you know the significance of this date?"

Kruger nodded. "It's the day the KGB split into the Federal Security Service and the Foreign Intelligence Service."

"Very good, my friend."

"JR and I have had a few encounters with disaffected former KGB officers."

"Well, you are about to have another encounter. Pavlovich did not return to Russia after the demise of the KGB. He stayed in Estonia and became a successful businessman as the economy of the small country prospered.

"The man became a billionaire in the early 2000s, about the time Estonia joined the EU. His company, with the help of a financial company called Northern Lights Investment Services, acquired a small IT firm called Odin Analytica a few years later. What was once a small but growing IT company doing work for numerous European governments became a thriving computer service enterprise with extensive influence throughout Western Europe."

JR frowned. "Are you telling us Pavlovich still works for the Russian FSB?"

Brutka shook his head. "No, we do suspect he maintains contacts in the Russian Federal Security Service, commonly called the SVR, but does not work for them.

That is the agency tasked with espionage activities outside the Russian Federation."

With a slight grin, JR said, "It is also the agency that sponsors hacking activities for Russia."

A nod from Brutka.

Kruger tapped his finger on his lips. "If Pavlovich is still connected within the SVR, that means Odin Analytica could be a possible extension of the Russian hacking program, or am I jumping to conclusions?"

"You are not, my friend. Odin Analytica is secretly involved in breaching computer systems throughout the world while maintaining its reputation as a legitimate IT consulting company."

JR asked, "Your whole tale started with how SolarWinds was breached. So, explain how your tale of Odin Analytica fits in with them."

"One man."

"His name?"

"Kreso Markovic."

Both JR and Kruger stared at Brutka with wide eyes and raised eyebrows.

Brutka continued. "I take it both of you have heard of this man."

With a nod, JR said, "Yeah, we have."

"I am curious, how?"

"Long story, Sergey." This from Kruger.

"I am, as you Americans say, all ears?"

Taking a deep breath, Kruger let it out slowly. "It occurred over a year ago. It was my last case as an FBI agent. It started out with an investigation into a serial killer targeting successful members of ethnic groups."

"Rich?"

"No, not really. However, they were highly successful in their professional careers. Most notable was Alan Seltzer, the deputy director of the FBI and a close personal friend of mine."

"I have heard about this case. The killer turned out to be a mathematics professor. No?"

"You are correct. However, he was also involved with a bunch of white supremacists in Wyoming and Montana."

"White supremacists? How did Kreso Markovic fit in?"

"First let me ask how long you've been investigating him?"

"He came to Interpol's attention about a year ago. Why?"

"That's about the time he disappeared. We think he went to Canada."

"Interesting."

"I was asked to find him before I left the FBI, but couldn't get a line on him. Does he have another alias?"

"According to Interpol's files, he has many."

"Can you get me a list?"

A nod. "Now tell me how he was involved with white supremacists?"

"He recruited them in a scheme to cause a race war in the States."

"Ah. We do not know his place of origin. The name Kreso is Slavic, but we cannot determine where he was born."

"He's from New York City, particularly Queens. His parents were from Serbia and brought him here as an infant. He became a naturalized citizen when he was young."

"That explains it."

JR asked, "Sergey, how was he involved with the SolarWinds hack?"

"We are not sure, but it seems he was romantically involved with one of their programmers."

Kruger furrowed his brow. "Markovic owned a Western wear store in Lander, Wyoming. How would he be able to date a programmer from a company in Austin, Texas?"

Clearing his throat, JR said, "You're thinking old-school, Sean. The majority of my associates work remotely."

Brutka laughed. "That explains a lot."

"What?"

"Interpol has hypothesized how the hack was made on SolarWinds."

JR frowned. "How?"

"It came from an employee's email. The programmer who was dating Markovic in Wyoming was probably compromised by her boyfriend."

JR's eyes widened. "Shit."

Kruger turned to him. "What, JR?"

"I just figured out that may be how my company got hacked. Through an attachment from a remote computer."

"But you've fixed that, haven't you?"

With a nod, JR turned back to Brutka. "So, why was this embarrassing to you Sergey?"

"I have never told anyone this."

"You're among friends. JR and I won't say anything."

"I did not learn all of this through my skills as an investigator, but through the warm embraces of a woman."

With a chuckle, Kruger folded his arms. "Let me guess. You hooked up with someone in Dimitri Orlov's office?"

Brutka nodded.

"Who?"

"Remember the woman in the café who was trying to determine if I was watching Orlov?"

Kruger nodded. "I never saw her, but I remember you talking about her."

"She worked for Orlov as a secretary. When he returned to Moscow under the supervision of his fellow comrades, his business suddenly ceased to exist. She sought solace in my arms one night after she lost her job."

CHAPTER 32

Tallinn, Estonia

The email Tomas Pavlovich read for the second time caused an eyebrow to rise. Even though the wording revealed nothing of consequence a member of law enforcement would find suspicious, the meaning was clear. Two individuals threatened the success of his well-planned and, so far, perfectly executed project.

After contemplating the email's meaning, he replied with a suggestion the two men needed to speak on the phone. Ten minutes later, his cell phone chirped and he accepted the call. "Da."

Markovic spoke in fluent Russian. "So, what do you want done?"

"The situation requires a swift solution."

"I agree."

"Can you handle the arrangements from your location?"

"Yes."

"Make sure the results are satisfactory."

"Understood."

"Where is the woman?"

"New York City."

"That complicates things."

"Not for me."

"Ahh—I forgot."

"I know someone willing to take the job. However, it will be expensive."

"I am not concerned about costs at this time. Just the results."

"Once the arrangements are made, I will contact you."

"Very good. What about the other project?"

"The seeds have been planted. We are just waiting for them to sprout."

"Excellent."

The call ended, and Pavlovich smiled as he put the cell phone down. Things were progressing rapidly. He turned his attention to other matters.

***

Montreal, Canada

Kreso Markovic lowered the cell phone from his ear and returned to the interior from the balcony of his fourth-floor apartment. After closing the sliding door, he went to the kitchen and poured a cup of fresh coffee.

The other man sitting at the breakfast bar eyed Markovic with curiosity. "What did he say?"

"As I suspected, he wants Peters and the Belsky woman silenced. Peters is on his way from New York City and should arrive within the hour. Do you want to meet him?"

"Yeah. I have unfinished business with him."

Markovic raised an eyebrow. "Such as?"

"I drove the truck that hit the kid. He's never paid me."

"He seems to be making a habit of not honoring his

commitments. It is unfortunate Peters abandoned the woman in New York. Not having them together complicates things on our end."

"Not really. If I meet him in a secluded spot, it's not that complicated."

Markovic nodded. "I can—" His cell phone rang, interrupting him. Seeing the ID, he answered. "Yes?"

"It's Peters."

"Where are you?"

"Plattsburgh, Vermont getting gas."

"Are you familiar with the Refuge faunique Marguerite-D'Youville area?" Markovic looked at the man standing next to the breakfast bar sipping coffee. He nodded in agreement with the location.

"Yes."

"There's a small bistro on the southwest corner near where the Chateauguay River empties into the St. Lawrence River."

"I know where it is."

"Meet me there in two hours. I'll be standing outside the café."

"That's a bit out of the way, isn't it?"

"The area has isolated walking trails. I need to talk to you where we won't be heard by others."

"I'll be there."

The call ended, and Markovic placed the cell phone in his pocket. "As I was saying, I can take care of the woman in New York. You take care of Peters."

***

After positioning the rental car in the parking area facing the small bistro, Peters did not exit the vehicle immediately. No one stood in front of the Bistro. The small hotel, café, and a public pavilion for picnics and hikes, all appeared to be abandoned. The absence of Kevin Marks made him nervous. *Why did he want to meet in such an isolated area?*

He stepped out of the car, kept the door open and stood behind it. He looked around and suddenly realized why Marks did not show up. The hairs on the back of his neck stood as the realization of a trap became apparent. Just before stepping back into the car and driving away, he sensed someone behind him.

"Well, looky what I found."

Peters turned to see a man with a gun pointed at his midriff. He was three inches shorter and possessed broad shoulders with a narrow waist, giving him the appearance of a Y. The man also appeared extremely angry. "What are you doing here, Russell?"

"A better question would be, where's my money?"

"Annika was supposed to pay you."

"Well, she didn't, and I don't see her around. So, that makes you responsible."

"Take it up with Kevin Marks."

Franklin Russell smiled. "I've known Marks a lot longer than I've known you, asshole. Marks has never screwed me. You, on the other hand, have. Now I want the money."

"I don't have it here."

The shorter man with broad shoulders stepped closer and smiled. "No, I don't suppose you do." He shoved Peters back into the car and as he fell across the middle console, his head hit the passenger door.

Franklin Russell pointed the suppressed pistol at him and pulled the trigger twice. Smiling as he observed his handiwork, he checked to see if anyone might have seen the confrontation. The parking lot remained empty. He calmly shoved the dead man's feet inside, closed the car's door and walked away.

***

Kreso Markovic walked down a specific street of his old neighborhood in the Ridgewood section of Queens. He ducked into a small tavern near the corner of Wycliff and Menahan. The dimly lit interior contained numerous hushed conversations which ceased when he entered the room. He walked up to the bar and said to the man behind it, "What's up, Janko?"

"I was told you might show up. What the hell are you doing in Queens?"

The various conversations of the other patrons behind him resumed at the previous volume.

"Visitin' the old neighborhood. Is Tommy here yet? I'm supposed to meet him."

Janko motioned with his fist and thumb toward the rear of the bar. "He's in the back. When he told me you might stop by, I thought he was joking."

Markovic made his way around the various tables, nodding at a few old acquaintances he recognized as he moved toward the rear of the establishment. He moved a dark curtain aside and entered the adjacent room. On the other side, he saw a round table with four chairs, all vacant except one. Tomislav Valdic stood and offered his hand. "Kreso Markovic. I didn't think you knew your way back to Queens."

"Nonsense, Tommy. I've been busy."

"So, I've heard."

The two men sat down across from each other, both assessing the other. "What'd ya hear?"

"Things."

"Come on, Tommy. What things?"

"I understand you got involved with a bunch of white supremacists out West."

"Rumors."

"Makes no never mind to me. The ones I know around here are pretty good guys."

Markovic remained quiet as he studied his old friend.

"So, why the visit, Kreso?"

"I need a favor." When the man across from him did not respond, Markovic continued. "And, I will be happy to compensate anyone who can grant me this favor."

Valdic laughed out loud. "Then it is not a favor. It is a job."

"Okay, I need a job done."

The man leaned across the table. "What kind of job?"

"There's a woman being held in the Queens Central Booking unit. She has information others do not need to know."

"What's her name?"

"Annika Belsky."

"Russian?"

Markovic nodded.

"The fact she is a Russian will get you a discount. The fact she is a Russian woman, there are those who would do it just for the fun of it. But…"

"How much?"

Valdic held up five fingers.

"Your cut?"

The man shrugged. "Since it is you, I will cut my fee in half."

Markovic smiled and withdrew an envelope from his back pocket. From it he took a folded bundle of one-hundred-dollar bills and slid them across the table. "There's the five thousand." After Valdic retrieved them, Markovic counted out twenty more and placed them on the table. "For your children and your children's children, my friend."

"You are most kind, Kreso. Your job will be completed tonight."

CHAPTER 33

Lyon, France

The time approached noon as Kruger sipped coffee in his room trying to determine the team's next move. Since he was new to the US Marshals Service, he decided to check with the director before making decisions he usually made on his own while with the FBI.

Adrian Watson answered on the second ring. "Good morning, Marshal Kruger."

"Hello, sir. Sorry for calling so early, but I have a couple of questions."

"I'll try to answer them. If I can't I'll find someone who can."

"Thank you. If I need to take the team to Estonia—"

"You don't have to ask permission, Sean. I had a long discussion with Paul Stumpf the other day."

"How's he doing?"

"He seems to be improving. But it could be another two months before he's able to return to work. Anyway, my discussion with Paul confirmed one of the reasons you're now with the US Marshals. You think independently and strategically. Therefore, you don't have to ask permission to take your team to Estonia. Just do it. I might add, he's pleased you're with the Marshals Service."

Smiling, Kruger was beginning to like Adrian Watson. "Thank you."

"What was the other question?"

"Actually, it's a request. I need a federal arrest warrant for Kreso Markovich, aka Kevin Marks, aka Dominic Ruiz, and aka Miroslav Klaus. There is probably one out on Kevin Marks, but it needs to be updated with his alias. Interpol is issuing a Red Notice on him to back up the US warrant. They are also issuing a Red Notice on Michael Peters, aka Mikhail Petrov. I believe there is already an Illinois state arrest warrant out of Chicago on him. If you can have someone upgrade it to a federal one, that will help also."

"You've been busy."

"The conference was well worth it."

"You probably learned all of this over an expensive dinner?"

"No, I'm a cheap date, Adrian. It only cost me two beers."

The director of the US Marshals chuckled.

They discussed several administrative concerns Kruger possessed before the call ended. Checking the time, he determined Stephanie would still be asleep, so he chose not to call her. He finished getting packed for their midafternoon departure and headed down to the café to meet the rest of the team.

When he arrived, to his surprise, Brutka was already there talking to Jimmie. JR and Hannah were nowhere to be seen. As he sat, he saw a concerned expression on the larger man. "You don't look pleased this morning, Sergey."

Brutka said, "Sit down, there's been a development."

Frowning Kruger sat across from his Ukrainian friend

and said, "What?"

Jimmie answered the question, "Interpol is reporting that Mikhail Petrov was found shot to death at a Canadian wildlife refuge outside of Montreal late yesterday."

Kruger grabbed his cell phone to see if he had been notified. Nothing. "I just talked to Adrian Watson. He didn't say anything about it."

"He probably doesn't know." Brutka took a sip of his coffee. "Interpol has a very close relationship with the Royal Canadian Mounted Police."

As he said this, Kruger's cell phone chirped. He answered it immediately. "Kruger."

"Sean, it's Adrian Watson."

"Yes, sir. I just heard."

"How would you hear about it in France? It just happened at the Queens Central Booking."

"Uh, I didn't hear anything about that. What are you talking about?"

"Annika Belsky was found dead in her cell a few minutes ago. What are you referring to?"

"Royal Canadian Mounted Police are reporting Mikhail Petrov was killed in Montreal, Canada, yesterday."

"Ah-boy. Okay, let me get details on both of these incidents, and I'll have someone get back to you."

Kruger ended the call and looked back and forth to Brutka and Gibbs. "Annika Belsky was killed in her cell last night."

"What the hell is going on, Sean?"

"I don't know, Jimmie. But we're wasting our time here in France. Instead of going to Estonia at this time, we'd better divert back to New York." He turned to Brutka. "After we know more, I'll get back to you on going to Estonia."

The big man nodded.

***

The Gulfstream G650 cruised east at 36,000 feet for its six-hour flight to New York City. Since Lyon, France was six hours ahead of the city, it meant Kruger and company would add six hours to the length of their day. Kruger's disorientation by the constant jet lag was beginning to wear on his nerves.

JR sat across from him and leaned over the aisle. "Can we stop this international jet setting for a while? I don't know if it's morning or night."

Nodding, his eyes closed, Kruger said, "Now you see why I don't miss flying. It screws up your sense of time."

"You realize we took off in France at 2:35 a.m. and will arrive in DC at 2:45 to drop Hannah off and then we'll be in Springfield by four."

"Very much aware of that, JR. It makes for a long day."

"Okay, I'm done with my rant. What now?"

"The plane will be making a stop at La Guardia. Queens Central Booking is about six miles from there. Jimmie and I are going to interview the person they believe killed Annika. We are basically wasting yours and Hannah's time hanging out with us. We need you back at your computer, and Hannah needs to be working with the DOJ to get warrants prepared."

"So, what are you saying?"

With a big smile, Kruger said, "You get to go home."

JR returned the smile.

***

Queens Central Booking

Captain Clarita Mateo stood next to Kruger as they observed the female prisoner on the video monitor. She was sitting in an interrogation room waiting for Kruger and

Gibbs to interview her. Kruger asked, "What can you tell me about her, Captain?"

"She's a frequent guest, Marshal. Usually for drugs, soliciting, or petty theft. Serves a few months and then released due to overcrowding. She was picked up yesterday for shoplifting. Somehow, she was assigned to the same cell as the Belsky woman. We found her sitting in her cell smiling at us with the other woman dead in her cot."

Kruger frowned and looked at the captain. "Who assigned her to the same cell?"

"A sergeant who claims he was told to put her there."

"Who told him?"

"He won't say."

"Great." He paused for a second. "What's the woman's name?"

"Sonja Popovic"

Kruger frowned. "Russian?"

"No, she's from a Serbian neighborhood in Ridgewood."

The word Ridgewood gave Kruger pause. "Where's Ridgewood?"

"It's a neighborhood in Queens with a heavy Romanian, Serbian, Puerto Rican, Yugoslavian, and Slovenian population."

"How about Russian?"

The captain shook her head. "They don't like Russians in that neighborhood."

"You said Serbian, right?"

She nodded. "There's a large concentration of Serbs in Ridgewood."

Kruger stared at the woman on the video monitor for several moments. He turned to Gibbs and said, "Jimmie, I need to make a phone call before we interview her." Turning to the captain, he asked, "Is there a small room I can use to make a call?"

"Sure, you can use my office." She showed him the way.

When the door closed and he was alone, he searched his cell phone and found a formerly frequently used phone number. He hit the send icon and waited.

"I haven't heard from you in over six months, Sean. How are you?"

"Good, Ryan. How 'bout yourself?"

"Knee deep in the shit. Heard a rumor you got a presidential reprieve and are with the US Marshals Service. Any truth to the rumor?"

"Yeah, they created a new district and made me the marshal."

"Congratulations. Or am I being too presumptive?"

"Too early to tell." Kruger paused for a moment and then said, "I have a question."

"Sure."

"Do you remember the paperwork we found in Kevin Marks' office?"

"You mean about the Ford F-150?"

"No, about him being a naturalized citizen from Queens."

"Vaguely, why?"

"I need to know if he was from Ridgewood. It's a neighborhood in Queens."

"Okay, I can get the file. What else?"

"I also need to know if the name Kreso Markovic is Russian or Serbian. When we first found the paperwork, I assumed he was Russian. There's a chance he may be a Serb. If he is, I've got a whole new set of problems."

***

The interrogation room was small, but large enough for Kruger and Gibbs to sit across from the prisoner while Captain Mateo leaned against the door.

The first thing out of the Serbian woman's mouth was, "I want lawyer."

Kruger looked up from the file he was reading. "Excuse me?"

"I ain't talking to cops. I want lawyer."

"Why did you kill the woman, Ms. Popovic?"

"I want lawyer."

"Did someone pay you to kill the woman?"

"I want lawyer."

"You've made that perfectly clear. We just have a few questions first." Kruger narrowed his eyes, "Who is Kreso Markovic?"

Sonja Popovic's eyes widened, and she gasped.

Kruger smiled. "So, you know who he is?"

She shook her head violently. "No, I don't. Stop asking me questions."

Leaning forward, Kruger said, "Tell us about Markovic, and I will ask the prosecutor to work out a deal for you."

"I don't care what kind of a deal you work out. I'll be dead if I tell you anything."

"Is that why you killed, Annika Belsky?"

"They'd kill—" She stopped talking and closed her eyes. "I've said enough. I want lawyer."

Looking at Gibbs and the captain, Kruger stood. "After you talk to your lawyer and you change your mind, ask your lawyer to call me." He gave her a business card with his name and phone number on it.

She looked up as she tore the card in half. "You don't get it, do you?"

"Don't get what?"

"My lawyer will be paid by them. If I ask him to make deal, he will tell them. Then I will be the one who is lying in her bunk the next morning with her neck crushed."

"Who is them? Tell me, Sonja."

The woman folded her arms and pressed her lips together.

CHAPTER 34

New York City / Southwest Missouri

As the two men walked out of the Queens Central Booking facility, Gibbs said, "Where to now, Sean?"

Kruger looked at the ex-Navy SEAL and shook his head. "To be honest with you, this whole investigation feels like it's spinning out of control."

With a smile, Gibbs folded his arms. "I've been with you on several now. What's been your solution in the past when you felt this way?"

Chuckling, the newly installed US Marshal said, "Get everybody together in JR's conference room and hash it out. It's also time to bring Sandy into the mix."

Gibbs nodded with enthusiasm. "About damn time."

Glancing at his watch, Kruger grabbed his cell phone. JR answered the call immediately. "We're still at the airport. Don't say it. You need me to stay."

"Nope, not why I called. Tell the pilot we'll be there in thirty minutes. After we drop Hannah off at Joint Base Andrews, we're going home with you."

***

Early the Next Day
Southwest Missouri

Kruger stared at the coffee machine as the final drips stopped falling into the carafe. He poured a cup, replaced the glass container on the warmer, and stepped into the conference room. He was the first to arrive, having his own set of keys to the building and a passcode for the security system. JR was normally in his cubicle by six every morning, however, today was an exception. When they arrived back in town the previous evening, his friend's jet lag appeared worse than Kruger's. More than likely, he was struggling to get out of bed.

The second floor remained dark and quiet for another thirty minutes as Kruger gathered his thoughts and made notes on a legal pad. When additional lights started to illuminate the second-floor cubicle farm, he looked to see Jimmie and Alexia Gibbs walking around the perimeter of the large room. He glanced at his watch—fifteen minutes to seven, and JR still had not made an appearance.

When Jimmie and Alexia entered the conference room, she said, "JR sent a text message around three this morning."

"That explains why he isn't here yet."

"Yes, it does."

"What'd the message say?"

"He found something last night he needs to discuss with all of us."

"And he didn't tell you what that something was, did he?"

"No."

"Typical JR."

Just as he said this, he saw his friend appear at the top of the stairs on the opposite side of the second floor, his normal ramrod-straight walking posture replaced by a slouched, head down shuffle. When JR entered the conference room, Kruger immediately noticed the dark circles under his eyes.

JR said, "Sorry, I'm late."

Kruger smiled. "You look like shit."

"I feel that way, too."

"Get a cup of coffee and tell us what you found."

After depositing his laptop on the conference room table and taking his backpack to his cubicle, JR retrieved his coffee mug from a desk drawer. He returned to take his normal place in the meeting room. He swept his gaze around the room, "I had a thought last night. It seemed unlikely, considering how many security cameras we found around the site where Danny Barton died, not one of them contained an image of the truck driver."

Taking a sip of coffee, Kruger nodded. "I hadn't thought of it that way, but it's a good assumption."

"Kinda what I thought. So, I hacked into the Cambridge Police Department."

Kruger closed his eyes and slowly shook his head. "JR, you didn't."

"I did. It seems they had numerous additional security camera videos we were never told about."

Jimmie Gibbs stiffened, and Kruger narrowed his eyes. "How many?"

"I found at least ten. None of which were logged in by Detective Bell. Plus, the file names did not identify them as part of the investigation."

"Then, how did you find them?"

"Date stamp on the files."

"Who logged them in?"

"Marlene Hoffman." He paused and took a sip of coffee. "The dates vary, but the first five were dated a day after we left, a few the next day and the rest four days later."

"Did you look at any of them?"

Another nod. He moved his mouse and touched the left button. "Here's what I found."

He turned the screen around so those across from him could see the image. Gibbs studied the picture, and a slow smile came to his face. "I'll be damned. That's Franklin Russell."

A slight grin appeared on Kruger. "This means our theory about Kreso Markovic is correct. Although, I thought Russell was in a federal prison somewhere."

JR turned the laptop back toward him and typed on the keyboard. "I thought so, too. So, I looked it up. He was released on bail prior to his trial and skipped out. He hasn't been seen since, until the image from the security camera."

Kruger said, "Which means he's a fugitive, which also means, as US Marshals, we are within our jurisdiction to pursue him."

Standing, JR walked out of the room and returned with two pieces of paper he retrieved from his desk. He handed the top one to Kruger. "On a hunch, I accessed the Canadian Province of Saskatchewan driver's license files in the capital of Regina. Guess what I found?" He handed one of the pages to Kruger."

It contained an image of a Canadian driver's license with the picture of Franklin Russell. Kruger looked at the name. "Forest Roberts?"

Gibbs said, "That was one of the aliases used by Russell if I'm not mistaken."

"You are correct, Jimmie." JR handed the other page to Kruger. "The reason I chose Saskatchewan is it has one of the easiest and quickest paths to permanent-residence status in Canada. Both Russell and Marks have status as Canadian citizens. Although Marks' is under the name Dominic Ruiz."

As he studied the pages from the SGI, Saskatchewan driver's licensing and vehicle registration department,

Kruger pursed his lips and looked up at the individuals sitting around the table. "Good work, JR. Our decision to return was the correct one."

A large man with bulging biceps entered the conference room. "Didn't know I was late."

Kruger smiled. "You're not, we got started early, get some coffee and take a seat."

Benedict "Sandy" Knoll, a retired special forces major possessed a large frame with muscles stretching the short sleeves of an untucked black polo shirt hanging over a narrow waist and faded blue jeans. He kept his dark-blond hair short, allowing streaks of gray to appear above his ears. His handsome, weathered face, permanently tanned from too many tours of duty in Iraq and Afghanistan, displayed a frown. He said, "What'd I miss?"

Kruger looked over his readers and said, "When did you start wearing bifocals, Sandy?"

"Since my last eye exam. I'm still not used to them."

"They look good on you." When the big man only glared at Kruger, he grinned and proceeded to summarize what the team learned prior to his arrival.

"So, we're finally going after Kevin Marks."

"If we're going to find out why Danny Barton was murdered, I believe we have to."

"So, how did Franklin Russell stay out of prison?" Knoll looked from Kruger to JR.

JR answered, "It seems his lawyer arranged for bail. After his release, he skipped, disappeared, and last showed up in a security camera shot driving the truck that killed Barton."

Standing and walking out of the conference room to warm his coffee, Kruger returned. "One thing I didn't mention, Sandy, is there are ten security camera videos mislabeled in the Cambridge Police Department files. My question is why. Unless—"

Tilting his head, Knoll asked, "What are you thinking?"

"It's highly unusual for a chief of police to log evidence in and then mislabel it. One, maybe. But ten? While I don't particularly care for Marlene, she never struck me as someone who would get involved with a crime. Much less a murder."

Kruger noticed JR not paying attention as he stared intently at his laptop screen. "What's wrong, JR?"

The computer whiz ignored the question as he continued to work on his computer. Finally, he sat straighter and looked at Kruger. "I didn't mention that when I tapped into the Cambridge PD computer, I left the backdoor open. I just checked the bank account Hoffman uses for her payroll direct deposit. She had a sizeable deposit made to her account the day after Danny Barton was killed. Source is a bank in the Caymans."

One eyebrow rose, Kruger asked, "How sizeable?"

"Upper five figures. She transferred it the next day to a brokerage account."

"Shit." Kruger paused for a second. "How much is in the brokerage account?"

"Haven't checked yet."

"Make a note to do so."

JR nodded.

CHAPTER 35

Cambridge, MA

Cambridge Police Department Chief of Police Marlene Hoffman studied the balance in her department 401k. The amount depressed her. The outcome of being ambitious and constantly breaking glass ceilings during her thirty years in law enforcement were personally rewarding. Financially, she possessed little to show for her efforts.

Five year earlier, with the realization she would never be able to retire to someplace warm, she made a decision. The money came in slowly at first, but now the balance in her private account located on a small island south of Cuba in the Caribbean Sea, contained ten times the amount in her current municipal retirement program set up by a well-meaning city council.

With the latest deposit in this secret account, she finally possessed enough cash to cut the cord with law enforcement and divorce herself from the constraints of her long-term career. A career she grew less enchanted with as each day passed. Never married, she did not have to consult anyone about her pending retirement. The only individual she needed to contact would be the city manager. The fact the current occupant of the office happened to be a woman, whom she argued with constantly, made giving her pending short notice for retirement even more satisfying.

She checked the time on her cell phone and noticed it was time to depart for her 4:30 p.m. appointment with the woman. As she closed her laptop and prepared to leave for the day, she received a text message from a familiar number.

Need to talk
Concerning?
Location of Bell
Unknown
Not a good answer
Only one I have
Find her
Did you know feds now involved?
No who?
Last name Kruger

A reply did not immediately appear. After a long three minutes, she saw.

FBI?
No DIA
Will check it out – Find Bell

Hoffman frowned at the last message. She decided not to reply and hurried to her meeting with the city manager.

***

City Manager Janet Powers finished reading the letter handed to her by Chief of Police Hoffman. She placed it on the desktop in front of her, removed her glasses, and smiled. "Marlene, congratulations on your decision to retire, but you aren't giving us much time to find a qualified candidate to replace you."

Returning the smile, she knew to be forced, Hoffman said, "You have several excellent candidates within the department."

"As a rule, we would need to post the position and allow four weeks for candidates to respond and then start the interview phase. It could take up to three months or longer to find someone."

Hoffman shrugged. "Four weeks is all I can give you."

Taking a deep breath for effect, Janet Powers let it out slowly. "Very well, I will forward your letter to HR and ask them to post the position. How much vacation do you have built up?"

"Four weeks."

"I assume you will be expecting a check after your last day?"

"I will be taking a week off, starting next Monday and expect a check for the remaining time after my last day."

With a nod, the city manager stood and offered her hand. "I wish you good luck."

Hoffman ignored the offer, turned, and walked out of the office.

Returning to her seat, Powers smiled, this time with pleasure. "Goodbye and good riddance."

***

Back in her office, Marlene Hoffman used her exclusive access to all levels of police records to copy the mislabeled security files from the main computer to a flash drive. She decided to leave the originals on the server, figuring no one would find them until she was long gone. Even then, she could plead innocence as the detective department would have been the ones who mislabeled them.

At seven in the evening, she made her way to the unmarked police car the department provided. As with everything else, with her current position, she would not miss having to drive a vehicle with over a hundred thousand miles and a persistent unidentifiable odor.

The drive to Hoffman's small suburban house north of Cambridge on Route 28 normally took thirty minutes in light traffic. Tonight, light traffic allowed her progress on the two-lane section of road to proceed at the posted fifty-five miles an hour. She noticed a large vehicle rapidly approaching in her rearview mirror. Traffic moving south was more congested with numerous tractor-trailer units spaced in among the SUVs and cars heading into the city.

As the approaching vehicle grew closer, she recognized it as a large pickup truck. At first, she did not give it much attention, but as it grew closer without slowing down, she prepared to take evasive action. As the truck approached, it swerved to her right as if to pass her on the highway shoulder. She looked at the southbound lane and saw a large semi approaching. With the big Ram 3500 pickup now side-by-side to her right, she slammed on her brakes just as it struck her car in the front quarter panel. This action forced the police car to skid into the oncoming lane in front of the semi.

The resulting head-on collision between two vehicles, one with a mass of a ton and a half and the other over forty tons did not favor survival for anyone in the smaller vehicle.

Marlene Hoffman died on impact with the semi as the large pickup sped away north on Massachusetts Route 28.

***

Franklin Russell watched in the Ram 3500's rearview mirror as the police cruiser driven by Marlene Hoffman collided with the semi. After taking a quick glance to check the road ahead, he noticed no one preparing to chase him. With no traffic ahead and none behind, he sped up, leaving the reflection of the wreck growing smaller as the distance increased.

He pressed an icon on his cell phone. The call was answered immediately.

"Is it done?"

"Yeah, added bonus, they hit head-on. No way she survived that one."

"Good." The voice on the other end paused for a few moments. "We may have a small problem."

"What?"

"Remember the FBI agent from Wyoming?"

"Kruger?"

"Yeah."

"What about him?"

"He may be involved."

"How? Last I checked, he retired not long after, I skipped bail."

"During the last communication I had with Hoffman, she mentioned his name."

Russell did not respond right away. He checked the rearview mirror again. No pursuer in sight. Finally, he said, "If he is involved, what then?"

"We'll have to make sure he doesn't interfere with getting our money."

***

News of the horrific vehicle accident on Route 28 north of Boston spread quickly as local and national news media picked up the story regarding the death of the Cambridge chief of police. Media coverage intensified the following day as hints of a scandal concerning Marlene Hoffman grew from an examination of her office laptop and personal finances.

Because of his disdain for watching cable news channels, newly appointed US Marshal Sean Kruger went about his day unaware of the happenings in Massachusetts.

That all changed at twenty minutes after two in the afternoon when he received a call on his cell phone.

"This is Sean."

"Sean Kruger?"

"Yes."

"This is Detective Brad Parker with the Cambridge, Massachusetts Police Department. We spoke a couple of weeks ago."

"Yes, Detective. What can I do for you?"

"Uh—are you still involved with the murder investigation of Danny Barton?"

"As a matter of fact, I am."

"We've, uh—had a new development here in Cambridge."

"Oh, what kind of development?"

"Not good. Marlene Hoffman was killed in a head-on collision with a tractor-trailer rig last night."

"I'm sorry to hear that."

"We've, or I should say, I've been tasked with going through her computer. I found something that may implicate her in the death of the Barton kid."

Kruger remained quiet as the detective continued.

"You're a federal agent, aren't you?"

"Yes, US Marshals Service."

"That's what I thought, but I couldn't remember which one." He paused for a moment. "Hoffman had a flash drive in her purse that contained security camera videos copied from our evidence files. Did you have suspicions about the chief when you were here?"

"No, not really. But I suspected additional videos were available."

"Why?"

"Sheer number of security cameras in the neighborhood."

"I remember now. Ginger Bell felt the same way."

"That's correct. Has she been located?"

"Yes. She was staying with her parents. Apparently, she had a run-in with Hoffman and was threatened. Another issue I'm looking into."

"That's good to hear. I'm glad she's okay."

"She will be. Getting back to Hoffman, I was told she went to the apartment with you when the body of Kenneth Deloach was discovered."

"That's correct."

"Was she ever out of your sight during that time, Marshal?"

Kruger did not answer right away, deciding whether to reveal what he knew already. He chose not to tell Parker. "If I remember correctly, she stepped out of the apartment for about an hour. Why?"

"We found a few numbers on her cell phone we can't identify, with one being an international call."

"Uh—oh."

"Yeah, uh—oh."

"Detective, why are you telling me this? This should be an internal affairs investigation within your department."

"That's the trouble, Marshal. I don't know who to believe around here. Hoffman's been dead less than twenty-four hours, and the vultures are already circling for her job."

"Who hired her?"

"City manager."

"Is he still there?"

"Yes, but it's a she."

"Sorry, do you trust her?"

Kruger's answer was total silence. Finally, he heard, "Ginger told me you were a stand-up guy and that I could be honest with you."

Kruger frowned, trying to determine what he could say to the detective. Finally, an idea formed. "What do you need from me, Brad?"

CHAPTER 36

Southwest Missouri / Cambridge, MA

Stephanie Kruger sat on the bed watching her husband pack for the fourth time in two weeks. "How are you holding up with all this traveling, Sean?"

He looked up after folding a pair of jeans and placing them in the carry-on suitcase. "At first, the jet lag was getting to me, but I've slipped back into the groove of traveling with ease. A good night's sleep and I'm fine." He stopped and looked at his wife. "This is the most I've been gone in almost a year. How are you doing with it?"

"I'm glad to see you happy again. You've got a reprieve on your retirement for another two years. I can deal with it if you can."

"What if it lasts a few more years beyond that?"

She sat up straighter. "Could it?"

"It could, but I'm not counting on it."

Standing, she stepped over to him and put her arm around his waist. "Sean, I saw how miserable you were. You didn't do well being a retired person."

He nodded, returned the embrace and remained quiet as he held her. Finally, he said, "Eventually, retirement is going to happen whether I like it or not. I need to quit feeling sorry for myself and find something I'll enjoy doing."

She smiled. "Like what?"

"I could play golf every day."

"You hate golf."

He chuckled. "I was being sarcastic."

She tightened her hug and put her cheek on his chest. "It's not funny, Sean. I don't want to see you retire and slowly die from boredom."

Placing his chin on the top of her head, he closed his eyes. "Trust me. That's not something I want either."

They held each other in silence for a while. Finally, she said, "How long will you be gone this time?"

"Not sure. We've been running around in circles without a direction in this investigation for a week. I'm tired of it. Three of the principal suspects are dead, and now we learn Marlene Hoffman may have been involved. The only positive from our side trip to France was learning a few of the aliases Franklin Russell uses. Other than that, it was a waste of time."

"So, why go back to Cambridge?"

"I need to know how deep Hoffman was involved. Plus, I think it's time I dig a little more into Danny Barton's work and background."

A puzzled look crossed her face. "You're going alone?"

"No, JR's going, too. We leave early in the morning. We have several interviews lined up. One is with the Cambridge detective who called me. It's scheduled for tomorrow afternoon. The following day, JR's going over to MIT, and I'm going to talk with Danny Barton's fiancée."

"So, I have you for one more night?" One of her eyebrows rose as the grin on her face grew.

He returned the smile. "What'd you have in mind?"

"Let's get the kids settled then I'll show you."

***

Cambridge, MA

"Thanks for meeting me here, Marshal."

Kruger shook Detective Brad Parker's hand as they arrived at a table in the back of a popular coffee shop just off Harvard Square. "Brad Parker, this is my partner, JR Diminski."

The two men shook hands as JR sized up the detective. Of equal height to JR, Parker outweighed him by thirty pounds. The man kept his thinning gray hair short in an old-fashioned flattop. The steel framed glasses were situated low on a long thin nose. His brown eyes appraised Diminski over the top of the spectacles. "Nice to meet you, Marshal."

JR just nodded.

After they sat, Parker said, "You two want anything?"

Kruger shook his head and then asked, "Why such an out-of-the-way place, Brad?"

"Too many eyes around the office, if you know what I mean."

"I do."

A young woman with an angry scowl and blue hair deposited a coffee in front of Parker. Without saying a word, she walked away from the table. The detective watched her leave and then turned back to Kruger and JR. "Like I told you on the phone, the death of Marlene Hoffman has everyone popping champaign corks. She wasn't one to instill loyalty in her fellow officers."

Not wishing to add his own mistrust of the woman to the conversation, Kruger said, "Did you bring her cell phone?"

Parker nodded.

"JR is part of our cybercrime unit. Would you allow him to examine it?"

Looking around the room, Parker pulled a phone from a sport coat pocket and handed it to JR. "There's a frequently called number on it our tech team can't seem to identify. She called it five times on the day Deloach's body was discovered."

Taking the phone, JR thumbed through it. He looked up. "Uh—she didn't have a security code on it?"

With a shake of his head, Parker clasped his hands together in front of him. "That's a problem. It's against CPD regulations. All phones are to be secured with a passcode, hers wasn't."

"Odd." He put the phone down and extracted his laptop from his backpack.

While he did this, Kruger asked, "Has the vehicle that forced Marlene Hoffman's car into the path of a semi been located?"

Parker nodded. "Yeah, it was stolen. Forensics is crawling all over it. They pulled three sets of prints out of it, two of which belonged to the husband and wife who owned it, and the other we sent to the FBI. They haven't gotten back to us yet."

Kruger nodded. "Brad, when we spoke on the phone you mentioned your distrust of everyone in the department. Want to elaborate?"

Taking a deep breath, the detective nodded. "I have a few friends I trust, but I don't want them involved. It's the city manager I don't trust. She's the one who hired her."

"When?"

Parker looked at the ceiling for a few moments. "Uh—about five years ago."

"Do you remember where Hoffman was before the she was hired by the city manager?"

The detective shook his head. "I tried not to interact with her. Plus, she had a tendency to treat us in the detective department as peons. During the time she's been here, I've only had five conversations with her, none of them pleasant."

"Huh."

JR looked up from his laptop, "The number she called was a router."

Kruger said, "A router?"

Nodding, he explained. "Same concept as a phone operator at a business routing calls to the correct department. Only it's done electronically. She calls a number. The router recognizes the number calling and transfers it to a pre-programmed phone. The recipient could change his or her number every day as long as the router knows where to send the call."

Frowning, Kruger said, "A method for calling someone who uses burner phones."

JR's answer was a nod.

"Is there any way to trace it past the router?"

"Not from here."

"Hmmmm." Kruger narrowed his eyes. "Who's the city manager?"

"Her name's Janet Powers."

"How long's she been in her position?"

"Twenty years or more, longer than I've been in the department."

"Why don't you trust her?"

"Not sure. She's one of those individuals who makes you feel like taking a shower after dealing with them."

Kruger pulled a picture of out of his jacket. "Does this guy look familiar?"

Parker pushed his glasses up his nose and studied the photo. "Kind of, who is it?"

Raising both eyebrows, Kruger gave Parker a half smile. "Before I answer that, where did you see him?"

"I'm trying to remember." Parker closed his eyes. "Got it. He had a meeting with Hoffman in her office the day before Ginger Bell failed to show up for her shift and took off for her parents. We all thought it funny. After he left, the chief was in an unusually foul mood."

"Did Hoffman meet with Ginger that day?"

"Don't know. She might have. I left right afterward to check on a robbery." He paused. "Who's the guy, Sean?"

Taking the photograph back, Kruger stared at it for a few seconds then pursed his lips. "He goes by various aliases, but his real name is Franklin Russell."

"Never heard of him."

"That doesn't surprise me. Can you get me a copy of those prints from the stolen truck?"

"Sure, why?"

"JR can get them checked pretty fast. Russell is involved with the death of Danny Barton. How? We don't know yet. But if the lizard side of my brain is correct, I'll bet you a steak dinner the unknown prints from the truck involved in Hoffman's accident are his."

***

The meeting with Parker lasted fifteen more minutes, after which he left the coffee shop, leaving Kruger and JR alone at the table. JR said, "Well, this is turning in a direction I didn't expect."

"You and me both, JR. When's your appointment at MIT tomorrow?"

"Ten, why?"

Kruger pulled out his cell phone and found the number for Natalie Hart. He pressed the send icon and waited.

"Hello."

"Natalie, this is Sean Kruger."

"Hi."

"Are you still available to see me tomorrow?"

"Yes, my last class is over at eleven."

"Would you prefer to meet at your place or somewhere

else?"

She was quiet for a few moments, "Uh—I moved. There's a restaurant called the Vegan Palace just northwest of campus on Massachusetts Avenue, I could meet you there around eleven thirty."

"Perfect, I'll see you then." He ended the call and turned his gaze toward JR. "While you're poking around MIT, I'll talk to Natalie."

JR nodded.

Placing his elbows on the table, Kruger clasped his hands together. "There's a crossing somewhere between Danny Barton and Kevin Marks. Maybe she'll be able to tell us when it occurred."

CHAPTER 37

Cambridge, MA

Natalie Hart appeared thinner and frailer to Kruger than the last time he saw her. As they shook hands at the table she already occupied, he noticed a half-eaten bowl of rice and beans she appeared to be ignoring.

"Thank you for meeting with me, Natalie."

She smiled but did not respond right away. Finally, she said, "What can I do for you, Agent Kruger?"

"First, you can call me, Sean." He felt it unnecessary to tell her about his transition to the US Marshals office. "Natalie, I need some information about Danny. Hopefully it won't be too painful for you."

She nodded.

"How did he first learn about the job at the presidential campaign office?"

"His advisor."

"Max Keller?"

"Yes."

"Did Danny ask his advisor to find a job for him?"

She shook her head. "No, the campaign contacted the department first. Max knew Danny needed a job to help finish up his doctoral thesis. He already had numerous options for summer employment. The campaign gig was the one offering the most money and the least conflict."

"Since he was part of the national campaign, who hired him?"

"He had a phone interview with the director of the national campaign. I forget their name."

"Ruth Greer."

The young woman stared at Kruger with wide eyes then just nodded. "I think so. Danny only mentioned it once. In fact, he was a little apathetic about taking the job."

"Really?"

She nodded.

"Can you tell me why?"

"Money. He told me a few days after he started, he wasn't sure how ethical it was for him to be using his systems to predict elections."

"But he did the work anyway."

She shrugged. "Money can overcome a lot of moral quandaries, Agent."

"Please call me, Sean."

The woman blinked several times and nodded. "Like I said, the money solved a lot of problems. It gave us a clear path for financing his doctorate work without going into debt before our wedding."

Kruger could see tears welling in her eyes. He paused for a second. "Do you need a few minutes, Natalie?"

She shook her head. "No, but thank you for asking, Sean."

Glad she was finally calling him by his first name, Kruger proceeded. "Do you remember some of the other companies he interviewed with?"

"Oh, yes. He interviewed with some of the largest data companies in the world. But since this was to be a part-time position for him, they didn't offer a lot of money."

"What companies?"

"Oh, let's see, IBM, Salesforce, Google, Odin Analytica, Oracle…"

"Excuse me, did you say, Odin Analytica?"

"Yes, they actually offered more money than the president's campaign. But they also wanted him to sign a contract giving them proprietary ownership of any algorithms he developed while in their employ. He felt uncomfortable about the arrangement and decided to go with the campaign job."

Kruger stared at Natalie for several seconds before he recovered from her revelation. Maintaining a neutral expression, he asked, "Do you remember the name of the person from Odin he interviewed with?"

She nodded. "Normally I wouldn't, but the man became so rude and abusive after Danny turned him down. I'll never forget his name, Dominic Ruiz. He was from Canada."

Reaching into his sport coat pocket, Kruger retrieved the two pictures he carried with him. He laid them on the table facing Natalie. "Do you recognize either of these two men, Natalie?"

She tapped on the picture of Kevin Marks. "That's him."

"Does the other man look familiar?"

She shook her head.

"How long did Ruiz bother Danny about not taking the job?"

"If I remember correctly, we heard from the man at least once a day for two weeks. Danny got so frustrated with the calls, he finally contacted the Cambridge Police Department."

"What did they do?"

"Nothing that we knew about. But the man finally stopped calling."

"Do you remember who Danny spoke to at the police?"

"No, sorry."

"That's okay." The pieces of the puzzle started falling into place as Kruger gave the young woman a fatherly smile. "Thank you, Natalie. You've been very helpful. Would it be all right if I have any additional questions, to give you a call?"

She nodded and then said, "Why did you have a picture of Ruiz in your pocket?"

Looking at the grieving woman, he decided it was best to let her know. "We consider both of those men as persons of interest in Danny's death."

She covered her mouth with her hand as she stared wide-eyed at Kruger.

***

"I must say, John, Ravi was more animated than I have seen him in years after his short trip to your company. He hasn't stopped talking about all the malicious cyberattacks you've been able to stop."

JR stared at Max Keller for several moments before he said, "I'm glad he enjoyed his stay. He was critical in helping solve a major problem."

"Yes, he said he felt like a hacker for a few days."

Choosing not to verbally comment, he gave his host a smile.

"I know you're here to discuss Danny Barton."

"Yes."

"The department is planning to posthumously grant him a PhD and publish his work."

"That's good to hear, Professor. Would it be possible for me to look at Danny's doctoral notes? I'm interested in who he might have conferred with or if he was basing his findings on the work of another mathematician."

"Can I ask why?"

"As we discussed before, we believe he was targeted

because of the unique algorithms he developed. Both of us know many breakthroughs are reached when someone takes a new or different approach to a discarded theory."

Keller nodded.

"We want to explore if that's the case here."

The professor narrowed his eyes. "Do you suspect someone killed Danny out of professional jealousy?"

"Well—actually, no. At least, that's not the direction we're headed at the moment. Let me ask you a question?"

"Sure."

"How would a person or company not associated with MIT know what Danny was working on?"

"Anyone who subscribes to, or reads the *Journal of Mathematical Modelling and Algorithms in Operations Research*."

"Why?"

"Danny started publishing in the journal after he attained his master's degree. It's the only place he ever submitted his work."

"I would assume a list of regular readers to that publication would be short."

Keller nodded.

"Where could I get information on the recipients?"

"What do you suspect?"

"Someone was following his work. We need to know who."

"I can assist you with getting in touch with the publication's editor."

JR smiled. "Perfect."

***

As a rule, JR Diminski, seldom waited for *the proper authorities* to provide him with any information he sought. He simply hacked into the database and extracted what he needed. However, in this situation, he carefully pursued proper access. Since any information he gathered might be crucial as evidence in a future criminal trial.

A knock on his hotel room door startled him out of his concentration. Checking the clock at the bottom right of his laptop, he rose from the desk to admit his friend.

As he entered, Kruger said, "What'd you learn?"

"A little, you?"

"A clear connection between Danny Barton and Odin Analytica."

JR nodded as he sat at the desk and pointed to his computer. "Well, then we have two connections. Look at this."

Placing his half-readers on, Kruger asked, "What am I looking at, JR?"

"The reason Odin Analytica knew about Barton's research."

Kruger stared at the screen as a small frown appeared. "Not following you."

Pointing to a specific name on the list, JR said, "Tomas Pavlovich."

"The guy who owns Odin Analytica?"

"One and the same. He subscribed to the journal Danny Barton published his research in."

"Huh." Kruger paused and displayed a slight grin. "Guess who interviewed Danny Barton for a summer job?"

"Pavlovich?"

"Almost." Kruger sat on the edge of the bed. "Dominic Ruiz, aka Kevin Marks.

One of JR's eyebrows rose. "Who did he say he worked for?"

"Danny Barton interviewed with several large data companies for his summer job. Odin Analytica being one of them. Marks claimed he was the Odin Analytica's representative when he interviewed him for the job."

"So, that gives us two references suggesting Odin knew who Barton was and what his research was about."

"Correct. Now, what are we going to do with this information?"

"Since Sergey Brutka is a big shot with Interpol, I think it's time we have a Zoom meeting with him and Joseph."

Kruger checked his watch. "If we hurry, we can catch the eight-p.m. shuttle to Washington, tonight."

CHAPTER 38

Arlington, VA
The Next Day

The American Airlines shuttle flight from Boston Logan International Airport to Washington DC's Ronald Reagan National Airport arrived just before ten p.m. This allowed Kruger and JR a few hours of sleep before their eight-fifteen meeting the next morning.

The conference room next to US Marshal Director Adrian Watson's office buzzed with activity as the participants gathered for the early morning meeting. The video call, scheduled for eight-thirty Eastern Time with Interpol at two-thirty Lyon, France time, would mark the first time US Attorney General Dale Delgado and the current president of Interpol interacted.

JR turned to Kruger and said, "I don't feel comfortable leading the discussion."

Looking over his half-readers, Kruger said, "Why not?"

His friend's answer consisted of a shrug.

"You understand the computer aspects of our evidence

better than I do."

"If they ask, I'll answer, but they won't."

"Why wouldn't they?"

"Because it's boring, Sean. Besides, most of them probably don't understand or want to understand the mechanics of how anything on the Internet works."

"They don't need to know how to build a watch, JR. They just need to know what time it is.

"I understand that, but I'm still not comfortable addressing them."

Leaning over to speak close to JR's ear, Kruger said, "No one, and I'll repeat that, no one is looking for you anymore, JR."

"I'm aware of that, Sean. Old habits can be hard to break."

Blowing out a breath, Kruger nodded and turned to wait for the start of the conference.

Attorney General Delgado started the meeting by introducing everyone on his team. After finishing, he nodded toward Kruger who started his summary of the facts they knew so far. After his conclusion, he looked around the room and then at the flat screen monitor on the wall and asked, "Does anyone have any questions?"

Two individuals were visible on the screen from France: Sergey Brutka, who shook his head, and the president of Interpol, Ra Se-Yoon, who asked, "Marshal Kruger, Tomas Pavlovich is a well-respected member of several European commissions on cybersecurity. Getting anyone to believe he is working to undermine democratic elections across Western Europe could be difficult."

"I agree, President Se-Yoon. From what we've been able to determine, he keeps the fact he used to be with the KGB very quiet. However, as I mentioned, we do have a direct link of his knowledge of Danny Barton's work."

"Yes, you do. However, a good defense advocate could argue his receipt of the journal is merely a coincidence."

Kruger nodded. "He could. But a good prosecutor could argue the link of the interview by Kevin Marks under the auspices of Odin Analytica and Danny's subsequent murder were proof of Pavlovich's involvement."

"All circumstantial."

"Not if we supply proof."

"Marshal Kruger, I would welcome such an explanation."

With a grin, Kruger presented their evidence.

The meeting lasted another twenty minutes with United States Attorney General Dale Delgado agreeing to take the facts Kruger and JR discovered to a grand jury and to ask a federal judge to sign a revised arrest warrant for Kevin Marks and Franklin Russell, including all their various aliases.

In addition, a cease-and-desist order would be issued against Odin Analytica within the borders of the United States. Interpol would issue a new Red Notice on the two men and put Odin Analytica on a watch list.

Kruger realized none of these actions would bring immediate results. But it would raise eyebrows across Europe and cause legitimate companies to ask questions before signing a contract with Odin.

When the video call ended, Delgado said, "Sorry, Sean. It's not what you wanted, but at least it's a start."

"Mr. Attorney General, it's more than a start. It turns up the heat on Pavlovich and his company. Hopefully enough he will lash out and make a mistake."

JR leaned over toward Kruger and whispered, "Is it time to send the virus back to Odin Analytica?"

"Yes. Time to turn up the heat."

***

Tallinn, Estonia

Tomas Pavlovich looked up from his desk to see his assistant standing at his office door with a terrified expression. "What is it, Elie?"

"You have a call waiting. It is the prime minister."

Pavlovich frowned and picked up is desk phone. "Jurgen, what a surprise. What can I do for you today?"

"Tomas, are you aware your company is on an Interpol watch list?"

"I'm sure it is a mistake. Where did you hear this nonsense?"

"The Interpol representative in Brussels called me directly to inform me. He also told me they are cautioning all governments within the EU to be careful with any contracts they might be considering with your company. The EU has issued a strong suggestion to all members to cease using your services."

"Who is this representative? I will call him directly to straighten this out."

After the prime minister gave him the information and ended the call, Pavlovich clasped his hands together on the desk and stared at the phone. He remained in this position for several minutes. Finally, he stood, removed his cell phone from the top right drawer of his desk and walked out.

Driving east out of Tallinn toward Lake Maardu, where Pavlovich maintained a summer cottage on the scenic lake, he debated whether to call Kreso Markovic. The pro side of the debate won. He asked the hands-free device on his car to call the man in Canada.

"Yeah."

"Where are you?"

"Montreal."

"I need you to look into a problem."

"What?"

"Why, all of a sudden, did Interpol put Odin Analytica on an international watch list?"

The recipient of the call remained silent for several

moments. "Who told you this?"

"The prime minister of Estonia. That is why you need to look into it. Once I have more information, I can make a better determination of the potential damage."

"How could they possibly know anything?"

"Does it matter? Just find the answer." He ended the call and took a deep breath before letting it out slowly.

***

Kevin Marks stared at the now-silent cell phone. The urge to throw it against a wall subsided as he thought through the problem. His first inclination would be to dump the problem on Russell, but after further consideration, he decided to take care of it himself.

He used the phone to do a Google search on the death of Danny Barton. The results remained the same as the last time he checked. He then did a search for the latest information on Marlene Hoffman's death in Cambridge. The results caused him to read intently for most of the next half hour. A name from his past kept being mentioned in the news reports. The name kept being identified as a US Marshal. There was no way an FBI agent and a US Marshal would have the same name, including how it was spelled.

The name Sean Kruger had been etched in his brain over a year ago as he made a mad dash across the Canadian border. Now the name haunted him again. But were they the same man? He made a call on his cell phone.

"This is a surprise. I thought you were out of town for a week."

"I am, but I heard a news report on NPR that might affect your company, Lydia."

"What was the report about?"

"The DOJ and the Federal Election Commission are concerned about possible hacks on companies involved in state and municipal election tabulations."

"Kevin, don't worry about PEC. We have the best IT staff in North America."

"I know you've told me before, but, just in case, maybe you should call and ask what they know about it. I understand the US Marshals Service is involved as well."

"I don't believe that's necessary, Kevin. But I'll let Tim know. If he feels it necessary, he can call them."

"Okay, I gotta go. See you this weekend."

Marks ended the call and knew he was running a risk of PEC finding the virus. But if the information learned about Sean Kruger being involved were true, he really needed to know. At this point, the only loyalty he felt toward Tomas Pavlovich extended to his next paycheck.

***

Lydia McDonald grew concerned after the phone call from her friend, Kevin. She did not take him for being an alarmist. But if he was concerned enough to call, maybe she should be as well. She stood from her desk and walked down the hall to Tim Goodman's office. As usual, his door was open as he concentrated on his computer screen. She lightly tapped on his doorframe.

Looking up, he smiled, saw her expression, and immediately asked, "What's wrong?"

"I just had a disturbing phone call."

"From?"

"My friend, Kevin Marks."

Goodman waved her into his office. "Shut the door. What did he say?"

"He told me he heard on NPR that companies supplying state and city election equipment were being attacked by would-be hackers."

Another smile. "Lydia, we deal with those types of reports constantly. That's why we only hire the top talent in IT. If we had been hacked, we would know about it."

"I know, Tim, but he suggested we call the US Marshals Service. They are heading up the investigation."

Goodman frowned. "Normally that's the FBI."

She shrugged. "That's what he said."

"Thanks, Lydia. I'll talk to our CEO to see if he knows anything about it."

CHAPTER 39

Southwest Missouri

The cell phone on Alexia Gibbs' desk danced as it vibrated. Glancing at the caller ID, she smiled and said, "Hi. Where are you?"

"Getting on a plane in Washington, DC. We've done all the damage we can here. Sean and I are heading back."

"Good, it's been busy here. You can help relieve the overtime."

"Why's it been so busy?"

"Don't know. Phase of the moon?"

JR chuckled. "Funny."

"Oh, an old friend of yours called."

"Really? What old friend?"

"He said his name was Tony Chien."

A lengthy silence ensued. Finally, JR said, "Did you say Tony Chien?"

"Yeah."

"Did he leave a number?"

"No, he didn't JR. But he said he'd call you later in the

week."

"Huh."

"When will you two be back?"

"Late tonight."

"See you in the morning."

***

Joint Base Andrews

JR ended the call and turned to Kruger. "Do you remember me telling you about Tony Chien?"

"Yeah, the last time you saw him he was walking out of a conference room after they announced Abel Plymel bought your company."

"He called the office."

Kruger frowned and tilted his head. "How—" He furrowed his brow.

Shrugging, JR shook his head. "I have no idea. Alexia said he would call back later."

"I thought you hadn't heard from him since he walked out of the conference room."

"I haven't."

"It seems your guise as JR Diminski isn't the well-kept secret you thought it was."

"So. it would seem. That's why I think it's a scam."

"Which brings up two questions. If it's a scam, who's behind it? And if it isn't, why is he calling now?"

"That, my friend, is something I guess I'll have to wait to find out."

***

The Next Day

By eight the following morning the second floor of Ozark Security Company hummed with activity of another busy day. JR sat in his cubicle answering emails and calling back clients who insisted on talking to him and only him.

At exactly nine-seventeen, an instant message appeared in the lower right-hand corner of JR's middle computer monitor. *Call for you on line 3.*

Without thinking about it, he picked up the phone and pressed the blinking light on his desk phone. "This is JR."

"Hello, John."

The familiar voice sent a rush of memories flooding back. Three friends working on code late into the night to finish a project in grad school, marathon weeks of writing software and little sleep, the exhilarating rush of submitting their first invoice to a new client and getting paid, the celebrations of hiring their first employee, the dizzying euphoria of surpassing one million dollars in billable services, and the utter deception of the hostile takeover by a private equity company.

"Hello, Tony. Kind of surprised to hear from you, after, what—a decade?" JR's voice dripped with the betrayal he felt toward his once-trusted friend.

"Still pissed at me, aren't you?"

JR didn't answer the question. "Why the call?"

"Guess you are." He paused for a second. "Could we meet somewhere and talk?"

"About what? Old times?"

The call went silent. JR really did not care if the person on the other side had ended the conversation. Finally, he heard, "I need your help, John."

JR closed his eyes and tried to keep from hyperventilating. "I charge three hundred an hour for consultations."

He heard a heavy sigh on the call. "Very well, John. You have every right to be angry."

"Angry isn't the correct word, Tony. Steve Wilson took

his own life because of your actions. I changed my name and relocated to the middle of the country because of your greed. So, the word angry doesn't really describe my mood."

"I still need your help."

"I have an opening at three this afternoon. There will be two of us, myself and a colleague."

"I can be there."

"Very well, I'll put you on the schedule."

The call ended without another word. JR bowed his head and closed his eyes. Unused to the strong emotions he felt, he took a deep breath and exhaled slowly as he dialed Sean Kruger's cell phone.

***

Kruger arrived at two. After reaching the second floor, he stopped at the coffee service and poured himself a cup. JR wore his computer headset as he spoke to a client on the phone. He acknowledged Kruger's presence with a wave and pointed toward the conference room.

Five minutes later, JR sat across from him and said, "Thanks for coming. Not sure how I'm going to react to this meeting. I need you to keep me calm."

Chuckling, Kruger nodded. "Okay. What do you think he's going to discuss with you?"

"I have no idea. He just said he needed my help."

"Did you ask him how he knew where to find you?"

"No, to be honest, I really didn't care."

"Okay, what's my role here."

"As a US Marshal."

"Ah—about that."

JR took a sip of coffee and stared at his friend. "What's that supposed to mean?"

"Steph and I discussed it last night. I'm tired of being something I'm not. I still feel like an FBI agent, only without the credentials. So, after we finish up this little escapade, I'll hang it up and join Jimmie and Sandy's company. They've got more work backed up than they can handle. Some of it fits my expertise."

"Isn't this a little sudden?"

"I've been thinking about it for a while. I made the decision after Jimmie called last night."

"What did he say?"

"He told me about all the contracts they have backed up. He and Sandy needed to bow out after we're done with the Kevin Marks business and get busy with their company. They also asked me to join them. Again."

With a nod, JR said, "I think that's a good idea."

"I'm curious, why?"

"You didn't seem to be enamored with being a US Marshal."

With a shrug, Kruger took a sip of his coffee. "I was honored the president thought enough about my service he's tried everything he can to keep me in the game. But it's time to stop this agency hopping. Time to try something different. The discrimination by the federal government toward individuals my age is a sheer waste of experience, in my opinion. Just because someone is of a certain age, doesn't mean they're incapable of doing the job. Besides, I'd have to retire from my current assignment in two years anyway.

"Working for Jimmie and Sandy will allow me to keep going as long as I feel I'm capable and can contribute to the company. I like the idea of retiring when I feel ready. Not when someone in HR thinks I need to."

JR smiled. "You'll be happier."

"I know. Steph's on board, too." He paused, "So, why the hell did Tony Chien call you?"

"That, my friend is a question he'll have to answer before I agree to help him."

Kruger glanced at his watch. "Guess we'll know in

twenty minutes."

With his attention directed to the cubicles outside the conference room, JR said, "Nope, he's already here." He pointed to a figure walking toward the conference room on the periphery of the second floor. "That is Tony Chien."

***

Kruger shook the man's hand and introduced himself. "I'm Sean Kruger, Tony."

"Nice to meet you." Chien's attention rested on JR who stood on the opposite side of the conference room with his arms folded. "It's nice to see you again, John."

"Before I start the clock on your hour of consultation, why now after all these years?"

"Where do you want me to sit?"

"Wherever you want."

Chien sat on the left side of the table a few chairs from JR. Kruger sat across from him and fixed his eyes on the man.

"You have a nice operation here, John. I—uh—have been following your progress, and I'm happy for you."

"Let's stop the pretense, Tony. How'd you find me?"

"It wasn't easy. Actually, it was by chance."

JR just glared, not responding.

Chien looked at Kruger and then at JR. "A little over four years ago, I was at Black Hat in Las Vegas and saw you and your friend here across the lobby. I hurried to catch up with you, but by the time I got through the crowd, you both were long gone. I inquired about you with the hotel concierge. They told me they didn't have a John Zachara registered."

Shaking his head, JR mumbled, "I am never going to Black Hat again."

Kruger chuckled.

With a questioning look, Chien said, "Excuse me?"

"Nothing. Go on, Tony."

"Anyway, it took a while, but I found someone who identified you as JR Diminski. Once I knew that, it was easy to determine more about you. I figured you had your reasons for changing your name, so I went back to St. Paul and kept tabs on you over the Internet. You are now considered one of the foremost cybersecurity experts in the country."

Not responding to the compliment, JR said, "So, what happened to you? Last time I saw you, you were walking behind Plymel going out the door of the conference room."

"After making the bad decision to sell to Abel Plymel, I left New York and went home to St. Paul. I didn't sell my stock right away, and when it crashed, I—well let's just say I didn't come out too well. Lesson learned."

"I did that."

Chien looked puzzled, and Kruger hid his smile with a hand.

JR continued. "I got him back, Tony. Plymel was running a Ponzi scheme and cheating thousands of investors." He nodded toward Kruger. "Sean used to be an FBI agent. I met him during his investigation of the man and helped him expose Plymel for who he really was. That's when the stock crashed."

"What happened to him?"

Smiling for the first time during their meeting, JR said, "He's not cheating people anymore."

Kruger changed the subject and asked, "You indicated you went back to St. Paul, Tony. Did you start another company?"

"Yes, I started one called Premier Elections Concept. We offer equipment and election services to state and local governments to help with their vote counting."

JR returned to his scowl. "So, why do you need my help?"

"I think we've been hacked."

CHAPTER 40

Springfield, MO

JR frowned. "What do you mean you've been hacked?"

"I can't put my finger on it, but we issued a software update a few weeks ago. We've done several quality checks on it now that it's live, and there's something off. My guys can't find it. John, you're the best software debugger I have ever come across. I was hoping you could take a look at our system and determine if we have anything to worry about."

Kruger straightened in his chair. "How big is Premier Elections Concepts?"

"After our last merger, we're in about thirty states."

Looking at JR, Kruger saw him return the glance.

Leaning forward, JR asked, "Exactly, when did you push out the update?"

"Two weeks ago."

Kruger stood and stared to pace. JR looked at him and said, "That's about the right time, Sean."

"I know. I generally don't believe in coincidences, but this might actually be one."

Chien frowned. "What are you two talking about?"

JR turned his attention to Chien. "Sean still works for the federal government as an investigator, I assist at times. Our current assignment is investigating the death of a young grad student at MIT. His work dealt with algorithms used to predict human behavior. His theories resulted in predicting elections to about 95 percent accuracy. He was murdered to gain access to his computer. Over the past few weeks, I've had the opportunity to examine his concepts. They're fascinating and, in my opinion, dangerous to democracies."

The blank stare JR received from Chien almost made him chuckle.

Kruger stopped pacing and leaned over the conference table and supported himself with his hands. "Tony do you, by chance, have an office in Montreal?"

He nodded. "That's the location for our main Canadian branch."

Straightening, Kruger looked at JR. "The ball's in your court, JR. What do you think?"

After taking a long deep breath, JR glanced at the ceiling and then focused on Chien. "I need one question answered before I agree to help you."

"Sure, John."

"After you left the conference room that day, you never responded to any of my phone calls or emails. Why?"

Tony Chien clasped his hands together and studied the top of the conference table for what seemed like minutes. Finally, he said, "I was embarrassed. I consider myself fairly intelligent, but I fell for Plymel's BS. He seemed generally interested in helping us take our company to the next level. When I discovered he was basically a snake in a suit, I didn't know what to say to you and Steve. So, I took the coward's way out and chose not to get in touch with either of you."

JR blinked several times, and a slight smile came to his

lips. "Kind of what I suspected." He turned to Kruger. "Time to help Tony with his problem."

Kruger nodded.

***

Once JR had access to the PEC server, Kruger touched Chien on the arm and said, "He'll be in a zone for a while." He motioned toward the conference room. "Let's talk in there." With a nod, Chien followed Kruger. When they were seated again, Kruger said, "Tell me what you suspect happened."

"As the company grew and we increased the number of remote offices, the opportunities for having our system compromised grew exponentially. So, we took that into consideration by beefing up our firewall and hiring more IT specialists. We installed a VPN, so interoffice and intraoffice communications would be as secure as possible. I've been around computers long enough to realize whatever you devise to protect yourself against being compromised, there is always someone smarter who will figure out how to get around your protections."

"You think that happened here?"

"I do. Like I said, I would put our cybersecurity efforts up against any private or government entity. If John finds we've been compromised, it will be an inside job."

Drumming his fingers on the tabletop, Kruger stared at Chien for a few moments. "Why come to JR now?"

With a slight grin, Chien said, "How long have you known John?"

"A little over seven years."

"With college and our company, I was around him for almost fifteen. He is by far one of the smartest individuals I have ever known."

"I agree."

"Also, he's probably one of the most unpretentious and

humble men I've ever met. He's comfortable with who he is and doesn't have the need to tell the world about his intelligence. I've always admired that about him."

"So do I. However, you haven't answered my original question."

"I know. The reason is complicated."

"Emotions are complicated; reasons generally aren't."

Chien nodded slightly. "I needed someone outside the company to confirm the compromise."

"Why?"

"Because I don't want to alert whoever did it."

"In other words, you don't trust anyone in your company at the moment?"

Chien sat back in his chair and folded his arms. His eyes bored through Kruger. Then he relaxed and said, "No, I guess I don't."

At that exact moment, JR rushed into the room with a huge smile. He looked directly at Kruger and said, "We now have proof Montreal is the center of everything."

***

With Kruger and Chien gathered around his cubicle, JR pointed to the left screen on his desk and said, "There is a piece of software buried within PEC's last update which we call a trojan horse. It won't activate until certain conditions are present."

"What conditions?"

He glanced at Chien. "When the system is being used to tabulate votes."

Kruger asked, "Why did you say Montreal is the center?"

"The malware was introduced into the PEC server from internal emails. Once I knew what to look for, it was easy to backtrack to which office it came from. The first email with the virus originated from the email address of an assistant to Tim Goodman." JR paused and looked at Chien. "The malware attached itself to all emails with the domain of @PEC.org. Goodman got the virus from an email sent to him from his assistant. He then sent one to everyone at his level about the upcoming software update and copied you, Tony. From there it infiltrated every computer in the entire PEC network. When the update was pushed out, the trojan horse went along with it to every client your company serves."

All color drained from Chien's face as he stared at JR's computer screen. "Oh, my gawd."

JR continued. "The coding on the thing is familiar."

Chien was speechless, so Kruger asked, "How so?"

"It's the same coding style as the virus that infected my own servers a few years back."

"Russians?"

"At this point, I can't be certain, but my guess would be yes. I think it might behoove us to have the Royal Canadian Mounted Police pick up Lydia McDonald and have a chat with her."

***

The three men who approached the home of Lydia McDonald on Thursday evening wore jeans, polo shirts, and windbreakers with the letters RCMP in bold letters on the back. Neighbors pointed and telephone calls ensued as one of the three knocked on her front door.

Ten minutes later, the three plainclothes police detectives escorted a sobbing Lydia McDonald to an awaiting black Chevy Tahoe with black wheels and no insignias. One of them carried her laptop in an evidence box, and another carried a similar one with files gathered from her home office. Twenty minutes after their arrival, the quiet neighborhood still buzzed with the unusual occurrence of a long-time resident's arrest.

***

Friday Morning
Montreal, Canada

Kruger shook Bentley Thatcher's hand as they stood outside an interrogation room. Thatcher said, "She hasn't stopped crying since her arrest last night."

"Really. Does she have an attorney yet?"

The RCMP Supervisor and long-time acquaintance of Kruger's shook his head. "No, she keeps asking why she was arrested and refuses to have a lawyer because that would prove she's guilty of something."

Kruger rolled his eyes. "Oh, good grief. Have you heard from her boss, Tim Goodman?"

"Apparently he is in consultation with the CEO of his company and not willing to talk to us without a lawyer present."

"The only evidence we have suggests her computer sent the original email with the Russian malware. We need to find out how." Kruger stared at the frightened woman and had an idea. "Find a female Mountie, I want her to accompany us into the room."

"You've got it."

***

Kruger sat across from the frightened woman with Bentley next to him and a female Mountie standing by the door, her arms folded. Kruger said, "Ms. McDonald, are you sure you don't want an attorney present while we ask questions?"

She violently shook her head. "I haven't done anything. Why would I need a lawyer?"

"You are accused of a cybercrime against your

employer."

The sigh emanating from her sounded as though she deflated. "How?"

"That's what we want you to tell us."

She narrowed her eyes, and her demeanor changed instantly. "You are talking in circles. How can I tell you how I did something if I don't know what it is I did?"

With a slight grin, Kruger asked, "You're not married, are you, Ms. McDonald?"

"No, I live by myself."

"Boyfriend?"

"Yes."

"Are you sleeping with him?"

"I don't believe that is any of your business."

"Oh, but it is."

"How?"

"If you have a boyfriend who stays over at your house and has access to your computer, he might be the person I need to talk to."

She furrowed her brow and bit her lip. "Uh…"

"Do you mind if I ask his name."

She shook her head slowly. "His name is Kevin Marks."

Maintaining his neutral expression, Kruger resisted the urge to jump out of his seat. Taking a deep breath, he reached into his suit coat pocket and pulled out two pictures. He laid them side by side on the table, positioned so they faced Lydia. "Can you identify either of these two men?"

When the woman's eyes widened, and she locked her gaze on the picture to Kruger's right, he knew she recognized the man.

She did not respond for almost a minute. Finally, she pointed at the picture as a tear flowed down her cheek. "That's Kevin."

Kruger turned to Bentley and said, "Ms. McDonald is innocent, but I suggest she be put in protective custody."

CHAPTER 41

Southwest Missouri

JR listened as Kruger summarized his findings in Montreal. "As it turned out, Lydia McDonald was dating our Kevin Marks. The Mounties conducted a raid on the address where he told her he lived."

"Let me guess, no such person?"

"No such address."

"What do you mean?"

"The place was total fiction. It didn't exist."

"How could she date a person for almost a year and not know where he lived?"

"Good question, JR. Lydia told us he was always out of town on business, and they always either met at a restaurant or he picked her up. She really never thought too much about it."

"So, they've had PEC in their sights for a long time?"

"It would appear so."

"Where are you on this?"

JR blew out a breath. "I've written an update for PEC to

push out that will neutralize the malware. Plus, I've got it isolated in their server. I was waiting to hear from you before I do anything."

"We need to shake the tree a little to see if we can rattle Marks."

"How do you do that?"

"Don't know, but I'm working on it."

JR chuckled. "So, you have no clue?"

"Somehow, I need to draw him into a trap."

"Does he know the woman is in custody?"

Kruger was silent for a second. Then he said, "Guess we need to find out, don't we?"

***

Kevin Marks read the text message from Lydia McDonald and considered not responding. With her usefulness a thing of the past and his permanent departure from Montreal imminent, he did not feel the need to see her. But she could identify him. Finally, he replied to her message and told her he would pick her up around seven that evening.

After pressing the send icon on the text message, he dialed another number. Franklin Russell answered immediately. "Yeah."

"Need a favor."

"You're always needing a favor. What is it this time?"

"I need a loose end tied up."

"Thought you were leaving for a meeting overseas."

"That's why I'm calling. My flight leaves in three hours."

Silence ensued on the call. Finally, Franklin Russell said, "What loose end?"

"The woman whose computer I used to download the package can identify me. And we don't need those kinds of complications, do we?"

Russell picked up on the implied threat. "No, I suppose we don't."

"The woman will arrive home from work about five-fifteen. She'll take a shower as soon as she gets there. If I were you, I'd be waiting inside the house when she gets home. You can take care of business while she's in the shower. Make it look like an accident."

"It'll cost you."

"I figured that."

"When can I expect my money?"

"That's why I'm going overseas, to get our money."

"I look forward to seeing it in my bank account. Don't disappoint me."

"I have no intention of doing so."

The call ended, and Kevin Marks finished preparing for his trip to Estonia.

***

With the help of three US Marshals, imported from the Boston area, and six Mounties, Kruger and Thatcher were situated in the living room of a house across the street from Lydia McDonald's house a little after three. As Thatcher observed the street through binoculars, he said, "What are you expecting?"

"Not sure. It would be nice if, after we arrest Marks, he expresses remorse for his actions and tells us everything. But I'm a realist. That won't happen."

After a chuckle, Thatcher said, "No, not in my experience either."

Kruger used his binoculars to survey the street north and south of the house. "Uh, oh."

"What?"

"Where'd the guy jogging south of the house come from?"

Thatcher looked in the direction indicated by Kruger.

"Shit." He picked up a handheld radio. "There's a man in blue running shorts and white Nike T-shirt jogging toward McDonald's house. Where'd he come from?" He listened as the response came through his earbud. He then turned to Kruger. "Outside the neighborhood. Why?"

"Because," Kruger pointed to the man, "That is Marks' accomplice Franklin Russell and he's wearing a fanny pack. Nobody wears one of those these days, unless you have a weapon in it. Advise them he's armed."

Thatcher said into the radio, "Heads up, lads. Keep an eye on this one. He's wearing a fanny pack and a possible weapon."

As the two men watched, the jogger crossed the street and disappeared into the backyard of Lydia's house.

A US Marshal by the name of O'Brian came on the radio. "He's working the lock on the back door." A moment of silence followed. "He's in. Do we take him now?"

Thatcher looked at Kruger. "Well?"

Kruger nodded. "Let's not let him get too comfortable."

Keying the mic, Thatcher said, "As we discussed, Group A through the back door, Group B take the front. Assume he's armed." He then said, "Shall we join them?"

Tightening his ballistic vest, Kruger pulled the rim of his US Marshals ballcap down and smiled at Thatcher. "Let's."

***

Russell closed the back door and listened. The only sound he heard came from the refrigerator in the kitchen next to the dining area where he stood. Extracting his Sig Sauer P226 from the fanny pack, he proceeded to search the house, making sure he was alone.

Satisfied, no one else was there, he approached the front door. Through the window, he saw dark-clad individuals wearing ballistic vests and Kevlar helmets, with weapons drawn, approaching the house.

"That son-of-bitch Marks set me up." He watched as they grew closer. He turned and ran toward the back door. When he approached, he saw shadows dancing on the curtains covering the mostly glass door. In the span of a heartbeat, he made his decision and raised his Sig Sauer.

The Mounties at the front door heard gunfire. The man carrying the breaching tool swung it, and the front door yielded to the force of its forty-pound mass. Five Mounties sprang through the now open space and rushed in.

More gunfire and then total silence. Kruger stepped through the front door as he heard the words, "Suspect down," shouted from the back of the house. When he arrived in the kitchen, he saw Franklin Russell on the floor, his back against a wall and blood on his white T-shirt, his eyes open, following Kruger's movement.

One of the Mounties secured a weapon lying several feet from Russell.

Kruger asked, "Anyone else hit?"

A US Marshal walked up to him and said, "One of our guys took one in the chest, but the vest stopped it. He'll be okay, sore, but okay."

With a nod, Kruger turned his attention back to Russell, who still stared at him. He then heard Thatcher on his radio requesting an ambulance.

Russell said through clenched teeth, "I should have taken care of you a long time ago."

Kruger gave the wounded man a smile. "Well, you didn't. Where's Marks?"

"Where you can't touch him."

Pointing to his hat, Kruger smiled and said, "I'm a US Marshal. I can pursue a fugitive anywhere I want. Now, where is he?"

A shake of Russell's head was his only response.

Thatcher stepped up beside Kruger. "You know this man?"

"Unfortunately, yes. I've dealt with him before. He's wanted in the US for jumping bail and the murder of five FBI agents."

Russell's scowl turned to a frown.

Kruger said, "Bet you thought I forgot about that, didn't you, Franklin?"

"I take it you'll want to extradite the fellow?"

"As soon as he stops bleeding."

***

Kruger checked his wristwatch. It was late in France, but he decided to call Sergey Brutka anyway. He pressed the send icon and waited. On the second ring he heard a groggy "Oui."

"Guess I caught you napping. It's Kruger, Sergey."

With a growl, the Serbian said with a heavy accent, "It's midnight here, *Kruger*."

"Yes, but a law enforcement officer is truly never off duty."

"Bah!"

There was silence for a few seconds, then Kruger heard, "What is you want?"

"Did you know that when you are tired, Sergey, your English deteriorates."

"If you want to insult, me. I will end call."

"We've had a development here."

The Interpol superintendent suddenly sounded alert. "Tell me."

"One of the fellows we spoke about when I last saw you may be headed to Estonia."

"How do you know?"

"I had a little run-in with his partner in crime over here, and he let it slip Marks was where I couldn't touch him. We know he has traveled to Tallinn several times over the past year. I think he's there now."

"Can you confirm he is?"

"I'll ask JR. If he can, is it possible for you to meet me there?"

"Once you confirm it, I'll catch a plane."

"I'll call you when I know for sure."

"Sean, call me in the morning."

As Kruger ended the call, he chuckled to himself.

CHAPTER 42

Southwest Missouri

"He's flying under the name Miroslav Klaus, Sean."

"Is he there now?"

"No, he has a layover in Amsterdam and then on to Tallinn." JR listened as his friend went silent. Finally, he went on. "I'm going to meet Sergey in Estonia. My guess is he'll be visiting Odin Analytica at some point."

"Do you need any of us to join you?"

"No, just stay by a phone. I'm at the airport now."

"What, no private jets heading your way?"

"As a matter of fact, Joseph arranged for my transport." He paused for a second. "JR, do you have the virus you spoke about ready?"

"Yes."

"Do you have a way to send it to Odin Analytica?"

"I do."

"I think it's time."

"So do I. Call me when you land."

***

JR ended the call and sat back in his chair, staring at the three computer screens in front of him. The left one showed Kevin Marks' itinerary on Lufthansa Airlines. The middle one displayed details of the credit card used to buy the ticket. It was linked to a bank account in the name of Miroslav Klaus. The bank, a mid-level financial institution in total deposits, bore the name BES EU and maintained a headquarters in Tallinn with branches all over Estonia and Western Europe. JR stared at the screen, index finger tapping his lips. Something was off with the bank.

He sent an instant message to Alexia's monitor, and she appeared next to him a few minutes later. He pointed at the screen with the banking information. "Ever hear of a bank called BES EU?"

"Yes."

He looked up. She stood there, her arms folded and a huge grin on her face. "You obviously know more than just a yes. Want to enlighten me?"

"Why are you interested?"

"They issued a credit card to Kevin Marks in the name of Miroslav Klaus."

"The bank is owned by Russian Mafia."

JR's eyebrows rose. "Huh." He looked at the screen again. "Openly or behind the scenes?"

"Definitely behind the scenes. One of the reasons I had to suddenly leave Paris at midnight years ago was because of BES EU."

"You aren't explaining yourself, Alexia."

"Because it's complicated, JR."

"Okay, give me the fifty-thousand-foot version."

"Who's the top politician in Russia?"

"You're kidding."

"No. Without his approval, nothing happens at BES EU." She studied JR's computer screens. "Sean always says, there are no coincidences, only connections. If BES EU issued a credit card to Kevin Marks, and Marks is associated with Odin Analytica, then a connection exists between the bank and the data company."

He continued to stare at the computer screen, his finger tapping an imaginary tune on his lips. Suddenly, he straightened in his chair, and his fingers danced on the keyboard. "Sometimes, I can be unbelievably dense."

She did not reply as she watched the direction of his inquiry. A minute later, his deep dive into the inner workings of BES EU began showing up on the screen. He stopped typing as a list of companies appeared on the right screen. He pointed to one name in the middle of the list and said, "We know this is the company that provided the major source of financial backing for Tomas Pavlovich to acquire Odin Analytica."

Leaning over she read the name. "Yes, you've mentioned Northern Lights Investment Services before. What about them?"

He stared at the screen with a slight smile. "They are a wholly owned subsidiary of a company called Financial Path, and guess who's the majority shareholder of Financial Path?"

"BES EU."

"Exactly."

"Sean is walking into a hornet's nest, JR."

"I know. Call your husband. I need to call Joseph, immediately."

***

Joint Base Andrews, while always busy, seemed a bit more hectic on this particular midsummer afternoon. The constant din of multiple-engine aircraft taking off and landing blended together to produce one continuous sound as he waited for his ride. The plane, the same Gulfstream

G650ER he traveled to Lyon, France on, had yet to arrive. He glanced at his watch for the seventh time in the past two minutes. Unfortunately, frequently checking the time did not make it pass faster.

During the time he stood outside the FBO, he watched Air Force One take off. This brief distraction caused him to wonder where President Griffin was headed. After the big plane shrank to an unseeable dot in the western sky, a young airman stepped up to him. "Marshal Kruger, the Gulfstream you're waiting on is making its final approach. We should be able to have you on board within the hour."

"Thank you, Airman."

Fifteen minutes later, the white plane parked on the tarmac outside the FBO. Kruger retrieved his small duffel bag and waited for the airstairs to descend from the plane. The pilot waved him to get on board as a refueling truck pulled up to the aircraft to service it.

As Kruger ascended the short flight of stairs the pilot leaned over to talk so Kruger could hear over the loud background noise. "Good afternoon, Sean. Make yourself at home, and we'll be taking off as soon as we have enough fuel."

"Thanks, Dale." Kruger entered the plane as the pilot descended the stairs and disappeared into the FBO. To his surprise, the plane already held two passengers. Jimmie Gibbs and Sandy Knoll. Both grinned at him as he found a seat on the right side of the cabin. "What the hell are you two doing here?"

Knoll smiled and stood to shake Kruger's hand. "Orders of the president. Joseph convinced him you needed backup in Estonia."

Kruger frowned. "Didn't know Joseph was aware of where I was going."

Gibbs said, "JR and Alexia found something and called him. That's why Sandy and I are involved."

Kruger asked, "How bad?"

"Don't know yet. We're supposed to get a briefing after we take off."

The pilot returned and raised the airstairs. "Ready to go, gentlemen?"

***

An hour into the flight, Kruger's cell phone notified him of an incoming call. After placing the device in speaker mode, he accepted and said, "Hello, Joseph."

"Where are you guys?"

Knoll said, "Somewhere over the Atlantic. What's the big mystery?"

"I don't have specifics right now. You'll be making a stop at Heathrow to pick-up Sergey Brutka and a member of MI5. Her name is Serene Watson, one of their best cybercrime experts. This is a joint Interpol, United States, and British operation."

Kruger asked, "Why the Brits?"

"We don't know all the details at this point, but the president and the prime minister are concerned enough about Odin Analytica they formed this little investigative team."

"Joseph, you're evading the question. What's going on?"

"Like I told you, Sean, JR found something and called me. It concerned me enough I took it to the president. After consulting with the British prime minister, he's asking for you and your new team to confirm."

"My new team?"

"Yeah, you keep getting field promotions."

"Joseph, just what the hell did JR find, and what are we supposed to confirm?"

"There is a direct money pipeline to and from Odin Analytica to the Kremlin."

"That means, Danny Barton's death and the hack on the

PEC election systems were directed by Moscow."

"That's how it appears at the moment. We need to talk on a landline as soon as you land at Heathrow."

"I think that's a great idea."

**

When Kruger, Knoll and Gibbs arrived at the conference room secured for them by MI5 at Heathrow, they found Brutka and Inspector Serene Watson already setting up a laptop for the video conference call. Kruger's first impression of the woman, as he was introduced by Brutka, was that of a hardworking, independent, and dedicated professional. She was in her mid-forties, and dressed in dark slacks and jacket over a white blouse. Her light brown hair was clasped at the nape of the neck in a ponytail. As they shook hands, her green eyes surveyed him with the same scrutiny he applied to her. A few inches shorter than Kruger, she was tall by European standards. He liked her immediately.

She said, "I am pleased to meet you, Sean Kruger. Your reputation precedes you to Britain."

Kruger smiled and said, "It's nice to meet you as well, Inspector Watson. Hopefully it was a positive reputation."

"Indeed, it was." She returned the smile, but did not comment further.

Brutka said, "Now that we all know each other, let's get to business. Serene, it is time. Would you initiate the video conference?"

A large flat-screen television dominated the wall at the front of the room and allowed the London participants to observe the meeting. When Watson initiated the Zoom call with her laptop, Joseph Kincaid appeared almost immediately in one panel by himself. JR and Alexia joined the meeting in a separate one at the top right. Watson's boss, a man named Kilby, whose first name Kruger forgot the minute he heard it, appeared in the bottom right frame. Since Brutka was the main intermediary from Interpol, no one else appeared from the organization.

JR and Alexia were introduced by Joseph. When finished, the national security adviser asked JR to start the meeting.

Their image was replaced by a PowerPoint flow chart. JR said, "To make this as clear as we can, here is a representation of the relationships we have derived from our study of Odin Analytica, BES EU Bank, and Moscow."

Kruger took a deep breath as Knoll leaned over and whispered to him, "Damn, Sean, would you stop finding Russians under every rock you turn over?"

"It's getting old, isn't it?"

Continuing with his narrative, JR said, "A bank known as BES EU owns a controlling interest in a company called Financial Path. It is a conglomerate which owns, by our estimate, forty separate companies across Europe and Southeast Asia. One of those companies is an investment firm called Northern Lights. Northern Lights is the establishment that basically supplied all of the capital for Tomas Pavlovich to buy Odin Analytica and turn it into a giant hacking machine disguised as a computer-services company."

Serene Watson said, "MI5 has had suspicions about Odin Analytica for several years."

JR nodded. "I'm not surprised. Now we have proof of what they are doing behind the scenes. We have proof that BES EU Bank is the credit card issuer for directors and management personnel at Odin. We have documentation that a man named Miroslav Klaus is on the board of directors for Odin."

Kruger frowned, as he suspected what would come next.

"Miroslav Klaus is an alias for a man named Kevin Marks. Marks is wanted in the United States on charges of murder, domestic terrorism, and sedition. He has Canadian identification papers under the name of Dominic Ruiz. He is also the man who dated a woman in Montreal, Canada for eleven months just so he had access to her computer when he needed. The woman works for a company called Premier Election Concepts and the dating ruse worked. An email from her laptop contained a trojan horse which has now spread throughout the company. PEC is one of the largest election service companies in the US and Canada. The virus infecting PEC's computers is a more robust version of the one that compromised multiple elections there in England. Oh, did I mention that the top man at the Kremlin, through various cutouts, owns BES EU Bank?"

CHAPTER 43

London

JR said, "Any questions?"

The man from MI5 yawned and asked, "How do you know the virus you found in the PEC computers is similar to the one here in England?"

"Because I've analyzed each of them, and we know where they came from."

The man blinked several times. "I say, mind telling us where?"

"I don't mind at all, Commissioner Kilby. Odin Analytica."

"Are you sure?"

"Positive. I will send Sean Kruger all the details, and he can share it with your inspector. We also know how to neutralize it."

Kilby lowered his head and looked over his glasses at JR. "Come now, my good fellow. Not even our best men know how to neutralize this malware."

JR shrugged. "Not sure what to tell you. Once Marshal

Kruger gets the information I am sending, he'll have the solution for you."

Kruger covered his mouth with his hand trying to hide the smile he displayed after JR's comment.

Brutka said, "We need to locate this Kevin Marks fellow. He seems to be the key."

"Maybe."

"You don't agree, JR?"

"No, Sergey, I'm afraid I don't. My partner, Alexia, will explain."

The screen showing the business flow chart went blank and was immediately replaced by two photos appearing side by side. Alexia said, "The individual on the left is a twenty-two-year-old KGB officer by the name of Grigori Tomas Pavlovich. The image on the right, is the driver's license photograph of the same man who is now sixty-eight years old and the current CEO of Odin Analytica. His birthday is two months prior to the man who currently owns the BES EU Bank. They are the same age."

A new slide replaced the one of the young and old Pavlovich. "This is a class portrait taken of the 1975 graduating class at Leningrad State University. While the graininess of the photo makes it difficult to tell for sure, the two circled individuals standing side by side can be identified with clarity. The man on the left is Tomas Pavlovich, and the man on the right is the future president of Russia."

Another slide appeared. This one showed a telephoto lens shot of two men standing on a balcony. One was pointing toward a distant point, the other looking in the same direction.

"This is a photo taken in Dresden, East Germany in 1985. The man with his arm extended is Pavlovich, and the other is the same man as in the other photograph. They have known each other for years. Some say Pavlovich still works for him."

Kilby cleared his throat. "What is the source of these photos?"

Alexia smiled. "CIA archives."

The MI 5 commissioner's eyes widened, and he nodded once.

Brutka crossed his arms. "How do we get to this Pavlovich fellow?"

Knoll said, "Snatch and grab."

The man from MI5 frowned. "I beg your pardon?"

Kruger smiled and explained. "Commissioner Kilby, my associate is suggesting we have a clandestine discussion with Mr. Pavlovich without others knowing we are having the discussion."

"I cannot condone kidnapping."

"Technically, it isn't kidnapping. We won't be asking for ransom."

With an indignant snort, Kilby said, "Then what would you call it?"

"An arrest."

"On what grounds?"

"Violation of The Computer Fraud and Abuse Act, 18 USC. 1030, as a principal accomplice, the United Kingdom's Computer Misuse Act 1990, and the United Nations General Assembly resolution 65/230."

A small grin appeared on Kilby's lips. "Very well, Marshal Kruger, you've done your homework."

Kruger nodded once.

Kilby continued. "Mr. Brutka, you will be the observer for Interpol, correct?"

"Yes, sir."

"Then you have our blessings, gentlemen. Just don't get caught."

Kruger said, "Goes without saying, Commissioner."

The video conference ended, and Kruger looked at Knoll. "Now, would you explain to me how the hell we're supposed to do what you just suggested?"

The big man put his hand on Kruger's shoulder. "Piece of cake, Sean."

***

Tallinn, Estonia

Tomas Pavlovich sipped coffee as he read the executive summary for the previous day's activities and income statement for Odin Analytica. A knock on his door drew his attention away from the report. "Ah, Kevin, come in, come in."

Kevin Marks sat in one of the chairs in front of Pavlovich's desk. "We have a possible problem."

With raised eyebrows, the Odin Analytica CEO asked, "What might that be?"

"Russell has not responded to any of my emails or text messages."

"For how long?"

"Going on three days."

"Hmmm." Pavlovich frowned and kept his gaze on Marks. "Is this unusual for him?"

"Extremely. He normally gets back to me within hours, never days."

"Assume he is compromised or dead."

A nod came from Marks.

"Does he know any of the details?"

"No."

"Then, I see no reason to delay our plans. Is the software in place?"

"Yes, the distribution went far smoother than I anticipated."

"How many locations are available to us?"

"From what I can determine, twenty-five state governments and nine hundred and thirty state counties and parishes."

"I have never understood why they call them parishes and not counties. Why is that, Kevin?"

"It's a holdover from the days Louisiana was part of Spain and France. The Roman Catholic Church established church parishes across the state. When the territory was purchased by the Americans in the early 1800s, the boundaries of the church parishes were used to establish territorial governments."

"I see, another intrusion by the church."

Marks shrugged.

"Is that enough to swing the election the way we wish?"

This time, Marks nodded. "More than enough."

"Good. Don't worry about Russell. He was just a tool we used as needed." Pavlovich went back to reading his computer screen, ignoring Kevin Marks.

After half a minute of being ignored, Marks rose and left the office. One thought left him concerned. *If Franklin Russell was considered a tool, then I probably am as well. Best to keep that in mind.*

***

Kruger crossed his arms and stared at Knoll. "I wasn't in the special forces, Sandy. How's it going to be a piece of cake?"

"I don't have all the details worked out yet, but the best way is for us to fly into Helsinki, cross over to Tallinn by ferry, grab Pavlovich, cross back over to Helsinki, and fly out with him in custody."

"Where do we take him?"

"Hey, I'm just the snatch-and-grab guy. Logistics is for those of you in management."

Watson smiled. "We bring him back to the UK."

Liking the plan so far, Kruger said, "Okay, we have proof Odin Analytica meddled in the elections here in

Britain. What happens when the Estonian government learns Pavlovich is in London facing computer crimes?"

Jimmie Gibbs spoke for the first time since the end of the video conference. "Have JR reveal Pavlovich's connections to Moscow via a London newspaper. Estonia is extremely sensitive to being seen as a puppet of the Russian government. My guess is they'll keep their mouths shut."

Knoll chuckled. "How do you know that, Jimmie?"

"Studied Estonian history and politics on the flight over." He held up his cell phone. "Amazing what you can find out on one of these things."

CHAPTER 44

Gulf of Finland
Three Days Later

Kruger stared out over the waters of the Gulf of Finland. Scheduling a ferry had been easy enough, and the three passengers sat at a table in one of the restaurants on the boat. Jimmie Gibbs and Sergey Brutka had flown into Tallinn immediately after the video conference to establish surveillance on Tomas Pavlovich.

Serene Watson nibbled on a *pulla,* a Finnish type of cinnamon roll, while Knoll sipped a cup of coffee. "That's what I like about the Finns. They don't care for all those foo-foo café drinks. Just straight old brewed coffee. The only thing I can complain about is they always use light roasted."

Kruger turned his attention back to the table. "I take it you don't like the espressos they make in France, Sandy?"

As the big man sipped his brew, he shook his head. "Nah, last time I was there I couldn't wait to have a plain old American cup of coffee."

Smiling, Kruger turned his attention back to the gulf waters, his chin cupped in his hand.

"Sean, if you're worried about coming events, don't. Jimmie and Sergey have a good plan. From what they've told me, Pavlovich is a creature of habit. He goes to work at the same time every morning and returns at the same time every night. His driver resembles you in height and weight. You'll be driving the car, hopefully it will keep him off-guard until Jimmie and I join you. Just don't turn around."

Shaking his head slightly, Kruger said, "I'm not worried about that part, Sandy."

"Then why so quiet?"

"Thinking."

"About?"

"How's the defense contractor business going?"

Knoll chuckled. "Bullshit. That's not what was on your mind. However, it's going well. Thanks for asking."

"I've decided to take you up on your offer."

Knoll tilted his head. "What changed your mind?"

Watson stood and said, "Be back in a while. Don't go anywhere."

Kruger watched her until she was out of ear shot and said, "Jimmie called the other night and told me about all the work you two have lined up. Plus, I had a discussion with Steph before I left. I'm tired of the agency shuffle the federal government's been throwing my way. First it was the DIA, now the US Marshals Service. I appreciate everyone's efforts, but I need to concentrate on one opportunity. If the offer is still open, I'd like to take you up on working for your company."

"Hell, Sean, you're one of our partners. We've always wanted your input and experience." He reached his hand over the table, and Kruger shook it. "Welcome aboard. We don't have titles."

"Good. I'm tired of keeping track of all the business cards I've had recently."

Knoll chuckled. "We've got so many contracts lined up, we haven't had time or personnel to work on them."

"Then, why the hell are you traipsing around Europe with me?"

Knoll smiled. "Because we're a team, and that's what teams do."

***

Jimmie Gibbs observed Pavlovich's driver through Nikon Aculon 10x42 binoculars. He resembled Kruger in height and build. Kruger's hair was lighter which could be changed easily. The major difference he could decipher was in facial features. Where Kruger's face was oval and well proportioned, the driver's appeared round with a broad nose, squinty eyes, and short facial hair. The beard they could fix on short notice, but not the nose and shape of the face.

He turned to Brutka. "Last night I noticed Pavlovich didn't even look at his driver when he got in the car. What did you see?"

"Same thing. I have been around his type before. He feels everyone around him is inferior, so why waste time and energy on paying attention to somebody when they are beneath you? It will serve our purposes well. As long as Sean does not look back at the man, we should be able to fool him until you and Sandy join him in the car."

The cell phone in Jimmie's pocket vibrated. He retrieved it and read the text message. "They just docked. Let's get back to the hotel and get ready. We need to intercept the driver a few blocks from Odin Analytica."

***

Kruger looked at himself in the bathroom mirror. His week-old beard's normal color, a combination of dark-and-white whiskers, appeared coal black after Serene Watson did her magic on his hair color. Even his grey-streaked hair was now coal black. He said, "Don't tell Steph I colored my hair. She'll never let me forget about it."

Gibbs stood behind him, his arms crossed. "You look like a wise guy from the streets of New York."

Knoll stood outside the room and chuckled. "Makes you look ten years younger. Maybe you could fool this age retirement crap."

Shooting the big man, a *don't go there look*, Kruger said, "You aren't too far from your golden years yourself, my friend."

Laughing out loud, Knoll walked away from the door, allowing Gibbs to follow and leaving Kruger and Watson behind. She said, "Look at the driver's picture. He combs his hair a little different than you do. Want me to change yours?"

After studying the picture and then his image in the mirror, he repeated the process. "If I don't turn around, I should be fine. What do you think?"

"If you have to turn around, the different hairstyle will not matter." She smiled as she said this. "This man looks like a thug from Tottenham. You, on the other hand, are more sophisticated."

"Well, I've been called a lot of things, Serene, but sophisticated is not one of them."

She chuckled as she walked out of the bathroom to join the others. Kruger followed.

As he stepped into the open living area, he saw Serene hand Brutka a passport. "This was given to me by MI5 just before we left. We will need to use it to get him on the ferry for the return to Helsinki."

Brutka examined the contents. "Very impressive." He closed it and said, "How do we get him on board without him screaming his bloody head off he is being kidnapped?"

Gibbs smiled. "Leave that to me."

Raising his eyebrows, Brutka nodded and handed the passport back to the inspector.

Knoll said, "Hate to break up this little party, but we need to get going. Jimmie, are you and Sergey checked out of the hotel?"

Gibbs said, "I am; this is Sergey's room."

"Then, let's go."

***

An hour later, as the regular driver for Tomas Pavlovich paid for his coffee in a small café five blocks from the Odin Analytica building, a large man with bulging biceps stood off to the side and followed the driver toward the black Mercedes with dark-shaded windows. As the driver reached into his pocket for the keys, another man with an athletic physique walked up to him and, in perfect Russian, asked him for directions.

The driver, stunned at the use of his native tongue, stared at the man who now displayed a large grin.

He replied in the same language, "I beg your par—"

Knoll grabbed the arm with the keys as Jimmie secured the man's other arm and plunged a small hypodermic needle into his neck. The look of surprise on the driver's face lasted only a few seconds as the liquid from the syringe flowed immediately into his brain. His eyes rolled up, and he went slack. Without missing a beat, Knoll and Gibbs assisted the now wobbly man to a waiting van now parked behind the Mercedes. Brutka, at the van's wheel, watched as they loaded the driver in the back.

Kruger emerged from the van and took the keys from Knoll. "See you all in a few." He got into the Mercedes and drove toward the Odin Analytica building.

The tightness in Kruger's stomach intensified as he waited in the designated parking spot for Pavlovich's car. He glanced at his watch and noticed the CEO was five minutes late. He pressed an icon on the cell phone he held in his lap. The call was answered immediately.

"Hang tight, Sean. He was about ten minutes late the second day we watched him."

Kruger said, "Thanks for finally telling me."

He ended the call as their target walked out of the building, attention directed at a cell phone in his hand. Kruger started the car, as instructed, before Pavlovich opened the back door. When the man slipped into the back seat and closed the door, Kruger pulled the car away from the curb.

The van carrying the rest of the team pulled out in front of the Mercedes, and Kruger followed it toward the location where the take-down would occur.

As soon as they pulled out of the parking lot, Pavlovich said, "Viktor, I forgot something. Go back."

Kruger flashed the headlights. A prearranged signal something was wrong. At the same time, he made sure the back doors were locked. Before pulling up to the parking slot at the building, he'd engaged the child locks so Pavlovich would have no way to get out of the back seat once inside.

Looking in the rearview mirror, he saw Pavlovich still staring at the cell phone.

"Sorry, Grigori, can't do that."

The man's head snapped up, and he stared at Kruger in the mirror. "You're not Viktor."

"Great observation."

Kruger kept his attention on the van ahead as it slowed to a stop. He parked right behind it as Pavlovich tried to open the rear door. Knoll and Gibbs scurried out of the van and ran to both sides of the Mercedes. Kruger unlocked the doors, and the two men slid in beside Pavlovich.

"What's the meaning of this?"

With their target secured in the back, Kruger accelerated and followed the van.

CHAPTER 45

Gulf of Finland

As scheduled, they made the last ferry of the night. Viktor, left in the Mercedes at the dock parking lot, would sleep off his sedative until morning and then face the consequences of his boss being gone. The team felt confident it would be morning before anyone discovered the Odin Analytica CEO was missing.

Getting Pavlovich quietly on the ferry took a bit of sleight of hand by Gibbs. After he parked the van in the interior of the ferry, he stepped out to show his passport. During the examination, he chose not to tell the ferry personnel he had someone asleep in the back of the van hidden by boxes.

As the man checked his passport, Gibbs said in Russian-accented English, "I am tired. Am I allowed to sleep in the van while we cross?"

The man looked at Gibbs and then his passport. "Yes, but once the boat is underway, do not leave your vehicle."

"Do not worry. I am too tired."

With a nod, the man returned to inspecting the other cars in the hold. Back inside the van, Gibbs checked the pulse of their visitor. Slow and steady. With a smile, he climbed back into the front of the van and typed out a text message.

Two-and-a-half hours later, Gibbs drove the van out of the ferry's hold directly to the spot where he would meet the other members of his team.

When he arrived, Kruger slipped into the passenger seat and asked. "How's Grigori?"

"Still napping. What about the others?"

"Sandy will drop Sergey off at the passenger terminal. Then he and Serene will meet us at the Gulfstream."

Glancing at his watch, Gibbs said, "Two minutes behind schedule. Not bad for a bunch of amateurs."

"Amateurs? Speak for yourself, my friend. I am now a professional kidnapper."

Gibbs chuckled as he drove the van toward the airport. During the trip, Kruger sent a simple text message to JR: *Time to release.*

***

Over the Atlantic Ocean
The Next Morning

The disappearance of Tomas Pavlovich dominated the news in Estonia, most of Western Europe, and the United Kingdom. At noon, a report, broadcasted on BBC News gave a detailed explanation on how various elections were manipulated earlier in the summer. This report identified Odin Analytica as the primary source of the hack.

Speculation about the whereabouts of Pavlovich dominated social media. Officially, Odin Analytica stated Pavlovich was on holiday and not hiding from reports circulating about election meddling. He would be making a statement, but not a public appearance.

Gibbs read this on his cell phone and chuckled. "Sean, did you see this?"

Taking the device, Kruger put his half-readers on and scanned the report. He also chuckled as he handed the phone back. "Wonder how long it will take them to disavow any knowledge of our friend Tomas?"

Knoll sat behind them as the Gulfstream G650ER streaked west toward the United States. "My guess is he will be declared a persona non grata in Estonia by the end of the day."

The cabin settled back into silence between the friends. The only sound being the constant roar of the jet engines.

Fifteen minutes later, Gibbs said, "Sandy told me you're officially joining us."

Sitting with his eyes closed, Kruger nodded. "About time, huh?"

Gibbs continued. "I never thanked you for arranging the initial financing we needed."

"There was no need to. I didn't do anything."

"Not what I heard."

"Then you heard wrong."

"Sean, are you going to sit there and tell me you didn't talk to David Wu about financing our company?"

"I'm not going to tell you that at all. Joseph is the individual who suggested David give you guys the seed money."

"Who put the idea in Joseph's head?"

"Don't know."

"Well, I do. Joseph told Sandy and me you were the one who laid out the reasons Wu should do it."

"Urban legend."

"You can't accept a simple thank you, can you?"

Kruger opened one eye, grinned, looked at Gibbs, and said, "You're welcome."

***

Southwest Missouri
Late that Night

Stephanie Kruger slipped under the covers and snuggled against her husband. "Glad you're home."

"Me, too." He put his arm around her shoulders. "I talked to Sandy and Jimmie. They're anxious for me to come on board. Apparently, they have numerous contracts waiting for them to sign."

"Are you going to be out of town much?"

"No, the younger guys are going to do the overseas contracts. Sandy likes to supervise the domestic ones, and Jimmie seems to be excelling as the office manager."

"What are you going to do?"

"I will be in charge of the fraud division."

She raised up on one elbow. "Fraud division. What's that?"

"Well, it seems rich people get scammed more than most of us common folk realized. They hate going to the police or the FBI. Sandy tells me they're too embarrassed to do so. It makes them look less successful or something like that. Anyway, they have several contracts they plan to sign, and I will take over as the investigator."

"Aren't you going to need some credentials to do so?"

"Apparently not. My twenty-five years with the FBI seem to be all the credentials I need to do this sort of work."

She snuggled tighter. "Good. I'm looking forward to you being home and busy again." They were quiet for a few minutes, enjoying being together. He was about to drift off to sleep when she said, "Are you going to resign as a US Marshal?"

Without opening his eyes, he said, "I'll give my notice tomorrow."

***

Tallinn, Estonia

Kevin Marks read the headlines on his cell phone and frowned. Tomas Pavlovich's sudden disappearance could only be described as a serious problem for him. Cursing under his breath, he realized the likelihood of getting the money owed to him no longer existed.

As soon as he finished reading, he packed his bag, left the hotel and took a shuttle bus to the airport. Luckily, his open-end first-class ticket meant his return to Canada was already paid for. Offering the passport for Miroslav Klaus at the ticket counter, the attendant gave him a boarding pass and directions toward the security check-in area.

***

Southwest Missouri

Sleep, once again, eluded JR Diminski on this late summer night. Mia slept peacefully next to him, her gentle breathing comforting as he lay there, his eye locked on the dimly lit slow turning ceiling fan.

Abruptly his cell phone vibrated against the surface of his nightstand signaling a new notification. Relieved by a reprieve from his insomnia, he grabbed the phone, slipped his glasses on and studied the screen. Quietly pushing the covers aside, he got out of bed and hurried to his home office down the hall.

He lifted the lid to his laptop and clicked on the notification at the bottom right side. What he read confirmed what he had suspected would happen once Pavlovich disappeared.

Kevin Marks was on the move.

"Shit."

He glanced at the time at the bottom right corner of his laptop and sighed. Marks would be in the air until early in the morning, plenty of time to inform Kruger.

***

The effects of traveling through multiple time zones, haphazard meals and constant stress left Kruger exhausted and still in bed at eight-thirty-two the next morning. Stephanie chose not to wake him as she gathered the children and hustled them off to school and herself to the university for a full day of lecturing.

When he opened his eyes, the house was eerily quiet. The hum of the air conditioner was the only sound he heard. He reached for her side of the bed and found it cold and empty.

Swinging his legs over, he sat on the side of the bed, placed his elbows on his knees and held his head with both palms as he oriented himself to where he was. He remained in this position for several minutes until his cell phone buzzed with a call.

Rolling his eyes, he glanced at the caller ID and answered. "Kruger."

"Marks is on the move."

"Where?"

"He flew into Montreal and rented a car under the name Miroslav Klaus."

"Any idea where he's headed?"

"Not at the moment."

"Any updates on Pavlovich?"

"None. The Estonian government is disavowing any knowledge of the man."

"What about his friend in Moscow?"

"Total and utter silence."

"Huh." Kruger paused. "Just like Jimmie predicted."

"What are you doing today?"

"Well, JR, first I'm going to make a pot of coffee and try to wake up."

The computer hacker chuckled. "Sorry, did I wake you?"

"You didn't, just struggling to get going this morning."

"Are you coming by the office today?"

"Eventually. I have to turn in my resignation as a US Marshal this morning."

Silence dominated the call for an extended amount of time. "What brought this on?"

"I'm tired of the bureaucratic indecision coming out of Washington this past year."

"Understandable." JR paused for a few moments. "Uh—I spoke to Joseph this morning."

"And?"

"Paul Stumpf took a turn for the worst and suddenly passed away last night."

Kruger was silent for a long time. "Oh—no. I thought he was getting better."

"So, did everybody else."

"What happened?"

"Joseph didn't have the details yet. He also told me the president was planning on naming Ryan Clark as the new Director."

"You're kidding?"

"Nope."

"Well, that'll piss off half the current management team in the bureau."

"That's what I told Joseph. The president doesn't care, apparently, he's tired of the current state of affairs there."

"Any word on when Paul's service will be?"

"Haven't heard."

"Okay, I'll call Joseph. What about the package for Odin Analytica? Was it delivered?"

"Yeah, I'll tell you more when you get here. Uh—

Sean?"
"Yeah."
"Don't resign yet."
"Why?"
"Talk to Joseph, first."
"Again, why?"
"Just talk to him."

CHAPTER 46

Southwest Missouri

Kruger impatiently waited for the drip coffee maker to produce enough liquid in the carafe to fill his mug. As he took his first sip, he stood next to the sink and stared out the kitchen window. After a few minutes, the fog muffling his thoughts began to clear and he made his way to his home office. Having failed to unpack his backpack from the trip, he extracted his laptop and turned it on.

When he checked his email, he found almost a hundred unopened messages with 60 percent of them from former colleagues at the FBI. The vast majority of these were informing him of the passing of Paul Stumpf. After reading thirty, his depression got the better of him and he called Joseph.

"Good morning, Sean."

"Is it?"

"Well, probably not as good as it could be."

"JR told me about Paul this morning."

"Yes, I am sorry. I knew you were traveling so I reached

out to JR."

"Have they announced services yet?"

"No, it was so sudden I'm told the family is still trying to cope with it."

"I thought he was doing better."

"So, did everyone else. He and his wife were even planning a trip to see their son in California before he returned to work."

"That sucks. When did it happen?"

"Early the night before last. I was told he went to bed early complaining of a headache and when his wife checked on him, he was already gone."

"Ah—geez. I'll call her today."

"She would appreciate it." Joseph, cleared his throat and said, "Are you planning to attend?"

"Yes, Stephanie and I will fly in as soon as they announce arrangements."

"Plan on having a meeting with President Griffin while you're here."

"Why?"

"He has a favor to ask you."

"I'm not moving to Washington."

"He's aware of your reluctance. Just hear him out."

"Joseph, I'm not sure how many times I have to tell you people, but I am not moving."

"Let me know when you plan to be here."

***

After two cups of coffee and a shower, he arrived at JR's office building and found himself at the second-floor coffee service pouring his third cup of coffee of the day. Still weary, he stood next to JR's cubicle and watched his friend finish a call with a client. When done, he stood and motioned for Kruger to join him in the conference room. After closing the door, he said, "Sorry about Paul."

"Yeah, me too."

"Are you going to the service?"

"Yes, Steph and I will fly out when we know the details."

JR nodded.

Kruger titled his head slightly, "You were going to tell me how you gained access to Odin Analytica."

With a grin, JR said, "Oh, that. After I posed as one of the campaign data crunchers, they gained access to the computer we used. I, uh—used that path to gain access to Odin Analytica's system. That was how we downloaded our worm. Now it seems their website is off-line this morning. News reports out of Estonia are extremely quiet about it. With the disappearance of Pavlovich and the sudden disruption in the company's website, conspiracy theories are flourishing on social media."

Returning the grin, Kruger said, "What sort of conspiracy theories?"

"All the way from a plot by rival companies to accusing Pavlovich of being an operative for the deep state."

"Which deep state?"

"Take your pick, although, the person who posted it pointed to the cabal taking over the European Union."

With a chuckle, Kruger sipped his coffee. "Hadn't heard about that one." He paused and asked, "Has Britain announced Pavlovich is in their custody?"

"Not yet."

"Huh." He took another sip of his coffee. "What exactly did the virus do?"

"Well, I paid them back for the attack on my system two years ago."

"And that was?"

"I encrypted everything on their server and back-up. Then I replaced their website home page with a GIF featuring a laughing Jolly Roger."

"You're mean."

"I learned from the best."

Both of Kruger's eyebrows rose. "I'll take that as a compliment."

"As you should."

"So, any news about Kevin Marks?"

JR shook his head. "He's disappeared in the digital world."

"You think he's paying cash?"

"Don't know, but I have flags on all his known credit cards." JR titled his head slightly. "What if he disappears like he did last year? I'm sure he's aware Odin Analytica is out of the picture and probably knows Pavlovich is in custody somewhere."

"I'm a patient man, JR. He'll surface eventually."

"What if he's patient too, Sean."

Kruger's mouth twitched. "A man like Marks can only wait so long, JR. I'll be here when he makes a mistake, and then I'll finish the job."

***

Arlington, VA
Thursday of the Following Week

Sean and Stephanie Kruger stood next to Joseph and Mary Kincaid during the graveside services for Paul Stumpf. While the ceremony proceeded, Kruger's thoughts kept returning to all of the bureau friends and colleagues lost over the past few years. First it was Alan Seltzer, gunned down by a serial killer, Thomas Shark, killed by a militia group and now Paul Stumpf, dead of cancer. These events strengthened his resolve to move on to the next phase of his career of working with Knoll and Gibbs.

Stephanie held his hand and leaned over, looking up at him. "Where are you?"

With a grim smile, he whispered back. "Not here."

"I could tell."

They both grew quiet as the priest recited the 23rd Psalm and then offered a prayer. Afterward he asked for a moment of silence and then made the sign of the cross. While he spoke to the family, Kruger and Stephanie stepped back so other mourners could pay their respects to Paul's wife and children.

As they stood there, Joseph and Mary joined them. Joseph said, "I spoke to a doctor at Walter Reed before the service. Apparently, the cancer metastasized in his brain and his attending physician missed it."

Kruger frowned. "Does his wife know about that?"

"She will after this all settles down."

The only way Kruger could respond was to nod.

"Sean, you and Stephanie have been invited to the White House for dinner tonight."

With a frown, Kruger said, "Joseph, I am not in the mood nor do I feel the inclination to attend some kind of state dinner right now."

"That's not what it will be. It's just you and Stephanie and the president and First Lady. I'm not invited."

Kruger looked at Stephanie, whose wide eyes were locked on Joseph. He turned his attention back to his friend. "Let me pay my respects to Paul's family and then I'll let you know."

***

Dinner with the Griffins occurred in the private dining area across from the president and first lady's bedroom. The atmosphere lacked the formality of an official dinner as President Griffin considered Sean Kruger a personal friend. Cheryl Griffin greeted them at the north entrance to the Executive Residence and showed them the way.

"It is so nice to finally meet you, Stephanie. I've heard so much about you from Sean, I feel I already know you.

Please call me Cheryl."

Stephanie Kruger shook the First Lady's hand and smiled. "Thank you, uh—Cheryl. I'm honored to meet you and…" She looked around and continued, "Be in the White House."

The first lady returned the smile. "I prefer our home in California. Sometimes I have to pinch myself to think we live here. Roy's finishing up a few things and will join us shortly." She turned her attention to Kruger. "Sean, thank you for joining us tonight. I know today couldn't have been easy for you."

"We appreciate the invitation." He chose not to discuss the day's events.

"May I show you around the White House?"

Stephane's eyes grew wide and a large smile appeared. "Oh, please. That would be wonderful."

During the tour, Kruger followed the two women. As Cheryl noted numerous historic points of interest in the house, he listened at times and other times he fell deep into his own thoughts. When they arrived at the private dining room on the second floor, Roy Griffin stood outside waiting for them. The ever-present Secret Service agents hovered nearby. After exchanging greetings, the Krugers followed their hosts into the room.

Conversation during dinner varied with Griffin expressing genuine interest in Stephanie's career as an assistant professor. Finally, after the dishes were cleared, the president placed his elbows on the table and made a steeple with his fingers. "I'm sure you are wondering why we invited you tonight?"

Kruger said, "I figured you'd get to it at some point."

"Well, I won't lie, the main reason was to discuss something that affects both of you. The second reason was to spend a little time with two people who have absolutely no ulterior reason for dining with Cheryl and me."

Cheryl said, "It has been a breath of fresh air. The

novelty of the place wears off quickly and it grows tiresome."

Stephanie nodded. "I can see how it would."

The president turned to Kruger. "Paul's sudden death has created numerous problems and exposed a glaring lack of progressive thinking at the FBI."

"I don't know Todd Perkins at all, so it will be hard for me to comment."

"Did you ever deal with him?"

Kruger shook his head. "He came from the Human Resource side. I'd heard of him, but never interacted. I understand he is bit of a traditionalist."

The president sighed. "More neanderthal than anything. He wants to take the FBI back to the way Hoover ran it."

"Oh, dear."

"That was my comment."

Even though he knew the answer, he asked the question anyway. "Not that it's any of my business, but who are you considering to replace Paul?"

"Ryan Clark."

"An excellent choice. But expect a lot of sudden early retirements."

"I am counting on them."

Tilting his head, Kruger asked, "Why?"

"As much as I respected Paul's leadership, some of his recent appointments to management, within the bureau, were starting to raise eyebrows."

"Really."

"Even the Attorney General questioned some of Paul's decisions."

"Is there a possibility the cancer was already present?"

"That's my thinking, but I haven't shared that with anyone."

"I hadn't spoken to him for a year."

"That's about when we starting questioning his actions." He paused for a moment. "Which brings me to the reason I asked you here."

Kruger didn't respond verbally. He kept his attention on the president.

"I know you are not interested in moving to Washington. And after listening to Stephanie's passion for her teaching, I can understand your reasons."

"However..."

The president smiled. "Yes, there is always a however. Would you be willing to head up a presidential advisory commission on how to reorganize the FBI?"

Kruger's brow furrowed as he leaned forward, "Beg your pardon?"

"I need an independent expert on the bureau. Someone who has an intricate knowledge of the bureau, but someone who is not currently associated with them. That person would head up the commission. You have more than twenty-five years of experience with the FBI and are currently considered retired. If you accept, you will need to resign from the US Marshals Service. Plus, once Ryan Clark is confirmed as the Director, you'd be available to advise him."

Without answering the president, Kruger looked at Stephanie who smiled and nodded once. He turned his attention to the president. "I'd be honored, sir."

CHAPTER 47

Windsor, Canada

Geographically southwest of Detroit, the town of Windsor, in the providence of Ontario, provided Kevin Marks a sanctuary from which to obtain new identification documents. A small Airbnb, whose owner he knew from a previous visit, made an exception for Marks and accepted cash and no record of his stay.

This gave the fugitive from Canadian and American law enforcement a relatively safe place to cross over to Detroit. There, in a locality Detroit police were reluctant to patrol, resided an individual with the skills and technology to supply Marks with a new identity.

The time approached noon as Marks drove slowly through a neighborhood consisting of a hodgepodge of inconsistent architectural styles. Since his last visit, plywood covered more than 50 percent of the doors and windows in the neighborhood. Those homes without plywood, now had iron bars.

The address he sought appeared the same as when he

last visited. Its owner, expecting his visit, turned the porch light on to signal his visit was still welcome. At this time of day, parking on the street held few risks, only when the sun set did events in the neighborhood get dicey.

The cottage-style house, with large stone siding, sat on a narrow lot twice as deep as it was wide. Large mature trees dominated the front yard. Ivy covered the sides and a third of the front façade of the structure. Un-mowed grass, ankle deep, gave the place an abandoned feel. Marks parked in front and sent a two-word text message, *out front*.

The response to the text came when the porch light blinked out. He slipped out of the car and approached the front door avoiding the cracked sidewalk leading to it. As he stepped on the front porch, the door opened and he walked in without knocking.

The forger, Marks did not know his real name, nor did he want to, stood inside the dimly lit front room and said, "My prices went up since your last visit."

With a shrug, Marks said, "Not surprised. Neighborhood still looks like shit."

"Yeah, it does and that keeps the cops away. They hate to come into the area. Now what do you need?"

"Driver's license, passport and an American Express card."

"Hmmmm." The man folded his arms. "Don't have an Express one at the moment, how about a Discover?"

"Whatever, doesn't matter to me. How secure are they?"

"The owner won't be needing them any longer."

"How?"

With a shrug, the man said, "Don't know the details, I never ask."

"Okay, how much."

"Ten thousand."

"Eight."

The forger chuckled. "No way. Ten or we're done talking."

Marks gave the man a crooked smile. "Ninety-five."

The man folded his arms and stared at his client for a few moments. "Since it's you…" He nodded and said, "I'll need a new picture. I burned all the previous negatives."

"Good."

The man pointed to a set of stairs leading to a basement and said, "Give me twenty-four hours and you can pick them up."

Shaking his head, Marks said, "I need them today."

Tilting his head, the forger pursed his lips. "That'll cost you another thousand for while-you-wait services and it'll need to be in-advance."

With a sly smile, Marks extracted a bundle of hundred-dollar bills from under his untucked polo shirt. "Here you go, there's twelve-thousand, consider the extra five a tip."

The man looked over his glasses. "Thought I should mention if anything happens to me while you're still in the house, you won't be able to get out."

Marks' eyebrows rose.

The forger gave him a grim smile. "Had to take precautions after another client tried that shit."

Raising his hands with the palms toward the man, Marks shook his head. "Don't look at me, I've no plans to cheat you."

"Good. Let's get that picture."

***

Washington, DC

Kruger's official designation as a US Marshal terminated at the request of both Kruger and the president of the United States. A meeting with his old friend Ryan Clark occurred at dinner on the final day of their stay. He and Stephanie arrived at one of Joseph's favorite out-of-the-way bistros and joined the National Security Advisor and Mary at an isolated table in the far corner of the restaurant.

Kruger said, "I can remember sitting here several times, Joseph. Do you always get this table?"

Looking at Mary, who nodded in agreement with Kruger, Joseph said, "Not always."

Mary chuckled and interjected. "As long as we've been coming here, we have. He says the spot is aesthetically pleasing."

With a nod, Kruger said, "I think "strategically" pleasing would be a better word. You can see the entire dining area from here."

"That's what I told him, but he denies it."

Joseph shrugged. "Probably a bit of both. Old habits are hard to break." He paused and took a sip of his scotch. "Ryan called and indicated they would be a bit late. His wife got tied up on a story and got home late."

"That's okay, gives me time to talk to you."

Raising his eyebrows, he took another sip and said, "About?"

"You and I go a long way back, my friend. You were instrumental in getting me into the FBI. For that, I want to thank you."

With a nod, he said, "And the FBI was better for it."

"I would like to think so. I need your council once again."

Joseph smiled. "About joining Sandy and Jimmie's company."

Kruger chuckled as the waiter deposited a glass of Merlot for Stephanie and a glass of Chardonnay for him. "I take it you spoke to either Sandy or Jimmie?"

"It was Sandy, and it was yesterday."

"What do you think?"

"I think it's the perfect next step for you."

Letting out his breath, Kruger smiled. "That helps,

Joseph. I was starting to have doubts."

"Don't. The trend is for more government services to be performed by independent contractors."

"Why?"

"If you think about it, it makes sense. Our elected representatives look at the number of individuals working for the government as out of hand. The federal government employs over two-million Americans. Walmart employs more, but that includes worldwide employees."

"Didn't know that."

"The total number of individuals doing work for the government is now over nine million, which means a little over 75 percent of those individuals are independent contractors of some form. And it's only going to increase. So, are you making a good decision to join Sandy and Jimmie? Yes. The bonus for you is, they won't make you retire when you reach a certain age."

Stephanie said, "Thank you, Joseph." She turned to her husband. "Does that satisfy all those persistent doubts you've been having?"

A smile and a nod of his head were Kruger's response.

***

Ryan Clark and his wife, Politico reporter Tracy Adkins arrived exactly thirty minutes late. Both apologized profusely as they sat down.

Now in his late forties, Clark had been a detective with the Arlington, Virginia Police Department. During those years, he and Kruger worked several times together during Kruger's FBI career. Most notably investigating the Beltway Sniper in October 2002 and again six years ago when they chased a group of assassins across the United States. It was during this investigation of the assassins, Clark was wounded while protecting then-Congressman Roy Griffin. After his recovery, Kruger lobbied the director to make him an agent. Since then, Clark had made a name for himself as an FBI agent and rising to the position of both Special Agent in Charge and Assistant Director.

Ten years his junior, Tracy Adkins, an experienced journalist, who at one time worked for both the New York Times and then the Washington Post, was now a White House correspondent for Politico. She and Clark met with the help of Kruger and secretly married after he joined the FBI. An attractive woman with long dark blonde hair and blue eyes, she fostered a studious professorial look during any on-air reporting she might do.

"Don't worry about it, Ryan." Kruger took a sip of his wine. "Joseph and I had plenty to discuss before you got here. By the way, congratulations."

"Thank you, it was unexpected."

"But well deserved."

"I hope so."

As soon as Clark and Tracy were served their drinks, Joseph raised his glass and said, "Here's to a successful directorship for Ryan Clark."

After the toast, Joseph grew serious. "Before we order, I want to let both of you know the president wants to reorganize the FBI. He feels it has regressed over the past few years. He's afraid the cancer that claimed Paul's life manifested itself in a number of bad decisions over the course of the last year and a half. Such as naming Todd Perkins as Alan Seltzer's successor. The president feels Perkins has taken the FBI back to the Hoover era. Morale is low and we've heard through the grapevine a lot of senior managers will retire if Perkins becomes the new director."

Clark nodded. "I've heard the same rumors, only it's not just management, it stretches down into the rank-and-file street agents. While I've not heard it personally, someone told me the other day he wants agents to start wearing fedoras again."

Kruger said, "That's a bit over the top."

With a grim smile, Joseph said, "It's not a rumor. I saw the first draft of the memo. The president called the Attorney General and put a squelch on it. I believe that was the last straw for Roy. He decided Perkins wasn't up to the job and that the FBI needed a complete overhaul. The president asked Sean to head up a commission on reorganization, which he has accepted."

Clark's eyebrows rose and smiled. "I can't think of a better person to do so." He paused and frowned. "Won't Congress demand hearings on the reorganization?"

"Not after Sean and JR testify about the recent hack on PEC. The president followed the investigation very carefully. He wants both of them to testify before the Senate Judiciary Committee. He had a one-on-one conversation with the Chairman, John Bell. As you know Bell is the senior Senator from California and a staunch Griffin supporter. Perkins was too busy bringing the agency back to the Hoover era that he turned down the opportunity for the FBI to be involved."

Kruger grimaced. "Ah—Joseph, when will this testimony occur?"

"Probably early next week. Why?"

"Stephanie and I are scheduled to fly back home early tomorrow."

"That's okay, Sean. You and JR will be traveling here together on Monday, plan to stay for a week."

Kruger nodded and squeezed Stephanie's hand.

Joseph continued. "Your testimony on what you found and JR's solution will help pave the way for Roy's reorganizational plan." He paused and turned his attention to Clark. "The president will officially name you as his designee for the directorship tomorrow morning. He has been informed the confirmation will be fast-tracked through Congress."

"What about Todd Perkins?"

As he took a sip of his drink, Joseph said, "Who cares?"

***

Ridgewood Neighborhood of Queens

The flickering neon sign above the entrance to the nondescript store front near the corner of Wycliff and Menahan simply proclaimed the establishment as a *Bar*. Kevin Marks liked that about the place, nondescript with no pretensions. It was a place for hard men to drink, period. If someone wanted a hamburger, go elsewhere. Elegance and glamor were unknown words in this environment. Shoes stuck to the floor and the lights so dim, the battered tables and mismatched chairs went unnoticed.

The time approached noon when Kevin Marks entered the place. While not as loud as it would be after dark, the din of the various conversations surprised Marks. As he passed the bartender on his way to the back room, he said, "Are you always here, Janko?"

The man shrugged. "Usually."

The back room, as with his last visit, contained only a round table with four chairs. The man he needed to see stood next to a built-in waist-high buffet. Tommy Valdic poured coffee from an ancient Mr. Coffee machine. He looked at his guest and pointed toward the table. "Want coffee?"

"No, thanks, Tommy."

Valdic finished and sat across from him and sipped the dark liquid. "Surprised you're back."

"Why?"

"Your name is a little radioactive right now, my friend."

"Yeah, I'm aware of that." He extracted his newly minted driver's license. "The individual you suggested does good work."

With a nod, Valdic narrowed his eyes. "What do you

need now?"

"Information."

"On?"

"A man, a former FBI agent."

Taking a sip of his coffee, Valdic's brow furrowed. "I have a strict rule around here, the less we screw with the feds, the less they will screw with us."

"I'm not asking you to do anything, I just need to know more about him."

"Why?"

"He's become an irritant."

"My dear, Kreso. I have never criticized your pursuit of revolutionary change, mainly because I find it a bit delusional. However, taking out your frustrations on a federal agent, retired or not, is a fool's errand. I cannot and will not condone it."

"Then you won't help me."

"I didn't say that."

Marks tilted his head. "Then what you are talking about?"

"I will not help you, but I can introduce you to others who share your frustration with the federal government."

CHAPTER 48

Washington, DC
One Week Later

"Mr. Diminski, are you telling this committee the threat of the computer virus you described has been neutralized?"

"Yes, Chairman Bell. Working alongside the owner of PEC, we have identified all the computer servers within state, county, and municipal governments originally infected by the malware."

"And you assure this committee that elections held by these government entities will not be compromised?"

"I am assuring your committee that elections measured by the forementioned computer servers will not be compromised by the malware designed by Odin Analytica and distributed by PEC. I cannot comment on any attack they may suffer from other malicious entities."

California Senator John Bell's first inclination was to smile at the comment by the computer expert, but he kept his expression neutral. The following question, worked out in advance by him and the president, would be the most important one of the hearing.

"So, you are telling this committee and the American people, the threat is not over. Am I understanding you correctly, Mr. Diminski?"

"Sir, the threat is greater today than yesterday. It will be larger tomorrow than today. In my opinion, it's just getting started. The need for the FBI to enhance and expand the cybercrimes division is critical. My company has experienced exponential growth over the past few years due to these types of computer attacks. It will get progressively worse, not better, in the coming years."

Bell took his glasses off and rubbed the lenses with the end of his tie. "There are those on this committee and in Congress who do not agree with you."

JR tilted his head slightly, thought about what he wanted to say for a few moments and then said it. "I understand that, Mr. Chairman. Sticking one's head in the sand and ignoring the problem will not make the issue go away. It's already here." He paused for a split second and continued. "Only a fool reacts to a crisis in that manner."

Half of the members of the committee grumbled loudly, and a few mumbled about an apology, but Bell clamored for order. He smiled at JR and said, "We appreciate your candor, sir. We also appreciate your appearance today in front of this committee."

JR just nodded.

"Since there are no more questions, this meeting will take an hour lunch break." He glanced at his watch. "We will reconvene at two."

Gathering his notes, JR stood and looked at Sean Kruger sitting just behind him in the gallery. His friend stood as well, and they made their way out of the hearing room. Kruger said in a low voice, "Nicely done. I thought you said you were nervous."

"I was until I realized most of them didn't understood a word I was saying and the rest were ignoring me."

"I liked the part where you called half the committee fools. Did you practice that observation?"

JR gave him a crooked grin. "It came to me listening to the rambling four-minute rant from the South Carolina senator. It was hard to tell if there was actually a question being asked."

Kruger chuckled. "I liked your one-word answer."

"As you have said many times, the word no can be a powerful response sometimes."

"Yes, it can be. I think you managed to scare them to death."

"Good, they need to be."

"At least our part of this is over."

JR looked over at him. "Are you done? I thought they reserved the right to call you back."

"Apparently, they don't need any additional information from me. I got a text message from Joseph. The committee is ready to advance Ryan Clark's nomination to the full Senate. He'll be confirmed tomorrow."

"Good. I'm ready to get out of this town."

"I would like that as well. However, I have been asked to attend the hearing tomorrow to advise Clark. After that, I'll be leaving, too."

"Want me to stay?"

"Nah, no point in both of us being miserable. Want me to buy you lunch?"

"I thought it was my turn."

"It is. That was my way of getting you to pay."

JR chuckled.

***

The walk to their rental car took about fifteen minutes. JR said as they walked through the parking lot, "I thought Missouri was hot in July. This place is worse."

"It's the humidity—"

The sound of tires squealing interrupted Kruger's statement, and he turned to see a large SUV bearing down on them, gaining speed. Grabbing JR by the arm, he basically threw him between two cars parked on the curb. His next reaction occurred almost simultaneously as the massive vehicle sped toward him. Withdrawing his Glock from the holster, hidden from view by his suit coat, he brought it up in a two-handed Weaver stance. Pulling the trigger rapidly, three times, he dashed to his left, and the truck missed him by a few inches.

The SUV swerved, sideswiped the rear bumpers of several vehicles and then accelerated away. Kruger made note of the license plate number and holstered his weapon. JR, having picked himself up from the pavement, stood next to him. "What the hell was that all about?"

"Apparently, someone didn't like our testimony."

***

Capitol and Metropolitan police swarmed over the parking lot, taking pictures and asking questions. Kruger and JR remained stoic and answered the ones they could. The Law Enforcement Officers Safety Act, enacted in 2004, allowed him, as a retired FBI agent, to carry a concealed firearm anywhere in the United States. He surrendered the Glock to the Metropolitan police, but it was returned to him after several witnesses told the police about the large vehicle attempting to run them over.

As the afternoon heat intensified, both JR and Kruger removed their suit coats and held them across their arms. JR said, "So much for lunch."

"Lucky you. You're still buying next time."

With a smile, JR glanced at his friend. "You realize that wasn't random, don't you?"

Kruger stared off into the distance. "Very much aware of it."

"Marks?"

"That would be my first guess."

"You know he won't give up."

"No, I don't suppose he will." Both men were leaning against the trunk of Kruger's rental car. He continued, "Are you still monitoring his credit card?"

"Alexia is. I called her while you were talking to the detectives. The cards we know about haven't been used for a couple of weeks."

"Then he's using cash, or he has a new one."

A Metropolitan Police sergeant walked up to them. "Just got a report about an abandoned Chevy Tahoe found about ten blocks from here. Lots of sideswipe damage on the passenger side and three bullet holes in the driver's-side windshield."

Kruger asked. "Was the truck stolen?"

The detective nodded. "They also found a lot of blood on the seat. You hit your mark."

With a grim smile, Kruger said, "At least I can still shoot." He paused, "Any reports of gunshot wounds showing up at the emergency rooms?"

"Yeah, we have a couple of guys on their way. If the blood type matches, we have the guy." With a smile, the man continued. "I didn't realize who you were until one of the USCP officers told me. I used to be with the Arlington Police department. Ryan Clark's a good friend. You're the one who talked him into joining the FBI, aren't you?"

Kruger nodded.

"That was a good day for all of us. He'll make the FBI a stronger organization."

"Those were my thoughts, also."

"You two are free to go."

"What about the driver?"

"Give me your phone number. I'll keep you posted."

"Thank you, Sergeant."

***

That Evening

"I appreciate the call, Sergeant." He paused. "No, I'm not leaving for a few days. Call me if you need to." Kruger ended the call and looked across the table at JR. "The driver is in critical condition and already has a lawyer running interference. His ID shows he's from Queens."

JR frowned. "Queens? Isn't that where Marks is from?"

"I don't suppose that's a coincidence, do you?"

"No, it isn't."

"So, now what, Sean?"

"I'm tired of playing defense." He took a sip of iced tea and then a bite of his hamburger. "Russell's been extradited from Canada and is in a hospital here in DC. I think it's time I have a heart-to-heart talk with him."

***

DOJ Attorney Hannah Martin and US Marshal Director Watson met Kruger in a waiting area at the Central Detention Facility located in Southeast Washington DC. They discussed their strategy about interviewing Franklin Russell.

Hannah said, "I have authorization to offer him a deal if he gives up Marks. That's from the attorney general himself."

Watson nodded and turned to Kruger. "It was your bust. What do you want to do?"

"Russell isn't going anywhere, and Marks is still on the lam. Do what you need to do."

With a small grin, Watson folded his arms. "Sean, there aren't any hard feelings about you resigning as a US Marshal. The president explained, and I have a tendency to agree with him. You would have had to leave the position in less than twenty months anyway."

"I appreciate that, Adrian. Russell's jumped bail before. He's a flight risk. If you can get him to talk without offering him a get-out-of-jail-free card, I'm all for it."

Hannah looked at Watson, "Your call, Director."

"Let's see what he has to say." He turned to Kruger. "Your prisoner. You want to question him?"

"I don't have the authority."

"Nonsense, he doesn't know you resigned. You take the lead."

Kruger only nodded.

***

Franklin Russell waited in the interrogation room, staring at the top of the table in front of him. He looked up as Kruger and Hannah Martin walked in. The Metropolitan Police officer guarding the prisoner nodded and stepped out as the two newcomers sat.

The first words out of Russell's mouth were, "I want a lawyer."

Kruger stared at the man and gave him a grim smile. "A wise request, Franklin."

"Well...?"

Hannah said, "Your identification shows you as a Canadian citizen. Something we know is not true. Technically, we can hold you on terrorist charges and as an enemy combatant. If we do that, you won't be entitled to an attorney."

Russell blinked twice, looked at the DOJ attorney and then at Kruger and then back to Hannah. "You can't do that." He pointed to Kruger. "He knows I'm an American citizen."

Kruger smiled. "Sorry, I don't know that to be a fact, Franklin. I don't really have a good grasp on who you really are. Until we know for sure, you could get lost in the system, be transferred to a federal prison facility and forgotten. Lots of possibilities and none of them good."

The prisoner leaned back in his chair and smiled. "Did you forget about my military record?"

"What military record?"

A smile appeared on the prisoner. "Okay, I see where this is going. What kind of a deal are you offering?"

Leaning forward on the table, Kruger glared at the man. "I want Marks. You give him to me, and you don't get lost in ADX Florence."

Changing his attention to Hannah, Russell asked, "That legit?"

She nodded.

"Okay, you've got a deal."

Kruger asked, "Where's Marks?"

"He's in Estonia."

Kruger folded his arms. "Probably not now. Tomas Pavlovich took an unexpected trip to England and is now being charged with interfering with their elections. Plus, Odin Analytica suffered a debilitating computer hack, and the government of Estonia seized their assets."

"Huh. Didn't know that."

"It's a fact."

"Then I doubt Marks is in Estonia anymore."

"Care to guess?"

With a conspiratorial smile, Russell said, "Why don't you let me call him?"

Hannah started to shake her head, but Kruger put his hand on her arm. "Good idea, Franklin. How will you go about contacting him?"

The prisoner frowned.

"Your statement indicates you know where he is."

Russell involuntarily gulped as his eyes shifted between Kruger and Hannah for a few seconds. Then he relaxed. "Guess you'll have to trust me."

"Something I am not inclined to do."

Narrowing his eyes, Russell sat back, his arms folded. "I know where he will be. Get me the deal and I'll tell you."

"Kind of what I thought. You have no clue where he is. After you figure it out, let me know." Kruger and Hannah stood to leave.

Sitting straighter, the prisoner said, "You forgot to ask how my wounds are doing."

As Hannah walked out the door, Kruger turned just before he exited. "No, I didn't forget. I simply don't care."

Kruger took Hannah aside upon leaving the interrogation room and asked, "What do you think?"

"I don't believe he knows where Marks is, she replied. "What about you?"

"I would have to agree. I have a funny feeling the man's disappeared just like he did a year ago."

"What now?"

"Well, until we have more to go on, it's probably time to put this investigation on hold and move on to other things."

She nodded.

CHAPTER 49

Ridgewood Neighborhood of Queens

"Kreso, you're bad karma." Tommy Valdic clenched the unlit cigar with his teeth. "I got a call from the people I sent you to, and they want nothing to do with you now."

"What happened?"

"Apparently the guy they sent to take care of your fed problem ended up in a hospital with three bullet holes in him. He's now cutting a deal to keep from being charged with attacking a federal law enforcement agent."

Kevin Marks glared at Valdic. "That's not my fault."

"No, but that won't keep them from blaming you." He paused and took the cigar out. "My suggestion to you is to figure out a way to draw this guy into a trap and take care of him yourself."

"This is the second and last time this particular federal agent is going to interfere." He stood to leave.

Valdic placed the cigar back between his teeth. "Here's a little health advice for you, Kreso."

"What?"

"You've worn out your welcome here in Ridgewood. Don't come back."

Marks glared at the man for several long seconds then turned and walked out of the office.

Traveling north on I-87 toward Montreal, Marks decided it was time to cash in on Lydia McDonald's hospitality, plus she'd received a large lump sum payment after her divorce. He knew where the money was and how to access it. Once she was taken care of, he would hide out north of Montreal and figure out how to pay Sean Kruger back for all of his meddling.

Satisfied with his plans. He set the speed control on his rental car and relaxed for the rest of his six-hour drive.

***

One Week Later

Life in the Kruger household settled into a regular routine after he officially joined KKG Solutions. During the mornings, he occupied himself attending Zoom video meetings with members of the commission looking into reorganizing the FBI. Since the members were scattered all across the country, video conference calls were the only solution.

Afternoons were spent either in his home office or at the headquarters of KKG at the Springfield-Branson National Airport. He was starting to enjoy working out of the airport office. The roar of jets taking off and landing gave him a sense of doing something completely different with his career. It was on one of these days Kruger was growing to enjoy that JR called his cell phone.

"Kruger."

"It's JR. You busy?"

"Never, for you. What's up?"

"Got a call from Tony Chien."

"Good or bad?"

"Not good. Is Jimmie in town?"

"Yeah, he's on a conference call. Why?"

"When could you two be in my office?"

Glancing at his watch, Kruger said, "How about three? That soon enough?"

"Yeah. See you then."

***

At three p.m., Kruger, Jimmie, and JR were situated in the soundproof conference room at JR's office building as he dialed a number.

"Tony Chien. How can I assist you today?"

"It's John."

"Huh—the caller ID says Melbourne, Australia."

"Yeah, one of my quirks. I don't like people knowing where I am."

"Thanks for calling. Are Sean and Jimmie there?"

Kruger said, "Yes, both of us."

"I need to hire KKG Solutions."

Jimmie's eyebrows rose, and Kruger smiled. "May I ask for what reason?"

"You may. I need your skills as an investigator, Sean, and I need Jimmie's experience as a Navy SEAL. Plus, I may need more help from John."

Gibbs asked, "What's happened, Tony?"

"Our Montreal office has suffered a terrible tragedy. Lydia McDonald has been brutally murdered and her house ransacked. We also have reason to believe all her financial assets have been stolen."

Kruger frowned. "Uh, Tony, this sounds like something the Royal Canadian Mounted Police should be investigating, not KKG Solutions"

"Who do you think asked for you? Your friend Bentley

Thatcher asked me to see if you'd be a consultant."

"Why?"

"Kevin Marks."

Closing his eyes, Kruger mumbled, "Ah—shit."

JR asked, "What do you need from me, Tony?"

"I would like for you to monitor our servers and make sure we are not attacked again. This needs to be on a permanent basis."

"You have a very robust IT staff. Why me?"

"Because they missed the first attack, I don't trust them to stop a second."

Raising an eyebrow, JR looked at Kruger, who shrugged, and Gibbs, who gave him a half grin. The former computer hacker said, "Okay, we can do that."

"Good. Then we are in agreement. What about KKG Solutions? Will you take the job?"

Jimmie visually checked with Kruger, who gave him the thumbs up gesture. Gibbs said, "Yes, Tony. We'll take it. When do you want us in Montreal?"

"Tomorrow, if possible."

Kruger stared at the Polycom conference phone and tapped his finger on the table. "We'll let you know our ETA."

"Gentlemen, I am not concerned about costs at the moment, this Kevin Marks person has caused my company and me way too much grief."

"Amen to that." Kruger's attention remained on the phone.

Details were discussed, and the call ended twenty minutes later. JR sat back and studied his friend. "Sean, are you okay with this?"

"I am." He continued to tap his finger on the conference table. Finally, he stopped. "We have to stop Marks once and for all. Too many individuals are dead because of him."

Gibbs said, "We have a green light to have Barnett involved. I'll have him pick us up with the jet in the morning. Say seven?"

Kruger stood and walked to the one wall with a window. He placed his hands behind his back and directed his attention to the outside.

JR said, "What's wrong, Sean."

"Nothing. I hope this is the last damn time I have to hear that individual's name."

CHAPTER 50

Montreal, Canada

The HA-420 HondaJet landed at Montreal Saint-Hubert Longueuil Airport at fifteen minutes after eleven a.m. Bentley Thatcher met them at the business FBO area with a black Chevy Suburban. Kruger sat in the front passenger seat with Gibbs directly behind him. Thatcher said, "I'd like for you to view the crime scene first."

Kruger buckled his seatbelt. Turning to Thatcher he asked, "How violent was the attack?"

Glancing at his friend, Thatcher wrinkled his nose. "I'll let you make that determination."

"That bad?"

"Unfortunately, yes."

Thirty minutes later, Kruger and Gibbs stood in the late Lydia McDonald's home. Surveying the senseless damage, he quietly walked around the living room, kneeling at times to look at an area closer. Finally, he stood and motioned with his head for Gibbs to follow. "What do you think, Jimmie?"

"This looks more like the aftermath of a terrorist attack than a home invasion."

"My thoughts, exactly. This was a message."

"For whom?"

"All of us."

When they entered the bedroom, even the battle-tested ex-Navy SEAL recoiled from the unsettling scene before him. Blood spatters covered every wall, and the red-soaked bedsheets betrayed the intense struggle Kruger surmised occurred there. He stayed quiet while he studied the area. Finally, he said, "In all my years of tracking serial killers and depraved personalities, this might be the worst crime scene I've ever encountered." He turned to Thatcher, who stood in the doorway. "I will assume you collected DNA samples."

"Yes. Quite a number, actually."

"How bad was the rape?"

"Medical examiner said it was the worst he'd ever seen."

"Kind of what I suspected." Turning to Gibbs, he said, "What are your thoughts?"

"I didn't realize Marks was this sick."

Kruger did not comment.

A Mountie sporting sergeant stripes stepped up behind Thatcher and whispered something in his ear. The superintendent nodded and said to Kruger and Gibbs. "We have a report of a body found in the Mont-Tremblant Park area. The ID indicates it's Marks, but the condition of the body isn't that great. Maybe you and Gibbs can help confirm the identity."

"Sure, let's go."

***

Mont-Tremblant Park, Providence of Quebec

Two hours later, the three men joined a group of RCMP investigators in a wooded area overlooking Devil's River. When Kruger and Gibbs were shown the body, both men said in unison, "That's not Marks."

Thatcher said, "How can you tell, the face has been obliterated by animals?"

Kruger looked at him. "Marks' face is round. This body has a narrower one, plus the height is wrong. Marks isn't that tall."

Surveying the scene, Kruger noted the area where the body lay, and overlooked the river some ten feet below. He turned to Gibbs. "With the higher elevations to the west and north this seems like the perfect place for an ambush."

Gibbs scanned the area. "I couldn't agree more." He pointed toward the north. "This clearing is part of a hiking trail. He didn't bother to wait for someone of similar build, he chose the first person to come by. No need to be picky about who it—"

Kruger jerked sideways as a bullet struck him in the upper shoulder, the report of the shot following a split second later. Training took over as Gibbs calculated the distance and direction of the shot while he rushed to Kruger.

Thatcher was next to be struck as the rest of the RCMPs took cover and returned fire with their pistols.

Gibbs grabbed Kruger and dragged him toward a grove of trees fifteen feet from their location. He checked the wound using his SEAL medical training and managed to slow the bleeding. "It hit high on your shoulder, nothing vital close to the wound."

With a grimace Kruger asked, "What about Bentley?"

"He's being attended to by one of the medical techs. Wound was high on his upper arm."

Looking Gibbs in the eye, the retired FBI agent said, "You up for going after him?"

A nod was his answer.

"Take my Glock as a backup."

Gibbs nodded and extracted the weapon from Kruger's belt holster.

Before he stood, Kruger grabbed his arm. "Jimmie, get this guy."

With a quick smile, the highly trained special forces sniper and tracker blended into the woods heading north.

**

The crack of another rifle shot helped Gibbs confirm he was heading in the right direction. Even with the echo of the shot reverberating off surrounding trees, he knew the course he needed to take. After stealthily traveling the mild uphill slope for what he estimated to be about a thousand feet, he stopped and listened. The earlier gunshots created an environment where birds and creatures of the forest remained quiet. Below and to his left, the unmistakable hiss and roar of a rapidly flowing river masked the sound of his trek through the wooded area. To his right, he knew the river's sound would be less noticeable. Squatting behind a large oak tree, he closed his eyes and listened. The faint rustling of leaves to the west caused him to turn his head and concentrate. Finally, he could distinguish a steady and regular swishing of leaves, like the slow steps of a man on the hunt.

Remaining perfectly still, he waited until he perceived the motion to be directly perpendicular to his current location. Keeping his position low, he strained his eyes and barely detected the outline of a shadowy figure, rifle in hand, moving slowly toward the south.

Raising the Glock in his right hand, he steadied it with his left and pulled the trigger rapidly three times. A grunt and a quick swishing of leaves back toward the north were his reward. Gibbs stayed perfectly still behind the tree and was rewarded for his decision by a rifle shot hitting a large oak several feet to his left. Another shot struck a different tree further to his right.

He rushed to his left, closer to the downslope leading to the river. When he had advanced, by his guess, another fifty feet, he stopped and listened again. Off in the distance, he barely heard the sound of a man breathing hard. Now crouching behind a large maple, he yelled from the right side of the tree, "Give it up, Marks. The place is crawling with Mounties."

His answer came with four rifle shots striking trees to his right. Moving to the left side of the giant tree, he rushed forward again, stopping ten feet ahead behind another maple. Two successive rifle shots hit the front of the tree where he hid. With more confidence of the man's position, he dropped to the ground and lay prone. With the gun stretched in front of him, he fired off another three rapid shots. As soon as he fired, he rolled back behind the tree.

This time only silence answered his attack. Standing erect, he leaned against the tree and listened. The distant murmur of multiple voices approached from his rear. This would be the Mounties following him. Above him he heard the unmistakable thump-thump-thump of a helicopter approaching from the south.

"Hear that, Marks? They're bringing in reinforcements. You can't get away."

His answer was the shuffling of leaves in the direction of a slope leading down to the river. A muffled grunt and the scream of a man in pain met his ears. Gibbs dashed toward the grade leading down. As he emerged from the tree line, he saw a man stumbling uncontrollably down the steep angle of the land leading toward the river. Just before the man reached the edge of the river, he slammed into a large boulder and cried out in pain. Gibbs started down the slope in hopes of getting the man before he slid into the waterway.

The figure lay still for a few moments as Gibbs grew

closer. Suddenly, he struggled to stand. A few feet from the river's edge, he wavered and fell into the swift-moving current. By the time Gibbs reached the water's edge, all he could see was the man's head bobbing up and down in the water as it rushed downstream.

Turning back to look at the boulder, where the man he assumed to be Marks, had crashed, he saw blood dripping toward the ground. Gibbs turned back to look downstream, but the fugitive was no longer in sight.

***

The helicopter turned out to be an Air-Evac unit out of the town of Saint-Jovite, to the south of the Mont-Tremblant Park. The Mounties who followed Gibbs were able to locate the rifle used by Marks. Later examination would reveal there were traces of blood on the gun which led to speculation one of the bullets fired by Gibbs struck its target.

Kruger was flown to a hospital, leaving Gibbs to return to Montreal with a patched-up Bentley Thatcher driving the Suburban.

As they drove south, Thatcher glanced for a second at Gibbs. "EMTs were a little concerned about Sean."

Looking at the superintendent, Gibbs asked, "How bad was he hit?"

"You saw the wound. They couldn't get it to stop bleeding."

"Where'd they take him?"

"Montreal General Hospital."

Gibbs pulled out his cell phone and checked the signal. When he saw he had one, he dialed JR.

***

Forty-Eight Hours Later

Kruger sat in his office, right arm immobilized by a sling, trying to type an email with his left hand. He failed miserably.

Stephanie stopped on her way to the kitchen and leaned against his doorframe. "You are one stubborn man, Mr. Kruger."

He looked up and smiled at her. "Why do you say that?"

"A little over two days ago, you were clinging to life, with a gunshot wound, while being flown in a helicopter out of the middle of nowhere. Now you're typing emails."

"I was not clinging to life. I lost a little blood."

"That's not what Jimmie Gibbs told me."

"Jimmie Gibbs is known to exaggerate." He stood and walked over to her. "I'd hug you, but it might hurt too much."

She patted him on his good shoulder. "Excuses, excuses." Folding her arms, she continued. "The doctor told you no work or stress for a few days. Let your body heal, Sean."

"And do what, watch TV? No, thank you."

"Read."

"That I can do."

"JR called a few moments ago and said he was coming over. He has some news."

Kruger smiled. "If he's bringing bad news, he needs to stay home."

Stephanie Kruger shook her head and continued her trip to the kitchen.

JR showed up two minutes later, and they retreated to the back deck overlooking Kruger's backyard. JR said, "Sean, when are you going to stop getting in the way of bullets?"

"Funny, JR. Steph said you had some news."

"Yeah, they haven't found Marks' body yet."

"Damn." Kruger grew quiet for a few moments. "When did you hear this?"

"I called Bentley this morning to see how he was doing, and he told me."

"How is he?"

"Better than you. He had the good sense to at least try to get out of the bullets' way."

"You're a riot, JR."

The computer expert smiled. "Want a beer?"

Kruger looked over at him and nodded. "Should be some Boulevards in the fridge."

JR returned and handed his friend a bottle. "If Marks survived, this isn't over, is it?"

Taking a sip of beer, Kruger stared out over the lawn. "No, I'm afraid it isn't."

EPILOGUE

Southwest Missouri
Two Months Later

Kruger walked around the peripheral of the second floor of JR's office building and motioned for his friend to join him in the conference room.

"This is a surprise. What's going on?"

Kruger slid a sheet of paper across the table. JR, read it, and grinned. "Where'd they find the body?"

"Tangled in some weeds on one of the meandering arms of Devil's River. About five miles downstream from where he shot me. A fisherman found him. DNA from the body matched samples from the McDonald woman's home and the blood on the rifle they found above the river."

"How do you feel about it?"

"Relieved, mostly." He paused and clasped his hands together. "Unfortunately, a lot of unnecessary deaths occurred because of him."

"Don't blame yourself, Sean."

"I don't. I can't. It'd drive me nuts if I did."

JR nodded. "Did you hear what happened to Pavlovich?"

Kruger snapped out of his funk and smiled. "No, what?"

"France, Portugal, and Spain have charged him with interfering with elections. Two of the countries are trying to extradite him from Britain. He's not going anywhere for a while."

"Good."

"You never have mentioned anything about the report you wrote for reorganizing the FBI. What happened?"

With a chuckle, Kruger said, "What do you think happened?"

"Don't tell me, it's on somebody's desk in the middle of the ignore pile."

"Sitting on the desk of the Judiciary Committee chairman. Clark called a couple of days ago to check on me and told me all about it. The president is livid. I'm surprised the news media hasn't gotten wind of it."

JR gave Kruger a half grin, "I'm surprised Ryan's wife hasn't written about it."

"She probably won't. They have a strict rule about those kinds of stories."

"She's not the only reporter in Washington, Sean."

"What've you got in mind?"

"Someone might have to send an anonymous email to someone at CNN."

"Just don't get Director Clark involved. He likes his job and is already trying to make a lot of the changes we suggested. At least the ones that don't have to be approved by Congress."

"I won't involve Ryan."

"Speaking of getting involved, I understand your company has a contract to take over the IT department for PEC. When did this come about?"

"Who told you?"

"Who do you think? Alexia told Jimmie and Jimmie told

me."

"I forgot about our internal gossip path. Yes, Tony talked me into it. I only agreed to it as long as his best people joined my company."

"Isn't that more expensive for him?"

"A little, but he said it was his way of trying to pay me back for his bad decision ten years ago. Besides, Tony and I are talking on a regular basis now. I like that."

"Good." Kruger stood to leave.

JR looked at him. "We might have a problem."

Frowning, Kruger returned to his seat. "What?"

"I heard a rumor the other day that when Estonia raided and confiscated the assets of Odin Analytica, all of the company's computers and servers were missing. Supposedly, a few key members of their IT department also disappeared."

"Why's that a problem?"

"Because those computers were used to make devastating computer attacks all over the world."

"I though you neutralized their systems."

"I did, to an extent."

"What do you mean to an extent, JR?"

The computer expert studied the tabletop for a few moments and then looked over his glasses at Kruger. "Let's put it this way. Odin Analytica was nothing without their IT team. They're the ones who wrote the code and figured out how to launch the attacks on other computer systems. I didn't neutralize them. All I did was stop them on a temporary basis. The code they used would still be intact on the company's computers."

"So, the world hasn't seen the last of them. Is that what you're saying.?"

"That's exactly what I'm saying."

And now, a sneak peak of
the next Sean Kruger story:
The Hidden Trail
By J.C. Fields

THE HIDDEN TRAIL, BOOK 8

CHAPTER 1

Fayetteville, AR

The youngest granddaughter of former President of the United States, Lawrence Osborne's, day started uneventful. Stephanie Osborne, a second semester junior at the University of Arkansas's Fayetteville campus, woke at her normal time. After making a cup of coffee in a well-used Keurig and putting the finishing touches on a paper for her International Law class, she listened to the weather forecast before dressing for her morning run. As a starting forward on the women's soccer team, she ran a minimum of five miles every morning during the off-season, sometimes more.

Stepping out of the front door of her apartment building east of campus, she looked at the slate gray sky and found the weatherman to be correct, an overcast sky, drizzle and temperatures hovering in the low forties. She adjusted her Under Armour ear-warmer headband and with a shrug, set out for her run.

A course meandering through the Mt. Sequoyah Woods Trail was her go-to place, despite the mist and cold temperatures she would experience today. The densely wooded hiking trails, with their hills and valleys, made her legs burn with exertion. This always brought a smile to her face as she pounded along her normal route.

As the fourth grandchild of a former United States president, she was not entitled to Secret Service protection, nor did she want it. Her political views were agnostic at best and the only strong opinions she held revolved around equal opportunities for women. The fact that her grandfather had been president when she was young had impressed her then, but now he was just her grandfather. A good grandfather, but yesterday's news.

As she topped the highest peak on the trail, a strong sensation of being watched swept over her. With such a profound feeling, she stopped, bent over and placed her hands on her knees to catch her breath. Straightening, she swept her eyes slowly across the tree line on both sides of the trail. Seeing nothing out of the ordinary, she smiled to herself shrugging the sensation off as a random movement of one of the many creatures inhabiting the wooded landscape.

***

The man dressed from head to toe in woodland camo froze as the woman's gaze swept past his position. Forest colored binoculars and a camo balaclava pulled over his face, helped to obscure his presence within the heavily wooded landscape.

Once the woman continued her run and descended the downward slope, the visibly obscured man spoke into a tactical throat mic hidden under his face covering. "Just passed this location."

He heard two clicks in his ear buds, which he knew to mean, *roger*.

After she disappeared from his sight, he trudged toward the path to follow her to a spot in the valley below. There she would be subdued and rendered unconscious by four similarly clad men.

As he walked toward this location, he checked his watch. Two minutes early. He took his time. He would arrive at the spot by the time she would be unconscious and ready to transport. As the leader of the group, he would be the one to make the decision on where to take the woman. There were plenty of back-water locations in Arkansas where the authorities would never find them while he negotiated her ransom. Half way there, he heard a muffled scream.

Coming up on the abduction location, a chaotic scene met him. The woman lay prone on the trail, bleeding from a spot low on her chest and unmoving as the abduction team stood over her.

The larger of the four men said, "Bitch put up a fight."

"What happened?"

The thinnest member of the group, a guy called Issy, held his hand to his eye as blood streamed down his face. "She jabbed her thumb in my eye." He nodded at the man next to him. "Ben shot her with the suppressed twenty-two."

The leader looked at the man called Ben and took a deep breath. "This wasn't how this was supposed to go down, gentlemen. Give me the gun."

He looked down at the young soccer player. "Prop her against that tree." He pointed to the trunk of a large oak just off the trail.

Two of the men positioned the woman's back against the tree, her head propped against the trunk.

The leader felt her neck and found a faint pulse. He also noted her shallow and irregular breathing. "Damn. Everyone, get out."

The others scattered and melted into the dense underbrush.

He pulled up his balaclava and bent down to look the young woman in the face. "Sorry, Stephanie, you would have been more valuable to us alive."

He stood, placed the suppressed twenty-two against her forehead and pulled the trigger twice.

***

Because of the cold temperatures and now steady rain, the Mt. Sequoyah Woods Trail experienced no additional traffic. Stephanie's roommate, Dana Shannon became concerned at thirty minutes after twelve when she returned home from morning classes. She found her friend's backpack and laptop still on the kitchen table. She went into Stephanie's room and did not see her running shoes nor did she find any running clothes in the washing machine.

Calling her roommate's cell phone resulted in no response. Her next thought was that Stephanie might have hurt herself on the trail and could not get back. Knowing her roommate's path, she dressed against the weather and set out to check the route, a path they had ran together many times. With her cell phone in hand, she set out to search for her friend.

Reaching the top of the tallest peak on the trail, she looked down and saw her friend's familiar bright yellow running jacket against a tree several hundred yards down the trail. Being careful not to slip in the wet mud, she hurried toward the figure praying to find her okay.

Thirty yards out, she called her name, but received no reply. Concern caused her to increase her pace. She stopped in front of her friend and gasped at the gruesome sight.

Her scream shattered the rhythmic patter of the falling rain.

ABOUT THE AUTHOR

J.C. Fields is an award-winning and Amazon Best Selling author. He is a full member of The Missouri Writers' Guild and active in numerous other writing groups.

With a degree in Psychology, five years in the computer industry and a long career of dealing with individuals possessing quirky personalities, J.C. has incorporated these experiences into his writing.

The Sean Kruger Series has won numerous awards, including multiple gold and silver medals in the Readers' Favorite International Book contest. *The Imposter's Trail* was awarded Best Mystery/Thriller at the 2017 Ozark Indie Book Fest.

In March of 2020, his novel, *A Lone Wolf,* became a #1 Amazon Best Selling Audiobook. His second novel in the series, *The Last Insurgent* became a #1 Amazon New Release in January 2021.

He lives with his wife, Connie in Southwest Missouri.